I0584172

REFUGE IN THE STARS

REFUGE IN THE STARS

ENEMY OF MY ENEMY BOOK TWO

TIM MARQUITZ   MICHAEL ANDERLE
CRAIG MARTELLE

DISRUPTIVE IMAGINATION

Refuge in the Stars (this book) is a work of fiction.

All of the characters, organizations, and events portrayed in this novel are either products of the author's imagination or are used fictitiously. Sometimes both.

Copyright © 2018 Tim Marquitz, Michael Anderle and Craig Martelle
Cover by Tom Edwards tomedwardsdesign.com/
Cover copyright © LMBPN Publishing

LMBPN Publishing supports the right to free expression and the value of copyright. The purpose of copyright is to encourage writers and artists to produce the creative works that enrich our culture.

The distribution of this book without permission is a theft of the author's intellectual property. If you would like permission to use material from the book (other than for review purposes), please contact support@lmbpn.com. Thank you for your support of the author's rights.

LMBPN Publishing
PMB 196, 2540 South Maryland Pkwy
Las Vegas, NV 89109

First US edition, August 2018

The Kurtherian Gambit (and what happens within / characters / situations / worlds) are copyright © 2015-2018 by Michael T. Anderle and LMBPN Publishing.

REFUGE IN THE STARS TEAM

Thanks to the JIT Readers

James Caplan
Peter Manis
Mary Morris
John Ashmore
Daniel Weigert
Keith Verret
Kelly O'Donnell
John Ashmore
Micky Cocker

If I've missed anyone, please let me know!

Editor
LKJ Bookmakers

CHAPTER ONE

The months after the accidental Wyyvan invasion of Krawlas were a whirlwind.

Taj stared out over Culvert City, but her mind couldn't quite square what she saw with the city she'd grown up in. It was so...different.

After the desperate move of crashing the Wyyvan ship, the *Monger*, into the dead center of the old town to kill off the enemy, the destroyer having pulled everything into the labyrinth of tunnels beneath the city, there was nothing left but memories where her home had stood.

The rebuilt town now rested five kilometers west of the original location in order to avoid the cavernous instability of the *Monger*'s impact crater. She and her people had filled in the secretive tunnels, given how they had mostly collapsed anyway, but they'd left a few of the entrances in place.

As it turned out, the alien destroyer hadn't been completely wrecked. While it would never fly again, much of its technology remained viable. Taj and her crew went to work right away, scavenging what they could from the ship, with Lina leading the effort.

"There is so much here we can use," Lina had muttered as she picked and pawed through everything, sorting bits and pieces and studying every one.

"You know what this stuff does?" Taj asked.

The engineer shrugged. "I'll figure it out. Most of it's pretty basic, bits and pieces of armor we can use to create defenses with, the guns we can mount as a sort of anti-ship or personnel devices around the perimeter of town." Her eyes scanned the treasure trove of the *Monger's* remains. "The biggest part of all this will be the data logs, if I can figure out how to crack them. That's what'll really help us when these guys come back."

Taj nodded, glad to have anything that would better their chances against the Wyyvan forces.

"Hey, Kal," Lina called out over the noise of their people poking through the wreckage. "Can I get you and Jadie to organize a collection and get all this stuff to my makeshift workshop? I need to examine it closer and can't do it out here."

"Sure," Kal answered, waving Jadie, Torbon's aunt, over from where she led a scavenging party sweeping the perimeter. "C'mon, Jadie, we've got a new job that needs doing."

Jadie chuckled and waved her crew to follow as she trotted over to Kal. "What are we doing now?"

Kal started to explain, and Taj turned her focus to the sky. She grinned as she thought about the Wyyvans' return.

She shook off the reverie of that day and glanced out at

the desert surrounding the newly rebuilt Culvert City, and she imagined the surprises she had in store for the cruel aliens when they set foot on Furlorian land again. Buried beneath the scrubby, sandy terrain, hundreds of makeshift mines and anti-personnel weapons lay ready to be activated, powered by the exact mineral the invaders were in search of. The Wyyvan soldiers wouldn't simply stroll into Culvert City as they had the last time. Taj smiled. No, they'd pay in blood for daring to set foot on Krawlas soil again.

On top of having prepped the city to defend itself, the crew managed to revive the *Paradigm*, the old Furlorian freighter that had brought Mama Merr, Gran Beaux, and the other survivors of Felinus 4 to Krawlas, fueling it with Toradium-42 and stuffing its cargo bays with more of the precious mineral.

Taj bit back a groan as she thought of the old Grans, both having given their lives to ensure their people made it to safety. A single tear ran down her cheek, tickling her whiskers.

But that was all she'd let fall.

She grunted and wiped it away in defiance.

Beaux and Mama Merr had entrusted her with the wellbeing of her entire race, and it was a burden that weighed heavily on Taj's shoulders, but she wasn't carrying it alone.

Her crew—even if the windrider, the *Thorn*, was now destroyed—was right there with her. Lina, Torbon, and Cabe were the backbone she could lean on, no matter what. She had friends, family, people she could count on in the direst of circumstances. They were there for her.

That thought chased the others from her mind, like a welcome sunrise burning away the morning's clouds. Taj grinned and let out a long, slow breath, clearing her lungs and mind at the same time.

She wasn't alone, and she never would be.

Her comm device chirped in her ear, reminding her of exactly that.

"Yeah?" she answered after a moment, letting her renewed confidence bolster her voice.

"You're gonna wanna see this," Lina told her. The static of the comm did nothing to mask the trepidation in the engineer's voice.

"Something tells me I really *don't* want to."

Lina grunted. "No, probably not."

Taj swallowed hard and nodded, even though she knew Lina couldn't see her. "Be right there," she replied, her feet starting off on their own. She knew better than to ignore the tone in Lina's voice. Something was going on, something bad.

She had a pretty good idea as to what that might be, too.

Taj made her way to the *Paradigm*'s bridge, out of breath from her forced run. Though the freighter had been pulled from its quiet cavern and was parked on the other side of the old Culvert City, it was still a few miles from where Taj had been. She'd arrived quickly enough, but there was no way to hide the exertion it had taken. Taj huffed and struggled to catch her breath as Lina met her at the bridge door.

"You're not gonna like this," Lina said.

"I already don't like it." Taj coughed and cleared her throat, her words raspy. "Tell me what's going on,"

The engineer led her to the array of sensors and displays that took up the front of the freighter's bridge. Without a word, she pointed to the screen set dead center in the console. Taj followed Lina's finger and her breath hitched in her lungs. A wave of lightheadedness washed over her and she clasped the seat back, then plopped into the monitoring chair with a grunt. Her heart didn't know whether to pound or stall. Instead, it beat an irregular rhythm in her chest, a drummer out of sync with the rest of her body.

"Bloody Rowl," she muttered. "There are eight of them up there."

"Nine," Lina corrected as yet another blip representing a spaceship appeared on the scanner monitor.

Taj looked closer, scanning the terminal's readouts as they scrolled across the old, green screen. "Seven destroyers." The words barely managed to escape her clenched lips.

"And there's another one." Lina came up behind her and set a hand on Taj's shoulder. Taj could feel it trembling. She reached up and clasped the engineer's hand in her own, offering reassurance. "And another. They keep coming, Taj."

Taj dropped into the captain's chair to think. Her tail fluttered and twitched, fury and frustration giving it a life of its own.

Cabe and Torbon came up behind the pair. She felt them staring over her shoulder at the screen.

"Uh, that's not good," Torbon muttered.

"Ya think?" Cabe asked, and though Taj couldn't see it, she knew he was shaking his head.

"Don't panic," Taj told them. "We didn't do all this work to cave now. This is what we've been preparing for."

"But we didn't plan for this many of them, Taj," Lina said. "The mines buried along the city perimeter might delay them, but they've clearly brought enough troops to overwhelm our traps."

"I really don't think that's gonna be a problem," Cabe mumbled. He reached past Taj and tapped the monitor with a claw. A massive black blip appeared right where he pointed.

"What the gack is that?" Torbon asked.

Lina gasped, and everyone spun their heads to stare at her.

"It's a…a…" she stammered.

"It's a what?" Torbon shouted, slapping his hands onto his hips.

"A dreadnought," she finally managed to spit out.

The word silenced the room, a heavy gloom settling over them as each of the crew thought back to their training holos and envisioned the monstrous battleship that went by the name of dreadnought.

"Rowl," Taj managed to say. A cold chill ran like spiders down her spine.

"We're gonna die," Torbon whispered, and despite how often he said it, Taj thought he might be right this time.

Then she shook the thought off. Torbon was never right.

There was no way she was going to let these gacking aliens come in and take over again.

"Why in the gack would they bring a dreadnought for a mining expedition? It's not like they don't have an army of soldiers sitting up there ready to..." Cabe paused, his hand flying to his mouth. "Oh." He seemed to realize the answer to his question.

A half-dozen more blips appeared on the screen.

"Oh?" Torbon asked. "*Oh* what?"

Cabe stared at the monitor for a moment longer, eyes wide, only seeming to wake up when Taj pinched his arm.

"Oh *what?*" she demanded. "What's running around in that skull of yours?"

"We are sooooo gacked," he answered. He tapped the screen once more, pointing out the dreadnought. "You apparently missed it in training, but that kind of ship has another name..."

Taj stared at the black blip and racked her brain, drifting back to the days of hunkering down in front of the holo vids, studying to impress Gran Beaux with her knowledge and aptitude. She flipped through her memories, chasing the elusive recall of the dreadnought. Taj had pushed that particular holo to the back of her mind as she doubted she'd ever come face to face with the monstrous ship, stranded on Krawlas as she was. But then it struck her.

"Worldbreaker," she mumbled, having a hard time getting the word out as its meaning sunk in.

Cabe nodded, and without another word, he reached over her again and tapped a code into the console. Red lights flashed on deck, bathing the crew in bloody crimson.

"Sound the city alarms," Taj shouted, "and get everyone mobilized. We need to get the bloody gack out of here. Now!"

Lina hesitated only an instant, but a buzzer sounded, reverberating throughout the bridge and spurring her into action. Taj swallowed hard, registering the flashes onscreen, which corresponded with the new alert. A cold emptiness clawed at her guts.

This wasn't what they'd prepared for, but she couldn't let that be a distraction. Her people were counting on her.

"Incoming," Cabe shouted. He raced for his seat, scrambling to buckle himself in. Torbon followed suit, muttering to himself.

Taj stared at the screen. She didn't like what she saw.

The Wyyvan invaders hadn't come to Krawlas to fight a guerilla war on the surface like Captain Vort had been forced to. No, they'd come to obliterate the Furlorians in one fell swoop and claim all the Toradium-42 for themselves.

What better way to do that than to blast the planet from orbit?

CHAPTER TWO

"Maximize shields overhead," Taj screamed, clutching the arms of her seat. Her chest ached from the flush of adrenaline searing through her. "Get us over the city. Now!"

The ship rumbled as the crew powered up the engines, ignoring the pre-flight beeps and complaints, and pushed the *Paradigm* into the air.

"What's going on?" Captain Vort asked from the doorway, pawing at the wall to keep himself steady as the Paradigm rose awkwardly. He stared across the deck at the scanner array, eyes wide as the first enemy fire struck. The ship rattled, the shields absorbing the crashing energy.

Taj snapped a glance at him over her shoulder. Kal, the young Furlorian she'd charged with guarding the Wyyvan captain, stood with him.

"What is he doing here?" Taj asked, returning her focus to the console in front of her.

"He demanded to know what was going on," Kal told her.

Taj sighed. "Demanded? What part of *prisoner* do you not understand, Kal?"

The alien captain interrupted. "Berate your crewmember later," he said, slurring the last with a sneer as he stomped forward to get a better look at the scanners. "Are those Wyyvan ships firing upon us?"

Cabe offered a sharp-edged chuckle. "Guess you're not as important as you thought you were, huh, Captain?"

"Your admiral definitely has a weird way of showing his appreciation," Taj told the captain, not bothering to hide the crooked smile that peeled her lips back. Much as she was sickened by the assault on her people, a tiny, cruel, and vindictive part of her flared happily at seeing the Wyyvan captain's sour expression at his betrayal. "Now, if you're staying, take a gacking seat, shut up, and stay out of the way. I've more important things to deal with than your hurt feelings."

Vort grunted and flung himself into a seat. He fought with the safety strap as Kal took a seat beside him and did the same, keeping an eye on the alien captain.

Since his capture, he hadn't been much of a threat. While still selfish, only offering what he knew when it suited his personal agenda, he hadn't once lashed out or caused trouble, playing the role of a model prisoner.

Taj figured he'd been waiting patiently for his people to arrive and free him. She cast a furtive glance at him and saw the defeat in his narrowed eyes, the droop of his jaw as he stared unflinchingly at the scanners. He looked more defeated now than he had when the whole of the Furlorian people surrounded him after crashing his ship.

Taj rather enjoyed that, too.

"We're over the city," Lina called out. "Hovering and dropping the ramp."

Taj wiped the petty thoughts of Vort's disappointment from her mind so she could focus on what was really important: the rescue of her people.

Culvert City already burned from the fury of the barrage. Below her, she could see her people gathering, instinctively running for the cover of the freighter's shields, but not all of them had made it. Scattered across the streets and sidewalks laid a dozen Furlorians, sightless eyes staring at the sky.

Taj swallowed hard and hissed at seeing them. Too many of her people had died already, and she wouldn't see more of them fall to the cruelty of the Wyyvan invaders.

"Give me the speakers!" she shouted. An instant later, a low beep told her that Lina had fulfilled her request, opening a channel outside of the ship. Taj cleared her throat. "Fellow Furlorians," she said, doing her best to control the tremor that threatened to rattle her voice, "the Wyyvan are upon us once more." She shook her head at the obviousness of her statement but went on. "Come to the *Paradigm* immediately. There's no time to gather your belongings. Get to the ship and get aboard now."

A dozen explosions emphasized her words, Wyyvan cannon fire falling from the sky. Smoke and debris filled the air, dust and dirt peppering the view screen. Taj snarled as she lost sight of her people in the chaos below. She had to rely on the ship's scanners, which only showed the

Furlorians as a blur of squirming black against the green background.

She spun in her seat. "Get them inside, Cabe! All of them!"

Cabe grunted, flung his safety harness aside, and shot off down the corridor outside the bridge. Taj watched him go, turning back when he disappeared. Comm still open, she hopped on the speakers and urged her people to hurry as more and more enemy fire rained down.

The *Paradigm* shuddered as blow after blow crashed into its ancient shields. Taj watched as the city they'd only recently rebuilt came apart in moments. An orange glow tinted the view screen as more and more fires erupted across the city, spreading quickly with no one there to curtail their advance. She could smell the bitter char wafting through the open hatch in the belly of the ship, the stench creeping its way through the ship.

It fueled the fire inside her.

"Hurry, people," she screamed, desperately urging them on.

A loud, harsh beep sounded, reverberating through the bridge. A half-dozen impacts rattled the ship right then.

"They're targeting us directly now," Torbon called out needlessly. Taj knew gacking well what was happening. Her only surprise was that it had taken so long for the enemy to do it.

"Double power to the shields," she ordered. "We sit here until everyone is aboard."

"Your misplaced compassion is going to get us all killed," Vort told her.

She snarled. "My compassion is the only thing keeping

you alive, Captain. So, unless you want to test my patience *and* my willingness to throw you out the hatch, I'd suggest you keep your mouth shut."

Vort harrumphed, but her threat didn't quiet him. "Forgive me for not trusting solely in your compassion to keep me alive," he replied. "My people's weaponry fires on a specific frequency," he offered. "While your shields appear to be holding, they would sustain the battery better if you tweaked their range in accordance."

Taj grunted and said nothing for an instant, debating the captain's offer. Much as she didn't trust him, she knew well enough that all he cared about was his own safety. The last thing he'd do is put the *Paradigm* and her people at risk right then because he would die right alongside them.

"Adjust the shields as he dictates," Taj called out to Lina, gesturing for Vort to go ahead.

The captain smirked and offered his knowledge, calling out the necessary adjustments.

Taj saw immediate improvement in the shield's function, but it still wouldn't be enough if they sat there for too much longer. "Hurry," she screamed into the comm again. "We need to move."

"Almost there," Cabe answered over their personal comm, his message only broadcasting to the crew. "It's seriously crowded down here. Having a hard time making room and getting everyone inside."

Taj nodded even though Cabe couldn't see it. "Do what you can, but do it fast. Better we pile live people on top of each other than leaving corpses."

She hadn't expected the Wyyvans to bombard the planet from orbit, hadn't even thought of the possibility, and that made her nauseous, a sure sign of her inexperience. Her people had spent all their time and resources preparing for a ground invasion, thinking the Toradium-42 too important for the invaders to do anything else but land and try to take it by force like Vort had.

Now, the fate of her people hung in the balance, a battered old freighter's shields and hull the only thing standing between them and annihilation. Taj's whiskers vibrated as her anger grew.

"Not without a fight!" she blurted.

"Shields at sixty-five percent," Lina warned. "Sixty-two percent. Sixty."

"Bloody Rowl," Taj muttered under her breath. "Push more power to them. We need everyone on board."

"Think maybe we can, I don't know, get this show on the road sometime soon?" Torbon asked.

"I concur," Captain Vort said, gesturing toward Torbon. "We remain much longer and my *dear* compatriots—" There was no mistaking the bitterness in his voice. "—will turn the dreadnought loose upon us. This—" He gestured toward the explosions rocking the ship. "—will be nothing compared to what we will endure if the dreadnought joins the barrage. No amount of shield tweaking will defy its power."

As much as Taj hated the alien captain, she knew he was right. She clenched her teeth and screamed into the comm, "Hurry up, people. We can't hold on much longer!"

She heard Vort sigh at what he considered to be her indecision and did her best to ignore him. She wasn't going to leave anyone behind.

Those were the decisions a real captain made, and that's

what she was now, like it or not. She was sitting in the big chair and making the big decisions. It was frightening, but exhilarating, too. "Prepare for max acceleration the second the last Furlorian is aboard, even if they aren't strapped in. Better bruised than dead."

"Almost done," Cabe called out.

"Better rush it, Cabe," Lina told him. "The dreadnought's weapon array is warming up. If we're still sitting here when it fires…"

Taj heard him mutter something across the channel about missing his nip, followed by a profound string of curses referencing the Wyyvans' mothers, and she couldn't help but concur with the latter.

More blasts echoed against the shields overhead, and she heard the emergency beacons kick on again, a horrible wail pinning her ears to the side of her head. She glanced over her shoulder at Torbon.

He met her eyes and shrugged. "You don't really need me to say it, do you?"

Taj sighed. She didn't. "Don't you dare."

"Done! Everyone's in," Cabe called. "Closing the hatch now."

Taj felt the knot in her stomach loosen the tiniest bit as she saw the hatch indicator signal its closure. "Hold on, everyone. Things are gonna get bumpy." She motioned to Lina. "Go! Get us out of here."

The engineer barked an affirmative. "Shields adjusted, full forward thrust."

Taj was pressed deeper into her seat as the *Paradigm* shot forward, angling low then darting upward. Culvert City disappeared behind them, and Taj groaned at leaving the only place she'd ever known as home behind. Her every memory centered around Culvert City and Krawlas, and now she and the whole of her people were abandoning it, hurtling into space with barely enough supplies to last a month, if that.

Though that wasn't her biggest concern right then.

"You do realize you are flying directly toward the fleet, correct?" Vort asked. "Seems counter-intuitive if your goal is to survive, but perhaps you have some tactical wisdom I simply don't comprehend, earned in all your years piloting a warcraft."

Taj growled at him, but once more, he was right. The Wyyvan ships were shifting their position, several of them turning to continue their barrage on the *Paradigm*. It would only be a matter of time before they cleared the atmosphere and ended up directly ahead of the whole Wyyvan fleet.

"Any suggestions?" she asked, squeezing the words out through her clenched teeth.

"Well, since not dying is at the top of my to-do list, I'd suggest you let me take the helm."

Taj jerked around, spinning in her chair to glare at the alien. "Are you serious?" she snapped. "You expect me to let you take control of the ship in the middle of a fight with your very own people?"

He shrugged. "Perhaps you haven't noticed, but no one aboard any of those ships knows I'm aboard this one, nor, as if it weren't even more obvious, does anyone appear to care about my safety or wellbeing." He jabbed a finger at the view screen. "As such, I am in every bit as much danger as you and your people. I'm also the most qualified regarding Wyyvan fleet tactics. So, unless you want to end up as charred debris floating in space, I suggest you stick a pin in your paranoia and allow me to take the helm."

"Gack me!" Taj cursed. She spun on the engineer. "Scoot over, Lina. Let him have the helm but stay close. He does anything funny, shoot him."

Wide-eyed, Lina loosened her safety harness and hopped to another seat, pulling her gun loose as Vort claimed her chair.

"I hope you know what you're doing, Taj," Lina told her.

"You and me both," Taj muttered in reply, wondering how in the gack she'd reached this point.

"We're all gonna die," Torbon muttered in the background, his lips moving as if he couldn't help himself.

Taj sighed. "You seriously need a new catch phrase, Torbon," she barked at him. "We're not gonna die. I won't allow it."

He grunted and sat back in his seat. While she didn't think she'd gotten through to him, at least he'd shut up.

That was something.

Not long after, as Vort had predicted, the *Paradigm* broke free of the atmosphere ahead of the fleet. She swallowed hard at seeing the array of destroyers splayed out before her. The dreadnought loomed large, ominous. Then the *Paradigm*'s engines kicked in with a rumble, pinning everyone to their seats. The whole crew gasped as one.

Then the *Paradigm* shot directly toward the dreadnought.

"What the gack are you doing, Vort?" Taj screamed. Her hand fought the surge of forward momentum in an effort

17

to kill power to the helm's console. "Lina! Get ready to shoot him."

"It's the only way to get clear," Vort answered as the engineer lifted her bolt pistol and pointed it at him.

Taj glared, finger over the console, ready to kill Vort's access. It was only the narrow-eyed, almost fearful expression on the captain's face that kept her from taking control from him.

"The rest of the fleet won't risk striking the dreadnought so this is the safest place we can be," he told them. "The dreadnought has no in-tight defenses, its focus solely on overwhelming offensive power, relying entirely on the fleet to keep ships from getting anywhere near it." He gestured to the view screen. "And since we came out of the atmosphere so close to the beast, the fleet is unprepared to defend it. That buys us several moments to maneuver past."

Taj continued to glare at the alien, but there was nothing she could do to alter their course, even if she did reclaim control of the ship. The nose of the dreadnought loomed in the view screen. Taj squirmed in her seat.

"You better know what you're doing," she said to Vort.

"If I don't, you've nothing to worry about," he replied. "Our death will be quick and painless."

"That's comforting," Torbon muttered. "Put that on my space dust headstone, if you don't mind. 'Torbon died, quickly and painlessly thanks to a stinky lizard's poor choice of tactics.'"

Vort shrugged. "Feel free to take the helm if you can do better," he told Torbon.

"Just do what needs to be done, *Captain*, and keep your mouth shut," Taj told him, cutting off any further banter with a sharp wave of her hand. "I really don't want to hear you right now."

To her surprise, Vort simply nodded as the dreadnought grew closer and closer. The dark gray steel of its armor filled the view screen. A few last explosions rattled the *Paradigm's* shields, the console reading 55%, and then they were flying only meters above the dreadnought's hull. The rattling impacts of enemy fire ended immediately like Vort had predicted.

Captain Vort chuckled. "Am I not a genius?"

"I hope you're not actually looking to get an answer," Torbon snarked.

The dreadnought hurtled under them, a blur of impending doom that grew less threatening with every passing second.

"Now what?" Taj asked as they neared the dreadnoughts massive engines.

"Now," the captain began, "we run like hell."

CHAPTER THREE

The *Paradigm* shot past the rear of the dreadnought, and Captain Vort veered the craft sharply, diving behind the hull of the enemy ship. Taj bit back a groan as the sudden change in direction pinned her to her seat, the old freighters equipment not quite up to the task of perfecting gravity within its confines.

"A little warning," Torbon shouted. "My tail nearly poked my eye out."

"This is no joyride, Furlorian," Vort answered. "Were I to warn you of every tactical maneuver required, we'd be back to discussing how quickly our deaths would be upon us."

"Knock it off, both of you," Taj shouted, waggling a clawed finger at Torbon. "Get us out of here, Vort."

"I endeavor to do exactly that," he replied.

There was another sudden shift of direction, and the *Paradigm* kept the dreadnought's bulk between them and the majority of the enemy ships.

Taj watched the monitors closely. For the most part, the alien fleet continued to bombard the planet, ignoring the escaping freighter now that it had slipped past them. Only two destroyers seemed to be engaged with the pursuit and even that seem halfhearted, neither ship pressing hard to catch them.

"Why aren't they chasing us?" she asked.

"Outside of satisfying Grand Admiral Galforin's ego and bloodlust, a ship full of escaping rodents is hardly high on his list of priorities. It's the Toradium-42 he wants, and his efforts at annihilating all life on the planet, to include my own, shows you how much he prizes the mineral over all else."

Taj swallowed her complaints at being called a rodent, simply grateful that the enemy wanted the precious mineral more than he wanted to kill off the escaping Furlorians. She sunk into her seat as Vort triggered the thrusters, doing his best to put as much distance between them and his murderous cohorts. She watched as the two destroyers slowed on the monitors, clearly content to let the *Paradigm* slip away.

She sighed and muttered a thanks to Rowl.

Of course, she should have known better than to trust a fickle goddess with her safety.

Out of nowhere, a sleek black craft appeared on the screen.

A metallic *thump* resounded through the bridge, and Vort cursed as the *Paradigm* trembled and slowed. The monitors showed the engines waning as something drained the power from them, a strange current shooting through the craft and overwhelming the systems.

"What the gack is that?" Torbon asked.

"We've been snagged by a small Wyyvan ship of some kind," Lina answered. "A boarding tube's caught our hull."

"What is this thing, Vort?" Taj asked.

The captain growled. "It's a leech ship," he replied. "Designed for boarding, infiltration. There will be—"

Another metallic *thump* interrupted him, followed by a second and a third.

"—more boarding tubes attached in a moment," Vort finished, offering a shrug for his delayed assessment. "Like those they're hooking up now."

"One near the bridge, two at the engines, and one attached at the midsection," Lina called out. "All power to the engines has been cut off. I'm trying to re-engage them."

"Cabe!" Taj shouted into the comm.

"Go!" he answered.

"I need people armed and ready to repulse invaders. Get them to the bridge and engine room, then I need some people arrayed at—"

"Wait," Vort said, clambering free of his chair and flinging his harness aside. "The extra tubes are a ploy, don't fall for them."

He ran over to where Taj sat and began typing a sequence onto her console. A holographic display of the leech ship and the *Paradigm* appeared, floating alongside each other, the boarding tubes visible. He tapped the spot where the tube connected to the bridge, then to those at the engines.

"Tactically, these three tubes are intended as feints. They'll be minimally manned, the forces stationed there intend to do nothing more than to hold your attention

23

while the true invaders—" He tapped the innocuous tube connected to the middle of the ship. "—board here, where you're least likely to deploy sufficient soldiers, and then they'll make their way to the bridge."

Taj growled. "How do I know you're being honest, Vort?"

The captain chuckled. "Because I don't want to die any more than you do, Furlorian, as I keep telling you," he answered. "Why would they raid your engines when they've already cut power to them? And why push straight at your bridge when they know you'll crowd the corridors and defend it with everything you've got? It would be suicide on their part."

He gestured to the leech ship floating alongside them outside of the hull.

"Their ship has a finite number of soldiers it can throw against your defenses, and they can't afford to mass up and risk being battled back while trying to navigate a narrow boarding tube. That's the reason behind the subterfuge. They'll engage you at all the tunnels, superficially, to keep you occupied, splitting your forces throughout the ship. That keeps you from mustering your people in time to hold the bridge from the true threat, which will catch you off guard, your attention turned away from them."

"Bloody Rowl," Taj muttered. She flipped on her comm. "Cabe! Belay my last. Get everyone armed and to the bridge. Now!"

He muttered an affirmative, and Taj lifted her gaze to meet Vort's once more. Her tail slapped hard against her thigh. "You better be right about this," she told him.

"If I'm not, then I die right alongside you," he answered

with a shrug. "Speaking of, perhaps you should have someone fetch Commander Dard. I've grown fond of him and would prefer not to leave him behind to the mercy of my former comrades."

"Wait! What do you mean by leaving him behind?" Taj asked.

The captain chuckled. "You don't actually think we'll be able to escape on this ancient clunker, do you? You saw how quickly the leech ship caught us, and there will be more on the heels of this one."

"I...uh..."

Vort shook his head. "Your lack of tactical acumen disturbs me, Furlorian." He tapped the monitor in front of her. The two destroyers that had backed off seemed to be closing on the *Paradigm* again now that it had stalled, a third, smaller ship leading the way. Vort pointed out the lead craft. "That's another leech craft, as I noted. It will attach itself to our port side, complementing the one on our starboard, and it will flood us with more soldiers than we can hope to repel or avoid no matter our understanding of their tactics. And should that fail, the destroyers will do their part and lay waste to us while we're dead in space."

A shudder ran through Taj, setting her hackles flaring. "What are you suggesting?"

"Not suggesting anything, Furlorian, I'm telling you what *must* be done. Simple fact, we push through the nearest boarding tube and the men defending it, and we surprise them by taking command of the leech ship. It's the only way we'll survive this. You do want to live, don't you? I know I do."

"You have got to be kidding," Torbon said, having come

up behind them.

"Have I shown you anything that suggests I have a sense of humor, Furlorian?" the captain asked.

Torbon sputtered, but Taj could only find herself agreeing with the alien captain. He hadn't once hinted at being capable of humor.

"We're so going to—"

"Don't gacking say it, Torbon," Taj told him with a growl. He raised his hands in surrender, unwilling to brave the fiery weight of her glare.

Right then, the clatter of footsteps filled the hall. Cabe stumbled onto the bridge, out of breath and clutching his ribs.

"We're all here, in position," he said through deep gasps, gesturing behind him with a thumb. Muttered conversations filled the corridor outside the bridge, the remainder of her people crowding the halls and preparing to repel the invaders.

Then another siren erupted in their ears.

"The enemy is piercing the hull at all the tube locations, cutting their way through," Lina shouted right after killing the alarm.

Vort jabbed a long green finger at Taj. "Amass a fire team at the tube entrance nearest the bridge and ready your people to cross over." He turned around and glanced off in the direction of the nearest boarding tube. "If we do this quickly enough, we can capture the bridge and disengage the tubes before the ship's captain realizes what we're attempting and calls his men back to reinforce the one we're traversing."

"That's the plan? Traverse boarding umbilicals under

fire and switch ships, all while hoping no one notices what we're doing?" Cabe asked. He shook his head, his shaggy fur flying about like a lion's mane. "I'm starting to think we should have stayed on Krawlas."

"You're more than welcome to remain onboard to greet your new overlords," Vort told him. "I wouldn't expect much in the way of kindness, however. If you thought I was cruel to your people, you should..."

Cabe sneered at the captain. "Keep talking about what you did to my people, and I'll launch you out the garbage chute in tiny little pieces, Wyyvan scum."

"Enough!" Taj yelled. "We don't have time for this." She yanked her bolt pistol from its holster. "Vort's in this as deeply as the rest of us, so do as he says, for *now*."

Taj grabbed her pouch, which she'd hung over the back of her seat, and flung it over her shoulder. She then pushed past Cabe and stormed into the corridor, marching down to where the Wyyvan leech ship's crew had already begun to cut away the hull.

"Keep some guns trained on the corridor behind us, and a couple on Vort and Dard, when he gets here, but I want everyone ready to charge the boarding tube when I give the okay. We need to push through hard and fast, giving them no chance to realize our intentions."

Right then, on the hull, a spark burst, the laser cutters on the other side beginning to break through the heavy steel armor of the freighter's hull. Taj slowed her breathing and watched as a molten red line appeared and slowly circled. It was time to lead.

She waved people to the side of what would soon be a makeshift opening in the *Paradigm's* hull, ensuring no one was injured when the door exploded inward, and gripped her pistol tight enough to make her hand ache.

"I hope you're right about all this," she told Vort as Commander Dard and the blind Wyyvan, S'thlor, were led through the crowd to stand alongside the captain. Ironically, Torbon's aunt, Jadie, helped guard them alongside Kal. Taj offered Jadie a quick smile, but Vort's roughened voice pulled her focus away.

"As do I, Furlorian," he told her. "Perhaps things would be better were you to give me a—"

"No guns for you, Vort." Taj cut him off with a wave. "Not gonna happen. Not now, not ever!"

He shrugged as if he'd expected that very answer and looked back toward the weakening hull. "Then I suggest you make ready. My former compatriots will be through the hull soon. Then the fun begins."

The ring of fire continued on its way, burning through the ship's side and hurling sparks at the waiting Furlorians.

There isn't anything fun about it, she thought.

Taj kicked herself mentally, wondering why she was standing there, following the alien captain's suggestion. He was a liar, total scum who cared about nothing but himself.

And that was exactly why it made so much sense.

His people hadn't shown the slightest interest in him or Commander Dard or any of the Wyyvans who might have survived the fight with the Furlorians.

At first, she'd thought they might have tried to contact him, letting him know what they were planning, but then Taj remembered Lina had salvaged the communication systems of the *Monger* and had been listening in, hoping to get a heads up when the Wyyvans would arrive. Had they bothered to reach out to Vort, Lina would have intercepted the transmission, and the Furlorians would have realized they were coming.

That was the biggest factor in keeping her in place, heeding his advice.

Entirely clueless to what had gone down on the planet, Vort's defeat and subsequent capture, the Wyyvan grand admiral clearly didn't give a damn that his soldiers were aboard the old freighter. For all he knew, they were alive and well on the planet, mining the Toradium-42 for their empire like good little minions, awaiting his arrival. The fact that he opened fire from space without hesitation told Taj he was even worse than Vort, and that he'd murder anyone who got in his way.

That reinforced her decision to remain steadfast. Vort had proven he'd do anything to stay alive, and that obviously included offering up Wyyvan secrets when it best suited him.

Taj gripped her bolt gun even tighter as the last of the hull was cut away and the molten-edged slab of steel fell away from the hull and clanged heavily into the corridor. Even if she'd wanted to change her mind, her decision had been made for her right then.

"Now!" she screamed. "Hit them hard and don't let up until we're through!"

The crew aimed their weapons down the boarding tube and fired without hesitation, following her lead. Bolts of energy screamed down the umbilical, met by surprised shouts and screams and a smattering of return fire.

All three of those wavered and faded away moments later.

Taj bit her lip as the sudden flurry of battle died away, the enemy falling back for cover. The coppery taste of blood filled her mouth, and she thought about casting a prayer to Rowl, then thought better of it. For better or worse, this choice was on her, and Rowl sure as gack wasn't going to help her make up her mind.

"Follow me," she hissed and clambered over the cooling steel of the makeshift doorway. She shot off down the tube, gun blasting, never slowing.

Pride filled her as the Furlorians spilled into the tube behind her. No matter what happened on the other side of the umbilical, they were in it together. She yowled and pressed on. Near the end of the short tube, she spied the scattered movement of hostiles, readying to meet her and the charging Furlorians. The barest of grins brightened her lips.

She'd thought long and hard about what she'd do if Vort was leading them into a trap, and she'd come prepared.

Her free hand dug in her pouch and pulled out a silver device. It sat heavily in her palm for a moment. Memories of Beaux lingered at the touch, him clutching two of the devices that ended his life, before she jerked her arm back and let it fly, sending the grenade flying down the tube and into the hallway beyond.

The surprised shouts of alien soldiers met its unexpected arrival. Terrified shouts sounded about a second later, the scuffle of boots following in its wake.

"Grenade!" she heard one scream, and all the dark-helmeted aliens who'd been crouched at the end of the boarding tube disappeared in a hurry, leaving the passageway clear.

Taj chuckled and bore down, running even faster. She burst from the tube as the aliens scattered, running for cover, their backs to her and the device bouncing across the floor.

The device she'd purposely not triggered before she threw it.

Her bolt pistol barked, ripping holes in the spines of the enemy soldiers desperately fleeing the grenade they didn't know was inactive.

Then her crew was there alongside her, firing their weapons the opposite direction and taking out the remainder of the soldiers tasked with guarding the tube. Seconds later, all the Wyyvan soldiers were dead, smoldering husks littering the floor of the leech craft.

"Kinda surprised Vort told us the truth," Torbon muttered, having edged in close to Taj so only she could hear him.

"Give him a gralfly for his honesty later, we've got more of his people to take out," Taj told him, snatching up her unexploded grenade and slipping it back into her pouch. "Which way to the bridge, Lina?"

"This way," the engineer said, pointing ahead of them, her weapon held high. "I think," she added in a mumble.

Taj's people spilled into the leech ship, Vort, Dard, and S'thlor in their midst. The captain offered Taj an arrogant smirk of satisfaction at having been right.

"Get these tubes disconnected as soon as all of my people are aboard, Vort," Taj told him, turning away when Kal grabbed the captain and pressed him to his task. "Cabe, Torbon, take enough people to clear the ship from bow to stern. I don't want any surprises popping out at us."

The pair gathered a group of armed Furlorians and darted off toward the rear of the craft while Taj collected others and stormed toward the bridge, leaving Kal and a few others with Vort and Dard. "Don't let them do anything stupid, Kal," she called back over the personal comm to keep the captive Wyyvans from overhearing.

He muttered an affirmative.

A short distance ahead, outside the bridge, Taj and her people ran into resistance.

Blaster fire seared down the corridor to greet them, sparking off the walls and floor. Taj and the others dove out of the way, pinning themselves against the wall and making themselves as small a target as possible. Bursts of green energy illuminated the hallway, a desperate ploy to keep them at bay, and Taj heard the howl of the wounded on both sides.

She watched as one of her people was shot in the arm. The Furlorian stumbled into the corridor and was shot again, a great black hole welling at his chest. He slumped without a sound, collapsing to the cold steel floor, dead before he even stopped moving.

Taj hissed, feeling her hackles rise. She'd seen far too much death of late, too many of her people being ground down beneath Wyyvan bootheels without a care. To see one more person die was more than she could handle.

"Incoming!" she screamed, digging out her confiscated grenade again. She figured, if it worked once, the ploy could work again. The enemy had no clue the Furlorians were there to steal the ship as opposed to simply clearing or disabling it. "Heads down!"

Taj made a show of the grenade, making sure the

Wyyvans saw it, and slid it across the floor, angling it to slip past the feet of the enemy soldiers in order to keep it out of the range of the blaster fire going back and forth. The last thing she wanted to do was have the device set off by a wayward gunshot.

That'd change the narrative in an ugly way.

She held her breath as the grenade skittered and bounced through the door.

Like before, the alien soldiers reacted as she'd hoped, screaming and scattering, several scrambling to corral the grenade and throw it back down the hall before it could explode.

"Idiots," Taj muttered and broke from cover, closing the distance between her and the bridge. Her people stomped after her, trusting she knew what she was doing.

She hit the doorway, crouched low and fired at the discombobulated Wyyvan soldiers. Lina came in behind her, followed by a half-dozen of the younger Furlorians. The Wyyvan crew barely even noticed their arrival, focused as they were on the grenade.

A moment later, they were nothing more than broken corpses scattered about the room.

Taj sighed and flopped into the captain's chair after pushing his slumped body aside. He'd held his post to the very last like a good soldier. Now he was just another dead soldier.

"Seal the bridge, Lina," Taj ordered.

The engineer scrambled to a seat, plopping down hard only to stare wide-eyed at the console. "Uh...we have a problem."

"What's wrong?" Taj asked. She rubbed at her temples. Now was not the time for more problems.

"I don't have a clue what any of this says?" Her hand hovered over the console, finger poised. "It's all in Wyyvanese, I'm guessing. Looks like a bunch of snakes crapped on the console and slithered through it. Maybe they call that a language."

"Didn't you figure all that stuff out with the command cube you took from the *Monger*?"

Lina shook her head. "That was all mechanical work, connecting circuits and whatnot, following the current. Didn't need to know what anything said to make it work. For this, though..."

Taj growled, triggering her comm. "Kal, as soon as those tubes are disengaged, get those gacking lizards in here. We *need* them right away." She hated saying the word but, while the primitive translators embedded in their head were a miracle when it came to understanding speech, they didn't do anything to help translate the written word.

The young Furlorian muttered something she took to be an affirmative, and Taj cut the connection, shifting the channel to reach out to Cabe.

"Status report," she said. "Give me some good news, Cabe."

"All clear," he replied. "Had a few stragglers in non-essential areas, and they put up a token fight, but they've been dealt with and now we have a collection of dead lizards in the hall."

Taj let out a satisfied sigh and lifted her gaze to the view screen. While she, like Lina, had no clue what the text said, she didn't need to know the words in order to recognize the three pursuing ships closing on them. As if to emphasize the point, an alarm sounded, and the room was suddenly bathed in iridescent red.

"I can't be certain, but I'm thinking that means we're being targeted," Lina said with a shrug.

"You think?" Taj mumbled, her eyes desperately scanning the console for some symbol or shape she recognized. "Today keeps getting better and better."

The console swam before her eyes, and it was getting close to having to just guess what sequence would engage the engines and turn on the shields and hope for the best because if she waited any longer, the Wyyvan destroyers would start using their stolen ship as target practice.

Kal and the captive Wyyvans burst through the open doorway to the bridge right then. Vort grinned at seeing their bewildered expressions as they stared at the foreign consoles.

"Having problems?"

Taj leapt from her seat and jabbed her bolt pistol into the captain's face. "Now is not the time for your smart tongue, Vort. You got us into this mess, so sit your tail down and get us the gack out of here before your admiral finishes the job he started on Krawlas."

"No need to be aggressive, Furlorian," he told her, wandering over to the pilot's seat and plopping down. Meaty fingers flew across the console, tapping keys. He smiled as he worked, and Taj felt a twinge of panic in her gut. No matter how much he wanted to survive, her mind just wouldn't let go enough to trust him.

All she wanted to do was blast a hole between his eyes

for what he did. Still, she understood the consequences of that and kept her cool.

If only for a second.

There was a sudden burst of energy outside, and the *Paradigm* glowed in the wake of it. Debris pattered against the stolen leech ship's hull, the wreckage obscuring the view screen for a moment as what he'd done started to seep into her head.

"What the...?" she cursed. "Why did you do that, Vort?" Her teeth clacked together as she screamed.

The leech ship's engines purred, and the alien craft shot off behind the cloud of wreckage that had, up until moments before, had been the *Paradigm*.

"A distraction, my dear Furlorian, nothing more," the captain replied. "The fleet has yet to realize we have commandeered their vessel and still believe us to be aboard your aged craft. They will think their leech ship was forced to fire to keep from being destroyed. That gives us a few extra moments to maneuver into a better tactical position before the ruse is discovered."

Taj watched as the old freighter listed and spun about without control, hurtling through space toward the two destroyers and the other pursuing leech ship. Her heart sputtered, beating an angry tattoo against her ribs at what Vort had done.

The ship was the last memory of Felinus 4, the final remaining piece of history of their home on Krawlas and all who had come before. Now it was nothing more than ruined junk floating lifeless in space.

Soon, it wouldn't even be that.

"Best strap in, Furlorian," Vort told her. "I'm about to

engage the drives. Wouldn't want anything...*untoward* to happen to you, now would we?"

Taj bit back her reply and did as he'd suggested, making sure the rest of her people on the bridge did the same. Then she cast one final glance at the view screen as the destroyers drew closer and opened fire on the drifting *Paradigm*. A low groan escaped her as momentum kicked in, her senses coming alive as she pushed deeper into her seat in defiance of the ship's atmospherics.

Everything she'd ever known was now disappearing behind her, the *Paradigm* drifting lifeless. She watched as Krawlas shrunk into the distance and become a blur. It was only when it had completely faded from sight that she peeled her eyes from the view screen.

To let go was one of the hardest things she'd ever had to do, but the past was the past. She only had the future to look forward to now.

She leapt from her seat and stormed from the bridge without a word or a glance behind her. For all the joy she knew she should feel that the vast majority of her people were safe, all she could think of was what they'd lost, what their survival had cost them.

Everything.

It struck her hard, welling up inside her, nearly unable to be contained. It would only be a matter of moments before she stormed over to Vort and snapped his neck with her bare hands if she didn't do something to circumvent the rage boiling over inside her.

So, she stomped off the bridge to keep from doing something stupid, something she'd regret.

No matter how good it would feel.

CHAPTER FOUR

The corridors of the leech craft were crowded with anxious Furlorians, a fact she'd only realized when she marched off the bridge. They were everywhere.

Taj bit back her errant emotions and growled low in her throat as she stepped around a clustered group of them, doing her best to keep from plowing into them. They nodded and offered her subdued smiles she wasn't ready to return yet.

She simply pressed on, finding a tiny space she could make her own.

Unlike the *Paradigm*, designed to ferry goods and people, the Wyyvan leech ship was a compact craft with little in the way of extra space. The corridors were narrow and sleek, utilitarian and sparse, and Taj could see her people sprawled out into the distance, making the best of their limited accommodations.

She groaned and, not for the first time, questioned the wisdom of letting Vort talk her into squeezing everyone into the tiny ship. Though, she had to admit, it wasn't as if she'd had much of a choice.

That didn't make her any happier about it, the thought only fueling her frustration with the whole of the Wyyvan invaders.

Taj fought the urge to smash a fist into the hull. A little pain would bring her thoughts into sharp focus, but she didn't want her people to see her out of control. They needed her to be strong, and she'd be gacked if she'd lend Vort more space inside her head than he already occupied.

Besides, I don't want to break my gacking hand.

She spun around a moment later, once she'd sufficiently reined in her fury. She returned the muttered thanks of her people with a wave as she made her way back to the bridge.

Captain Vort grinned at her as she returned.

She redirected her desire to punch him in his smug face by asking him a question. "This tin can have a name?"

"A rough translation from our language to yours would be the *Discordant*," the captain told her, looking as if he'd caught a fly on his tongue, his smile so wide it threatened to split his green cheeks.

"Of course that's what it's called." Taj grunted and shook her head. *Couldn't it be something positive like* Sunflower *or the* Invincible? *The* We're gonna Whup Every Gacking Wyyvans' Ass in the Universe?

No such luck.

"Kal," she ordered, having had more than enough of the captain and his second in command, even though Dard hadn't said a word this entire time. "Find someplace to lock these two up. Someplace small and uncomfortable and smelly would be perfect. Feel free to hurt them a little if they give you grief." Taj sneered. Vort and Commander Dard felt her vehemence wash over them. "And escort S'thlor up here after you're done stashing these two gackpiles."

Captain Vort chuckled at that and offered a lazy bow as he relinquished the seat he'd claimed, sliding out of it casually as if he'd been invited to dinner. "I'll take this to mean you won't be thanking me for saving your lives, Furlorian?"

Taj growled at him. "Be glad we didn't leave you to the mercy of your people back on Krawlas or on the *Paradigm*. That's all the thanks you'll be getting, gack you very much, so I suggest you be grateful for it."

Captain Vort shrugged. "You'll need me again, no doubt," he said. "Maybe next time you'll appreciate my efforts. Perhaps I might even make you ask nicely before I acquiesce to rescuing your hide again."

"Get him out of here." Taj returned to the vacant captain's chair and turned her back on the alien. Much as she knew he'd saved their lives with his advice and knowledge, she couldn't find it in herself to thank him or even pretend the one selfish act evened out all the atrocities he'd committed against her people.

Not even close.

Too many good Furlorians had died for there to be any chance of her forgiving or forgetting.

Kal did as he was ordered and ushered the captain and Commander Dard off the bridge in a hurry, Jadie assisting him, her gun pointed at the captain to keep him in line. Taj had no doubt the queen would blast a hole in Vort if he so much as looked at her wrong.

He was smart not to. Taj doubted Jadie had a quarter of Taj's restraint, which wasn't saying much.

The door to the bridge still open, Taj could hear Vort's incessant laughter carry down the corridor for another few moments before the sound finally faded into blissful silence.

Then Torbon arrived to ruin it.

"This ship is weird!" he shouted, stomping onto the bridge ahead of Cabe. "There's, like, one big barracks-type room at the center of the ship, a small mess hall and kitchen next door, and a few tiny, private rooms scattered here and there, but the vast majority of the space is taken up by the umbilical boarding tubes, the systems that operate them and, surprisingly, a fairly robust weapons system. There's even a plasma torpedo launcher." He grinned like a little kid with a new toy. "But because of all that, folks are packed in tight everywhere. It's like a coffin ship in here."

Cabe, who'd arrived right after Torbon, smacked him in the back of the head with a resounding *thump*.

"Hey!" Torbon howled, spinning about, pawing at his skull. "What was that for?"

"Maybe you should take a moment before you speak and, I don't know, perhaps think about what kind of drivel is gonna come out your mouth before you actually say it," Cabe told him, casting a sideways glance outside the bridge at the throng of Furlorians sitting there, listening in.

"And deprive us of the brilliant witticisms that spill out so often?" Lina asked. "How dare you suggest that, Cabe."

"We don't have time for this," Taj snapped, her voice edging into a growl. She hated her impatience, the frustration that came out so easily, but there was nothing she could do to draw it back. "Please...focus on the task at hand, okay?"

"Which is?" Torbon asked.

That was a good question. One she wasn't completely sure she had the answer for. "We need someplace to go, a safe haven for our people, somewhere the Wyyvans can't reach us."

"That sounds great in theory," Cabe told her, shaking his head, "but really, how do we do that? It's not like we have a clue as to where we are. Gran Beaux and the others never properly charted the galaxy. We need to plot some coordinates and go from there first."

She hated that he questioned her yet loved it at the same time. She was doing her best to stay strong, to lead, but she needed to be pushed, helped to make a decision she had no idea how to make on her own, and he seemed to realize that. He was pressing for a much-needed discussion regarding their future. "We need to..."

She sighed inwardly as Jadie returned right then, interrupting the start of the discussion as she led the captive Wyyvan, S'thlor, onto the bridge. Taj was grateful for a moment to let her whirling mind settle. Torbon's aunt took the alien over to Lina and left him alone alongside the engineer. He stood there stiffly, the slits of his nose wiggling as he sniffed at the air, probably trying to determine where he was and who was there with him.

"We're gonna need your help, S'thlor," Taj told him. "We don't know your language and can't read the consoles."

S'thlor chuckled. "You do remember I'm blind, right?" He cast a wounded glance vaguely in her direction.

Taj sighed, knowing gacking well he was blind, having been the one to take his sight from him. She regretted her actions now that things had changed, unable to blame it entirely on the fog of war that precipitated it. "What if Lina describes the symbols to you? Can you translate them?" she asked, not wanting to dwell on the momentary loss of restraint that had led to the alien's crippling.

"I can certainly try," he answered without argument.

Taj offered him a nod, biting back a chuckle when she realized what she'd done. "Do that then, please, and show Cabe the basic flight controls so he can pilot the craft as we don't want to rely on that gackspittle Vort," she said, moving alongside Lina and the captive alien. "And get the bridge door closed, Lina. We need to discuss our situation without an unintended audience," she whispered to the engineer, motioning with her chin toward the people still lurking outside in the corridor.

S'thlor obliged her wishes and described the manner to seal the bridge off. And though he wasn't a pilot, he admitted to having some small training in the field as the Wyyvan military apparently embraced the concept of cross-training, preparing their warriors in case replacements were needed in the heart of battle.

At least minimally.

Still, for that, Taj was grateful.

The less she had to call on Captain Vort to help them overcome obstacles, the better.

Fortunately, she and the other Furlorians had gotten closer to S'thlor after the remaining Wyyvans had been defeated. While he held an ember of animosity for her crippling him, he had grudgingly admitted, had the circumstances been reversed, he might very well have done the same thing.

Or worse.

As such, he'd surrendered to the circumstances and had joined the Furlorians' cause rather than fight against it.

He'd told Taj early on, his people had little compassion for the fallen or captured, and they especially had no concern for a wounded soldier such as himself. He was a liability to them, and they would just as soon kill him as look at him. So, rather than surrender to the cruel fate his people would impose upon him, he'd chosen to side with the Furlorians.

In the months between the Wyyvan defeat and their brutal return, S'thlor had even become something of a friend to Taj and her people, offering them what assistance he could manage, entirely without restraint or demands for recompense.

Taj grinned at remembering his first awkward attempts at assimilating into their culture. It had been hard on him, she knew, but he never complained.

Well, he didn't complain *too* much.

His roughened voice broke Taj from her reverie, and she glanced over at the alien, blinking away her memories.

"I've set the door to be opened manually, so you can do it yourself from either side with a swipe of your hand. It limits privacy and security, but I'm guessing convenience is more what you're looking for right now," S'thlor stated, gesturing in the general direction of a small panel set alongside the door. "I've also simplified and isolated the pilot's station controls, allowing Cabe to fly the ship much like he would any other standard craft. His station will be limited to maneuvering functions, but he won't require knowledge of our language to execute basic flight. However, navigation, control of the gate drives, and basically any other function but the simplest of flight requirements will need to be handled by another console. As of now, that's this one." He motioned to the one Lina sat in front of. "I'm working on pushing similar protocols to the captain's console so you can override at any point necessary."

"Thank you," Taj muttered as the bridge door hissed shut. She exhaled in relief, glad to be out of sight of all the hopeful Furlorians hovering on the other side of the door, all of them watching her flail about in her attempt to command.

Now, alone with her crew and the captive alien they'd befriended, Cabe able to pilot the ship without Vort's help, she knew they needed to discuss their future plans. She could only imagine it'd be a matter of time before the Wyyvans they'd left behind realized what had happened in the battle sought out their stolen ship. The Furlorians needed to be long gone by then.

"So, what's the plan?" Torbon asked as if reading her mind.

"We need to find a sanctuary, someplace to go where we can start over, like I was saying before," she answered, but she still didn't know how to go about finding such a place.

Before the others could question her vague declaration, she gestured to Lina, thinking back on what Cabe had said moments before. "Figure out how to access the scanners and get us some idea as to where we are and what habitable planets there are nearby. Any history on them would be nice, too. As much as you can find." Given their complete lack of knowledge, anything would help. "We need reliable intel before we can make a reasonable decision."

Lina grunted an affirmative and went to work, chatting back and forth with S'thlor, calling out symbols and tapping away at the console in an attempt to become comfortable with it.

"What about the Federation S'thlor told us about?" Cabe asked, reminding her of a conversation they'd had in the few moments between preparing for the Wyyvan return and recovering from said preparations. "Would they be willing to take us in? Seems like a good choice, seeing how much they dislike our scaly lizard companions." He glanced at S'thlor. "Present company excluded, of course. No offense."

S'thlor chuckled. "Only a little taken," he admitted.

Cabe joined the alien in his amusement, the two laughing quietly along with one another.

Taj grunted. She had no idea how to answer Cabe's question, having spent little time discussing the Federation with S'thlor after his capture. They'd had other priorities, like preparing for the ground invasion of their planet that never happened. She'd spoken with Cabe about it more than she had S'thlor.

Still, it made sense that the enemy of their enemy could be an ally, but what did she know about the Federation and its mysterious leader, Bethany Anne, who Vort and his people hated and feared so much? Would she and her people be a friend or another enemy to contend with?

"S'thlor?" she asked.

"If you're asking me if they'll befriend you, I truthfully have no idea," he admitted. "We Wyyvans have been at war with them since the Federation stumbled upon and invaded our space, the circumstances of which being barbarous and savage as recounted by Command propaganda.

"My people aren't the most forgiving of folks, as I've said before, so my entire career, short as it's been, has been spent listening to stories about the evils of humans and their ilk. Nothing I know of them is good, and many of my fellow soldiers have died at their hands in our various skirmishes. They are a powerful force with no love for those who oppose them."

"Which means they're probably our best bet," Torbon said. "Anyone so despised by your people has to be on the right side in the grand scheme of things."

While his statement was tainted by more than a bit of wishful thinking, Taj felt herself agreeing with Torbon, if only in spirit. If nothing else, the Wyyvans appeared to fear the Federation enough to perhaps leave Taj and her people alone were they to find their way to a Federation stronghold. *That alone would be enough,* she thought. *We could make a new start with no fear of anyone hunting us down.*

"Can you set us on a course to a Federation planet or stronghold?" she asked S'thlor.

He shook his head. "Command kept us in the dark as far as intelligence went. Can't have the grunts knowing anything substantive," he replied. "I can tell you how best to approach a Federation soldier, what weapons to use to try and kill one, what their home world is called—Earth, by the way, strange name that—but we were never given much in the way of details regarding their whereabouts, and I've never run across them personally before the drubbing that crashed the *Monger* on your planet," he said. "Our job was to fight and die for our superiors when they demanded it, not to ask questions or hold opinions outside of those handed to us by Command." He shrugged. "In that respect, I was a good soldier."

"Sounds...sad," Lina muttered.

S'thlor nodded. "Perhaps, but it was better than a life spent in the Toradium mines, eking out a squalid existence until a shaft collapsed on top of you or you became too infirm to lift a pick or shovel." A shudder shook the alien's frame, a repressed memory clearly surfacing. "They simply left the useless to rot and wither away in the mines until death became a prize to be sought. The workers dug up almost as many bones in the process as they did the mineral."

Taj clasped the alien's shoulder and gave a gentle squeeze. It was obvious he spoke from experience, someone he knew suffering the cold fate he'd described. Someone close from the sounds of it.

"I'm sorry, S'thlor," she told him.

He drew in a slow, deep breath and nodded, clearly repressing the memory once again. "Such is the way of life for my people. At least those with no great lineage or financial inheritance to lean upon." S'thlor straightened and lifted his chin. "But all that is behind me now," he said, forcing a halfhearted smile. "And though I cannot direct you to the Federation or their holdings on Earth, or elsewhere for that matter, I *can* set us on a course toward where they are rumored to have first appeared in Wyyvan space.

"Perhaps that will lead us to their doorstep, or at least somewhere that might provide us with better information, though I fear you might well be exchanging one enemy for another given their violent reaction to my people. He shrugged. "Still, what do we have to lose? We all die eventually."

Taj spent a quiet moment contemplating the alien's words before coming to a decision. "Make it so," she called out, remembering some ancient, grainy holo-program Gran Beaux had shown her once. The old, bald human in the vid made the line sound so gacking cool.

"So, this is what we're doing?" Cabe asked after having been silent for a while, likely running their options on his own.

"Have a better idea? I'm all ears if you do," she answered, not wanting to push him, but she needed some kind of resolution then, even if it was illusory.

He grunted. "No, not really, but if S'thlor is right, we're not doing ourselves any favors by seeking these people out. We are flying a stolen Wyyvan ship, which isn't gonna earn us any friends out of the gate. What happens if they fire on us before we get a chance to explain who we are and why we're there?"

"We go poof!" Torbon said, grinning like an idiot.

Lina growled at him, and he hunkered down and shut up.

"The situation's hardly ideal," Taj admitted, ignoring Torbon's antics, "but we're not exactly spoiled for choice, Cabe. I would absolutely *love* another option."

"I understand, but the Federation could be as bad, if not worse, than the Wyyvan military," Cabe argued.

Taj agreed. "They very well could be, but we'll have to deal with that when the time comes," she told him, doubling down on the decision in her head because she had no other ideas to fall back on. "What other choices do we have? Seriously, we don't have any, Cabe. We don't know anyone we can run to, and we surely can't go back to Felinus 4." She felt her breath hitch in her lungs at remembering the holos Beaux had shown her of the days before the great migration to Krawlas.

The planet was a ruin, smoke so thick the air was black, only the flicker of weapons fire breaking through the gloom. Bodies lay everywhere, charred and decayed, left where they'd died for there were so few Furlorians left to bury them.

She didn't want to think of what Felinus 4 was like these days, the oppressing Xeron army roaming the streets, their mechanical forms near-impervious to harm. They'd pressed for genocide and had nearly achieved their goal. Only the Grans defiance and courage had kept that from happening.

Deep down, she didn't want to believe the Federation could be anywhere near as evil as Captain Vort or the Xeron were. No one could be.

The stories S'thlor had shared had been tainted by the bias of his people and the willful propaganda machine of their command structure. *Of course*, the Federation was the worst thing to ever come their way.

The Federation was winning the war between them and the Wyyvans from the sounds of it, killing and taking out

Wyyvan soldiers across their own empire with apparent ease. To the rank and file soldiers like S'thlor, those on the front lines seeing death day in and day out, the Federation could be nothing *but* evil. They'd killed friends, and likely family, but that didn't necessarily define them as the bad guys as far as Taj was concerned.

Victory was always steeped in blood. That didn't mean it wasn't necessary or just.

Still, she didn't know enough to make an informed decision, and that nagged at her, her worries prickling the hairs at her nape. She was responsible for her people's welfare, for their safety, and here she was, leading them into the unknown with nothing more than the hope that things would turn out okay, that her people would be safe. It was hardly an ideal situation.

She needed to know more before they were too far along to turn back.

"Set the course S'thlor suggests, Lina," she told the engineer and strolled toward the bridge door. "Contact me over the comm should there be any developments."

"And where are you going?" Cabe asked.

"To beat some answers out of a smug lizard," she replied, storming for the door.

"Ask him if he has any nip while you're there," Cabe called out as the door hissed shut behind her.

CHAPTER FIVE

Taj tracked down Kal and found where the captain and commander had been locked away. She chuckled as she realized where her fellow Furlorian had secured the two aliens.

"A janitorial closet?" she asked.

Kal shrugged. "It was this or a latrine, but I figured that was too important to block off with gack like these two, no matter how fitting it might have been." Jadie giggled behind him. "Imagine the torment of us using the facilities with them locked in there with us?"

Taj grinned. She very well could imagine it.

Kal triggered the door locks, and Taj handed him her weapon before stepping inside the dimly lit room, if it could be called that. Little more than a tiny square, stretching two meters in each direction, the closet was barely big enough for the two aliens to sit casually without intruding upon each other's space. Their tails were bent crooked, twisted about their waists and curled in their laps to keep them contained in the tight space.

The door hissed behind her, and Taj felt a pang of guilt at the tiny confines but pushed it away. Neither of these Wyyvan deserved her pity or concern. They had killed a number of her people in cold blood, used them as leverage against the rest of the Furlorians, and the only reason the two lizards hadn't been shot into the cold blackness of space was because Taj felt she could use them to her advantage.

For now.

They had been the architects of Krawlas's fall, and as soon as they had been exhausted as resources, Taj would personally see them dealt with. Though, admittedly, she wasn't entirely sure what she'd do. She knew what she wanted to, but recurring bouts of compassion kept tripping her up.

No matter how angry she was, how disgusted at their actions, she wasn't a cold-blooded killer, no matter how much the two deserved to die.

I might have to reassess my stance, though, she thought as Vort grinned at her.

"Hello, Furlorian," Captain Vort said, still as smug as he'd always been despite his confinement. "I didn't expect to see you so soon after you kicked us off the bridge." He turned to the commander. "I wonder, Dard, could she perhaps *need* something from us? Why else would she be here?"

"Hmmm," Dard replied, rubbing his chin. "I also wonder. It's boggling. Perhaps we should ask."

"Cut the gack, you two," Taj said. "This isn't a game."

"I wouldn't be so certain," Vort replied, offering a toothy grin. "Games take on many forms. Some are fun and frivolous, some are far more dastardly, ominous. Dangerous even."

Taj wanted to knock his teeth from his mouth but managed to resist the temptation once again. She couldn't fathom where she'd found the restraint.

Not wanting to lose her temper, she got right to the point. The less time she spent with the aliens, the better. "Tell me about the Federation."

"Ah, so you *do* need something," Vort said, his grin growing even wider as he cast a glance Dard's direction before looking back to Taj. "I like when I'm right. It's quite the satisfying feeling, I have to admit."

Taj reached for her bolt pistol, remembering as her hand clawed at an empty holster that she'd given it to Kal for safekeeping. She bit back a groan at her decision. "We're in this together, Captain, so whether you like it or not, the safety of this ship and my people is as much a priority for you as it is for me."

"I beg to differ, Furlorian." He waggled a thick finger her direction. His tail slapped the floor. "My priority is only to keep myself and my commander alive. Directing you to the Federation hardly accomplishes that goal. Quite the opposite, in fact, especially seeing how we're stuck with you for the foreseeable future. There is no happy ending for either of us if you are serious about reaching out to the Federation. As such, you can expect no assistance from me in that regards."

Taj leaned in, growling in his face. "You think the

Federation will do anything worse to you than your own people will if they catch us?"

He shrugged. "I've no certainty of anything save that whoever gets their hands on me, I'm going to regret it. I simply know too much to be pacified and cast aside by either side without enduring a long, uncomfortable stay in one of their prisons. As such, I see no reason to cooperate with you beyond what is reasonable to keep us both hale and healthy." He motioned to Dard, indicating he meant the commander and him not Taj. "The sooner you realize that, the better."

She wondered what she could do to make Vort talk, knowing full well she didn't have it in her to torture him. Even worse, she hated the idea of bargaining with the alien captain, giving in to him in any way at all, but it looked as if that was what it might come down to exactly that if she wanted his assistance again. But what did she have to offer him? Better still, what was she *willing* to offer for the information he held buried in his head?

Not much, she thought. *Not much at all.*

For all his help, Vort was still the enemy, tried and true. No matter what he did to assist her, his intentions were always slanted in his own favor. Nothing he did was altruistic. His end goal was only to survive, and he'd do anything he could to make that happen, which meant any information he provided willingly was suspect as it would be geared toward his own advantage.

She would never be able to trust it fully.

All she could do was bluster and bluff. "Tell me what I want to know or I'll eject you through the sewage vent and you'll no longer have to worry about what side gets their hands on you."

"No, you won't," Vort replied with a chuckle, daring her to follow through. "You need me too much to kill me, as we've already established."

"We don't *need* you," Taj shouted, spittle flying. "We have S'thlor to help us."

The captain clutched his belly, letting loose a barking laugh that echoed inside the tiny closet. "Oh yes, the blind grunt is your savior, clearly." Vort clambered to his feet, grinning as he towered over Taj. "Were that even remotely true, you wouldn't be here, begging me for my assistance, now would you?"

He poked a finger into her shoulder, a stab of pain shooting through the muscle. "You know quite well his knowledge is restrained to little more than rumor and gossip and the basest of technical information, Furlorian, or you would have left us to die on your pitiful little planet. We're still alive because you're lost in uncertain space, in an enemy ship you have no idea how to pilot, and you have no idea where to go next, and your little pet alien can't help you beyond the most rudimentary of tasks. You *need* someone more capable." He lifted his chin and patted his chest. "That someone is me."

Taj sneered, baring her teeth, but she couldn't help but hate the fact that he was right. Again.

"There is so much you don't know, Furlorian, but there is much I *do* know." Vort dropped to a seat once more, his vile grin lighting up the room. "Treat us well, and I'll share my knowledge with you and, perhaps, we'll both see our way out of the jam we currently find ourselves in. If not, then myself and Commander Dard here are no worse off than we were before, and you are no better off."

That was when Taj had had enough.

She clenched her hand into a fist and lashed out, driving her knuckles into Vort's mouth with a satisfying *crunch.*

The captain's head whiplashed back, striking the wall, setting his eyes to whirling. He hissed and reached to clasp his aching head. A trail of blood trickled down his lip and across his chin.

The commander went to clamber to his feet, but Taj warned him off with a low growl that seemed to emanate from deep inside her. "Don't even think about it, Dard. I'll have Kal and Jadie come in here and blow a few of your less useful pieces off if you even think about standing up again."

Dard glared at her a moment, caught halfway between standing and sitting, then he dropped back down.

Vort licked his lips, drawing the rivulet of blood into his mouth, staining his tongue red. "Ah, so you do have some fire in you after all, Furlorian," he said, his grin returning to his swollen lips.

Taj was glad to see the smile didn't come naturally.

"I've more fire than you can withstand, lizard," she snapped back. "Whatever leverage you think you have, be warned it isn't near as much as you need to manipulate me." She spit at his feet. "Touch me again, Vort, and you'll find out just how willing I am to move ahead without you or your assistance."

Having had all she could take of the arrogant alien, she spun on her heel and slammed her fist into the door. It hissed open a moment later, and she stormed outside, ignoring the sting in her knuckles while the captain's forced laughter followed her.

Jadie shut the door to silence Vort while Kal stared at Taj with eyes as wide as saucers. She grabbed her pistol from him and marched off, not saying a word to either of them.

She realized then that, despite Vort being a hostage, stripped of his ship and his army and all the things that made him dangerous, he still held all the cards.

Sadly, both Taj *and* he knew it.

"Why do you provoke her like that?" Dard asked the captain after the Furlorian had stormed off.

Vort grinned, dabbing at his wounded lip. "She's no commander, no soldier, trained and taught to do what she must. The Furlorian is a child, nothing more. She is weak, uncertain, and the more I press her, the more she is likely to make the wrong choice."

"I fail to see how flustering her and causing indecision benefits us." Dard motioned to Vort's face. "It seems she is more than willing to reply in kind to your pressing her."

"This?" He shook his head. "This is nothing, a temper tantrum," he explained. "The more she fails in her quest to rescue her people, the greater the mistrust sown between her and her crew," Vort answered. "If she's getting Furlorians killed with her rash and ignorant decisions, she will be forced to deal with us, to cooperate in order to avoid further deaths. And even if her pride gets in the way of her doing so, her crew will force the issue eventually, which provides us with more opportunities for our eventual escape." Captain Vort jabbed a finger toward the commander. "She needs us, Dard. She needs only to realize that."

"And again, I'm not sure how that benefits us if her goal is to reach the Federation," Dard said.

"That may well be *her* goal, but it isn't ours, clearly," Vort replied. "S'thlor knows nothing and can lead them nowhere. Better still, my convincing them to abandon their freighter and flee in this leech ship only compounded their issues."

"How so?"

"There was no time for the Furlorians to organize an intelligent retreat from Krawlas or transfer between ships, my dear Commander," the captain told him, smiling all the while. "What supplies and Toradium-42 they had stored away on the freighter are now so much as space dust behind us, and this—" He motioned toward the leech ship as a whole. "—is a short-range craft dependent upon the fleet for its needs, most importantly of which is food." A crooked grin played across his tender green lips. "It won't be long until our Furlorian keeper must set down to resupply or watch her people starve. That provides us with the first of our opportunities."

Dard swallowed hard and met the captain's cold gaze. "Are you forgetting something, Captain? The tracker?" he asked. "There's no way these creatures have realized it's there or disabled it. Once the ship alights, our people will hone in on it and will come to reclaim the craft, having realized their prey has escaped them. Grand Admiral Galforin will not let such disrespect stand."

Vort shook his head. "That's exactly what I'm hoping for, Commander."

"But—"

The captain waved his second to silence. "Our dear Galforin will not spare a contingent to capture a rogue leech ship or a few escaped Furlorians, Commander, no matter how wounded his ego is. Not with the treasure trove of Toradium-42 splayed out before him on Krawlas. That will be his focus. He will task a local scout ship, or two at most, to do the deed, but he will not divert his resources from the mining operation that stands to make him the most important man on Belor Prime."

Vort bit back a growl at saying the words.

Had things worked as planned, Vort would have been the most important man on his home world, not the conniving admiral. But the worthless rodents bested him, all because he couldn't imagine them being his equal, being able to defeat him. How wrong he'd been.

Fury roiled inside, and he clasped his gut as it rumbled with displeasure, teeth grinding so hard his jaw ached where the girl had struck him. He'd allowed the Furlorians to win out because he'd underestimated them. Now, he and Commander Dard were trapped on a stolen leech craft with enemies on all sides, and it rankled.

Vort swore he'd not make the same mistake again. He'd make the Furlorian scum pay for this indignity and all they'd cost him, especially the Taj rodent for having dared to strike him.

"Still, there's a chance the recovery crew accomplishes their goal and defeats the Furlorians," Dard said. "What then?"

"It won't happen so easily as that," Vort assured his second. "Either the opportunity to escape and disappear in a newly empty Wyyvan craft presents itself or we make ourselves even more useful by helping the Furlorians extricate themselves from the situation and await the next opportunity to take advantage of." Vort spread his hands magnanimously. "Regardless, we will have options. Soon enough, we will be free, and then..." His voice faded as a broad smile spread across his features.

Dard stiffened, one eye widening to encourage Vort to go on. "And then?"

"And then, we figure out a way to repay Grand Admiral Galforin for his betrayal and reclaim our stake on Krawlas."

"And the Furlorians? What about them?"

Vort shrugged. "If they all die in the process of our escape, I won't mourn them."

CHAPTER SIX

Taj sat in her confiscated captain's chair, glaring at the view screen splayed out before her. The lack of comprehension as to the language everything was in frustrated her to no end.

At least she had the memory of punching Vort in his face to cheer her up.

While she'd been gone, the crew had moved a chair over for S'thlor so he could be near Lina and strapped him in to be safe, letting the two confer back and forth, a constant, muttered chatter filling the room. To her credit, Lina was a quick study, and she picked up much of what S'thlor taught her as they went along, but there was no substituting true knowledge for the bandage that was the alien's technical and linguistic advice.

He barely knew anything as it was, and the fact that he was passing that basic information on to Lina wasn't much of a confidence builder as far as Taj was concerned. They were flying through the middle of nowhere, in a ship packed with way more people than it was designed to hold or support. If they ran into trouble before they reached a safe location, it was a certainty that people would be hurt because there was simply no way to avoid it.

They couldn't secure everyone in reinforced areas, and Taj had begun to realize that that had been part of Captain Vort's plans when he'd tricked them onto the *Discordant* and blasted the *Paradigm* out from under them.

He meant for them to be cramped aboard this tiny craft, uncomfortable, awkward, all of which helped to sow her people's frustration with Taj, the supposed *leader* who convinced them all that this was what they needed to do to survive. And though no one had yet to approach her about it, she could see it in the eyes of her crew and the people crowded in the hallways, and that was pissing her off.

They were beginning to doubt her already, to question her decisions in their heads, and she wondered how long it would take before they started to voice their concerns. She didn't figure it would be long given how uncomfortable everyone was already.

She snarled, not looking forward to that moment but seeing it approach ever-faster as the bridge door hissed open and Torbon walked inside, shaking his head in a way that could only mean bad news. She'd known it would be before she'd sent him off to scour the ship's resources.

He cast a furtive glance over his shoulder and waited until the door sealed before saying anything. "It's like you thought, Taj. The stores onboard are sparse to the point of ridiculousness. This ship wasn't designed to support its people for long. There's barely enough food to last until the end of the week, *if* we ration strictly. A *lot* of people are

gonna go hungry if this journey takes any longer than that."
He glanced around surreptitiously, finally looking back at
Taj. "And don't tell Cabe, but there's not a hint of nip
anywhere to be found on this tub." He chuckled. "Nor is
there any contraband. These lizards might as well be
hermits."

Taj let her head loll back and *thump* against the headrest
of her seat. In her rush to get her people to safety, she
hadn't even thought about the supplies she'd left behind on
the *Paradigm*. Her concern had been bodies, getting them
onboard and getting them out of danger, keeping them
from being gunned down. She hadn't once remembered
the food or fuel stores or the stash of Toradium-42 she'd
packed aboard the freighter in case the Wyyvans did something she hadn't predicted.

And they had done exactly that, only it was something
even more unexpected than Taj could have imagined.
Leveling the planet started the cascade of surprises.

She had underestimated their ruthlessness and lack of
concern for their fellow soldiers, and the fleeing Furlorians
were paying for it now.

Worse still, she had let the chaos and terror dictate her
decisions. She'd given in and allowed Vort to direct her
actions, and though they'd been right in the end, in the
general scheme of things, she'd let him manipulate her into
being a fool.

And that was all on her, which only pissed her off more.

Her people now faced a real threat of starvation and no
guarantees of finding a source of food or the means to
procure it.

She needed to rectify that immediately.

"Gack!" she shouted, slamming her fists into the armrests. "We need a populated planet or space station if we hope to resupply." She spun her chair to face Lina. "Can you find us one closer than S'thlor's estimated coordinates?"

"I can try, but we've already got issues," Lina answered, and Taj could see the uncertainty etched into the engineer's features. "Neither me nor S'thlor know exactly where we are in reference to Wyyvan space currently, the *Monger*'s crash and subsequent panic having disoriented him, and we have no clue what's between here and the border where the Federation first appeared." She shrugged, her tail wiggling over her shoulder in irritation. "Scanners are picking up the gate the *Monger* used to get to Krawlas, but I can't read anything beyond it because of the limited scope of this ship's functions."

"It's likely the only chance we have of finding a populated planet is to use the gate," S'thlor told the crew. "This sector, as you well know, is mostly barren, Krawlas being the exception, apparently the only habitable planet. It leaves us little in the way of navigational beacons, making it nigh impossible to set an accurate course no matter what coordinates I recall."

Taj ground her teeth together, tightening her grip on her seat. Beaux and the others had chosen the galaxy for exactly those reasons: its sparseness and distance from populated neighbors. It had kept them alive all this time. Now, that same distance was going to kill them if they let it.

Taj would face Rowl before she let that happen.

"Make for the gate, and let's see what the gack is

waiting for us out there," Taj ordered, believing there to be no other option. *We can figure things out from there,* she thought, refusing to voice her concerns aloud. The crew had enough disappointments to deal with already.

There was no certainty of what lay ahead, but she knew exactly what lay behind so there would be no turning around. As such, there was nothing she could do but trust they were doing the right thing and hope things worked out for the best.

She'd sent her people into space with her decisions, and now there was nothing left to do but carry on and see what opportunities presented themselves to fix everything before it was too late.

A ragged chuckle rose unbidden in her throat, the inner voice of logic and reason sneaking out and scoffing at her. It was just one more thing tugging at her fur.

They needed food and fuel and maybe even a larger ship, but Taj knew all that was yet another challenge given their lack of resources. They had no money and nothing to barter with. The truth was, wherever they ended up, she suspected it would be their final destination.

They would have to sell the *Discordant* for a pittance, since it'd be clear it was stolen, and wouldn't get its full value. She couldn't hope to make much more from the sale than barely enough to set her people up someplace on the planet and maybe start new lives.

But life was life. As long as a Furlorian survived, then the Wyyvans failed.

Taj straightened in her seat, spinning back around to face the view screen. She met the eyes of her crew as she did, offering each a nod in turn.

They would make it. They had to.

Bloody Rowl! Mama Merr and Beaux had led their people across the vastness of space in their escape from Felinus 4, and Taj was sure she could do the same.

The Grans hadn't let their emotions get in the way of what needed to be done, and Taj swore right then to follow their examples. She would see her people to safety if it was the last thing she ever did.

She hopped up and headed for the exit, feeling her adrenaline finally tapering off. The bridge door eased open as she waved her hand over the control pad—Taj was glad S'thlor could accommodate that, at least—and she paused at its threshold, feeling the stares of her crew on her back.

She knew she needed to tell them something, that she couldn't storm off and leave them to wonder what she was thinking or they'd feed into despair and maybe think she was abandoning them.

That wasn't the case at all.

"Let me know as soon as we pass through the gate and scanners pick up a suitable planet for us to stop off at," she told them.

"What are you gonna do until then?" Cabe asked, his gaze seeking hers.

"I'm gonna try to get some sleep," she answered, stifling a yawn. "After that, we'll find us a new home." Taj offered him a genuine smile, glad that, despite it all, she could still find some happiness to project after all the anger and frustration.

"Maybe you can join me later," she said quietly, not giving him a chance to reply before she swept out the door.

Her grin beamed even brighter.

CHAPTER SEVEN

The shriek of alarms tore Taj from her slumber.

She bolted upright, eyes wide, heart pounding against her ribs, unsure how much of her swirling brain was due to the dream and how much was reality. The tiny room she'd curled up in was bathed in crimson, casting ugly shadows over the walls.

She rubbed her temples, causing the shadows to dance in her bleary vision. The communicator on the bedside table barked static, and Taj snatched it up, slipping it into her ear. Lina's mechanical-sounding voice cut through a moment later.

"Need you on the bridge, Taj," Lina said. "We've got trouble."

"Of course we do," Taj muttered, crawling out of bed and wiping the sleep from her eyes. "Be right there." She muted the comm and growled. "Gack, gacking, gackity-gack," she spit out, stuffing her feet into her boots as quickly as she could manage. "So much for sleep."

She'd slept fully clothed, expectant of trouble, and she regretted it now. Her uniform was twisted and damp from sweat, her tiny cabin uncomfortable since the life support hadn't been adjusted to accommodate the Furlorians yet.

She imagined she stunk nicely, but she couldn't be bothered to check, though she was half-tempted to pay Vort a visit and force her stench upon him.

Maybe even give the gackpuddle a big hug.

She chuckled at the image and fought the urge to do exactly that.

Instead, she finished getting her boots on and stomped from the room, ignoring the pins and needles assailing her right foot. She'd apparently slept on it funny, but there wasn't time to worry about it now.

"At least one of us slept well," she complained, wrangling her foot in line as she marched on, offering it no respite.

She stepped out into the hall and had to immediately dodge a number of Furlorians who'd made their *home* outside the door. "Sorry," she muttered, adjusting her awkward movement to keep from stepping on anyone. Once she was through the obstacle course of survivors and had a clear path where no one could overhear her, she triggered her comm.

"Shut that gacking alarm off, will you, Lina? I can't hear myself think."

The sound reverberated in her ears until her brain rattled, then it went mercifully silent. She breathed a grateful sigh and followed the gleaming red lights down the corridor, once more dodging wide-eyed Furlorians until she reached the bridge. The door was already open when she got there.

"What's going on?" she asked, her mind struggling to parse the images flashing across the view screen. "Is that—" Bursts of blue and green seared her vision, mixing with the strobing red coloring the bridge.

Cabe cut her off as he ushered her to her seat. She plopped into it as he answered, a little out of breath, his excitement clear in the wrinkled lines of his face, his pinned whiskers. "We received a distress call moments ago," he said, pointing a clawed finger at the screen. "Those two ships are assaulting that battered freighter. Doesn't look like it's gonna last much longer at this rate. It doesn't even look armed."

"Pirates?" Taj asked, leaning toward the view screen to get a better look.

"Not sure it matters," Cabe replied with a shrug.

No, I guess it doesn't, she thought.

Regardless what they were, it wasn't like she was prepared to go to war against a random enemy whose capabilities were a complete mystery to her. Gack, for that matter, her own capabilities were nearly as unclear.

She knew the *Discordant* had weaponry, as she'd watched Vort light up the *Paradigm* with them, but how effective they'd be in a fight, she had no clue. Even more concerning was her uncertainty as to her and the crew's effectiveness in combat like this. Despite all they'd been through on Krawlas, all the simulations they'd been made to run by Beaux, none of them had ever been in a space battle.

"What do you want us to do?" Lina asked. The engineer

hunched over her console, and S'thlor clasped his seat arms, the ragged scars about his eyes stretching as she imagined him trying to see what was going on.

"Run away?" Torbon volunteered from his seat, offering a shrug when they glanced his way. "What? I'm only saying what everyone is thinking."

Taj grunted. "That's actually not what I was thinking," she answered.

"I kind of was," S'thlor admitted.

"Oh, gack," Torbon mumbled. "You're not thinking about engaging them, are you?"

"We've been looking for some kind of opportunity, right?" She gestured toward the view screen. "Here's one right before us."

"An opportunity to die?" Torbon countered.

"Rowl, Torbon, everything we'd done since the Wyyvans showed up has put us at a risk of dying. This...this right here could be the key to the door of our future."

"Affirmation much?" he asked, shaking his head. "You sound like a gacking propaganda poster. See the stars, battle aliens, live a life of adventure...and die miserably."

Lina chuckled. "Not that that isn't an excellent recruitment slogan, I don't think you're looking at this the right way."

"Two enemy ships on one?" he replied. "I'm thinking I'm looking at it the only way we should be."

"Is there anyone alive on that freighter?" Taj asked, waving Torbon to silence.

"Can't tell," Lina replied. "Scanners are detecting living beings in the area, but with the closeness of the pirates, or whatever those little ships are, it's distorting the *Discordant*'s readings."

"These leech crafts suffer from both clarity and power when it comes to their scanning systems," S'thlor volunteered. "They rely on the supporting fleet for intel and tactical advice and are used largely as battering rams after all the command decisions have been made. None of the systems aboard are overly advanced, though they are quite fast and resilient. It's a reasonable trade-off given what they're meant to do: be cannon fodder."

"How wonderfully convenient," Taj said, imagining Captain Vort snickering in his makeshift cell as his plan to limit Taj's options played out perfectly.

Gack him! She'd prove him wrong.

She contemplated their options. The smart thing would be to turn tail and run as Torbon suggested, leave the distressed freighter to its unfortunate fate.

But she wouldn't do that.

"Raise shields and ready the weapons," she commanded. "We fought off a gacking army of Wyyvans back on Krawlas, so I'm sure we can blast a few pirates into space dust."

Cabe caught her eye and winked, and Taj bit back the flush of excitement that washed over as she made ready to charge into battle.

"Want me to get Vort?" Torbon asked.

"Not unless you plan to load him in a torpedo tube and fire him at the enemy ships," Taj told him.

"That's an option? Would have been nice to know that earlier," Cabe said.

Taj actually considered it a moment before shaking her

head. "I wish it was," she replied, doing her best to wipe the image of Captain Vort hurtling through space out of her mind.

She was already smiling.

"Torbon, get everyone settled somewhere safe, then hunker down with them until this is over."

Torbon unsnapped his restraints and leapt to his feet. "You sure about this?"

"I *hate* that question," she barked, baring her teeth. "Just do it...*please.*" She added the last to soothe the hurt look on his face that appeared after she had snapped at him, his whiskers laid back against his cheeks.

She was determined to see this through to the end. There was no way she could sit back and watch more people die, especially after all her people had endured. If she could save a few lives on the way toward their new ones, that was what she was going to do.

"Go, please. Do as I said," she repeated, and Torbon nodded. He shot through the door, his voice echoing down the halls as he shouted for the assembled Furlorians to follow him.

"Another distress signal coming through," Lina called out. "This one's clearer."

"Put it through." Taj growled as soon as the voice came across the speakers. The worry, the fear of the assaulted ship's crew member came echoed clearly through the comm.

It only reinforced Taj's decision to lash out at the pirates.

"This is the NVS *Prospect*! We are under attack by two unknown hostile crafts. We are an unarmed science vessel on a mission of peace on our way to the Voloran Galaxy under a flag of—" A rumbling explosion sounded in the background, cutting the desperate woman off, followed by a burst of screeching static. The signal dropped right after.

"Rowl!" Knuckles popped as Taj clenched her hands into fists. "We need to stop this, now. Are the weapon systems ready?"

"The guns are raring to go, but I'm not so sure about the gunner," Lina answered. Her voice was ragged, forced, sounding much like the occupant of the imperiled freighter than her usual self. The distress signal had clearly flagged her confidence.

Taj glanced to the engineer's station to see her trembling hands hovering over the console. Taj offered her a confident nod, hoping it conveyed her understanding of Lina's situation, but they had to act.

S'thlor offered quiet reassurances to Lina at the same time.

They were all nervous. It made sense. They'd only recently escaped their home planet, and now they found themselves about to engage in a fight for no reason other than it seemed the right thing to do.

Gacking morals. Thanks, Mama.

She glanced back to the view screen as the two pirate ships closed on their prey. Any further hesitation would see the occupants of the freighter die a miserable death.

"You're gonna have to deal with your reservations later, Lina," Taj pressed the engineer. "Take them out!"

The leech ship shot forward at Cabe's behest, the nose veering toward the engines of the rearmost pirate craft. Lina was only an instant behind him, to Taj's relief.

The engineer triggered the guns and sent searing bursts of energy toward the enemy craft. Taj held her breath as the blasts tore through the weaker shields near the rear of the craft—their focus on the ship in front of them—and scorched great black holes in the armored hull.

One of the pirate ship's engines sparked and flared out, and the ship began to list to starboard, its pilot clearly unprepared to counter the sudden loss of one of the ship's engines due to a sneak attack. Debris billowed out behind the ship as it drifted off course.

Another alarm rang across the bridge, but Taj ignored it, knowing it likely meant they were being targeted by the wounded pirate craft as it struggled to respond in kind. Beaux's voice echoed in her head, and she remembered one of the many lessons he'd given in an attempt to prepare her for exactly these circumstances.

"Hit them again!" she shouted, agreeing with Beaux's memory that overwhelming offense was always the best defense. "Hit them hard and don't give them a chance to fire back!"

Lina did exactly that, her confidence visibly growing as the moments passed.

More cannon fire rained down upon the wounded pirate ship, peppering the hull and tearing through its defenses as it struggled to shift its shields into the best position to repel damage.

Lina didn't give them the chance.

Behind the barrage of strafing energy blasts, she launched a plasma torpedo, S'thlor talking her through the process, his voice smooth and even.

Taj watched as the coffin-shaped missile hurtled

through the intervening space. It struck the pirate ship dead center and exploded, ripping through the armored hull. A flash of light momentarily blinded her before the view screen adjusted to its brightness. When she could see again, a massive, smoking crater now resided where the bulk of the ragtag pirate ship used to be.

Its other engine flared and burned out as the ship vented its atmosphere and cracked in half, the image ominously strange in the silence of space. The backside of the two pieces crumpled in upon itself, and the craft began to tumble, spewing oxygen acting as a makeshift engine they couldn't control.

The ship spun, end over broken end, its previous momentum usurped by the explosion and Lina's continued cannon fire.

The second pirate ship, obviously seeing its compatriot falling lifeless alongside its port side, broke off its attack on the science craft and came about, streaking toward the *Discordant*, ready to engage the more dangerous foe.

"Well, we have their attention now," Cabe muttered. "That's what you wanted, right?"

"Gacking right," Taj called out, resisting the urge to whoop. "Let's send them to join their friends."

The second pirate ship streaked toward them, its guns unloading first. The *Discordant*'s shields flared at the impacts, Lina having reinforced them on the port side. Despite that, the bridge trembled, and Taj saw red warning lights flickering on her console.

"I'm really starting to hate the color red," she complained. "How are the shields holding up?"

"She can take it," S'thlor announced. "For a time, at least."

"Optimism at its finest," Taj grunted as the pirate ship closed. "Can you turn us so we're facing them, Cabe?"

"We're too close to the wreck for my liking to do that. This guy's pushing us like a bully, keeping us broadside," Cabe answered. "We need some distance between us so he doesn't punch our shields. I'm initiating evasive maneuvers."

"About gacking time," Lina told him. "I was beginning to think you were trying to win the most damaged ship competition."

He snarled at her and started to respond, but Taj cut him off with a savage hiss.

"Wait!" she ordered. "Hold your course a moment longer."

She stared at the view screen, contemplating the intercept vector the pirate ship had plotted as an idea came to her.

"Seriously?" Cabe and Lina asked at the same time.

"I never thought I'd say this," S'thlor said, sinking lower in his chair, "but I'm glad I can't see what's going on right now."

"Take us right toward the wreckage of the first ship," Taj commanded a split-second later. "Straight at it. Don't deviate."

"You do realize that running headlong into another spaceship, no matter how broken it might be, has only one result, right? Us being splattered across its hull."

"That's what I'm picturing," she replied. "Sort of."

S'thlor grunted. "And here I thought she was on your side."

"Keep the shields at full all around, Lina, and be ready at my command."

"I'm not liking this," Cabe mumbled.

"You don't have to like it," Taj told him, "just be ready to do what I tell you, no hesitation."

He snarled as more cannon fire rattled the *Discordant*, hammering its shields as he followed Taj's order. The junked pirate ship loomed large in the view screen every passing second. They were so close that Taj could almost read the hull markings that had been scoured of color to mask its identity.

"Hold course!" she called out. "Hold it!"

"The only thing I want to hold right now is my ass," Cabe replied, his eyes narrowing as the wreckage drew even closer. Yet, despite his complaints, he stayed on course.

The second pirate ship wasn't much farther away than the first, and Taj felt each and every blast it fired as the *Discordant*'s shields began to buckle under the assault as it closed on them. The hull trembled, a low vibration traveling through the hull.

"Shields are flickering," Lina called out.

"Sometime soon would be wonderful," Cabe muttered. "We're getting awful close to that junker, Taj. I mean, *splat* close."

Taj held her tongue, watching the ruined ship draw ever nearer. It wasn't until it was a gray blur stretched across the view screen, its shape unidentifiable, that she felt ready to reveal her true plan behind the strange maneuver.

"Now!" Taj shouted. "Dive and take us under the wreck."

Cabe didn't waste any time following her orders. The *Discordant* dipped and barely avoided colliding with the ruin of the pirate ship, pieces of the wreck thundering against the shields and kicking off sparks that died as soon as they burst alive.

The pirate ship's scarred and scorched hull blocked the whole of the view screen as they darted underneath, the ruin testing the limits of the shields right above their heads.

Taj let out the breath she'd been holding. She'd been counting on the leech craft to be maneuverable enough to pull off what she'd planned, but the reality of the move drove her stomach into her throat.

The second pirate ship, too far above the Discordant to mimic its maneuver safely, shot upward to avoid the wreck of its companion. The two clashed silently, the pursuing pirate ship barely managing to redirect so that the impact did little harm save hammer its shields into near oblivion and send a ripple of warped metal down the length of the ship's lower hull.

Though Taj had hoped the two would crash into each other dead on, that being what she envisioned, she was still happy to see the pilot had been forced to pull back hard on the throttle and kill all the enemy ship's forward momentum.

"Now climb," she shouted as they cleared the wreck,

barely able to get the words out. "Straight up! Bring us around over top of the wreck."

The ship responded perfectly to Cabe's touch, with none of the *Thorn*'s hesitance, and the *Discordant* changed direction and circled the far edge of the burnt-out pirate ship. The other ship, having only just avoided being a bug on the view screen of its dead companion, did the best it could to regain thrust and turn to meet the Furlorians.

Taj saw the enemy ship's shields flicker, moving to deflect the angle it was most likely the *Discordant* would hit them from.

That played directly into Taj's plan.

Before they had cleared the husk of the first pirate ship, its broken frame still between them and the other pirate, Taj shouted, "Blast the wreck full-on in its side, Lina!"

And while Taj could tell Lina hadn't realized what Taj was going for, she did as she was told. The *Discordant*'s cannons opened up, slamming into the unshielded lump of the ruined pirate ship to brutal effect.

"I have no idea what you're trying to—" Lina started, then her eyes popped wide as realization clearly hit home. "Oh!"

"Oh indeed," Taj answered, grinning.

"Whoa!" Cabe muttered, eyes wide.

The wreck shifted under the force of the *Discordant*'s weapons, spinning about. Its fellow pirate ship, focused on redirecting its course and readying for the *Discordant* to appear above it, found itself directly in the path of the wreckage.

No chance to veer off or redirect its shields, already

committed, the remaining pirate ship could do nothing but hold its position. The ships crashed into one other. Their hulls crumpled with the impact, metal shredding as the broken husk folded its companion nearly in half in a fatal hug.

The *Discordant* shot up and over the destruction as the two craft, now forever entangled as a wad of twisted steel, spewed and spun away into the distance, trailing debris.

A muffled distress call echoed through the comms, panic in the voice, but Taj only grinned in response.

The beings on those two craft had gotten nothing less than they deserved. She had no pity for them.

"Are we still alive?" S'thlor asked.

"I'll let you know once my heart stops trying to strangle me," Lina told him, and she slumped into her chair, exhaling hard, her head lolling back against the headrest.

"Bring us around and scan the freighter," Taj ordered, not wasting a moment in celebration or reflection. "The pirate ships should be far enough away now to get a better reading, right?"

"I think so," Lina replied as Cabe changed course and angled the *Discordant* toward the listing science ship. "Scanning now."

Taj sank into her seat as the rest of the crew focused on the task at hand. She let the adrenaline run riot through her veins, closing her eyes and reveling in the feel. It was intoxicating.

Scared as she had been when they'd first engaged, it didn't take long for the thrill of combat to win over and wash away lingering misgivings. While she still held some residual doubt in training, her lack of experience a concern, she couldn't help but feel she was born for this.

"I'm picking up a lifeform," Lina announced.

Taj straightened and opened her eyes. "That's great. How many?"

"Uh, *a* lifeform."

"Wait! Only one?" Taj asked, leaning forward in her seat, glaring at the engineer. "Are you serious?"

"That's what the scanners are reading." Lina nodded. "It's kind of weak, too. The being might be too far gone to save by now."

"Can you confirm, S'thlor?" Taj asked the captive alien.

"So it would appear," he replied, "if Lina is describing the readout correctly. A single signal is being returned."

"We did all that for one person?" Cabe shook his head and groaned.

"One's better than none." Lina let out a quiet sigh. "Right?"

"Bloody Rowl, it is." Taj glared at the view screen. The science craft drew closer and closer as they examined it. "Bring us around so we can board. We need to find that survivor before he or she is no longer a survivor."

"We're doing this?" Cabe spun in his seat to face her.

"Seems wrong to go through all that and leave someone stranded on a dead ship, prolonging their agony, doesn't it?"

Cabe grunted. "I'm thinking we're wasting our time, seeing how Lina says the signal is weak, but if that's what you want to do..."

"It is," Taj told him, leaving no room for argument. "And we didn't waste anything. There are two less predators out here attacking people. That counts for something no matter what happens now."

She leaned back in her seat and thought of Gran Beaux and Mama Merr. She was sure they'd want her to make the attempt, no matter how it worked out. And even if she weren't able to rescue anyone, the more rational side of Taj reminded her that her people needed food, fuel, and supplies. If nothing else was accomplished by boarding the craft, there had to be something they could scavenge from the ruined hulk of a freighter.

She'd made the right choice and her conscience was clear.

Now, she only had to prove that to the rest of the crew.

CHAPTER EIGHT

The boarding umbilical floated across empty space until it *clanged* against the science ship's hull. The tube sealed its connection and pressurized, then a red warning light flashed.

"Cutting through the hull now," Lina called out as she manipulated the tube controls. S'thlor stood beside her, walking her through the process. "Breaching now."

Taj stood in front of the small porthole in the door that led to the boarding tube, watching as the device flared and worked its way through the armored plating of the listing freighter. She was surprised by how fast the cutter—she saw it as being a kind of laser-scythe—sliced through the metal. After a few moments, a great slab of hull collapsed inward, crashing silently into a corridor inside the science freighter.

"Impressive," Torbon said, nodding in appreciation. "I wonder if we can use that thing as a weapon somehow."

Taj thought about the possibilities for a moment before

dismissing them. There wasn't time for flights of fancy. They had a person, possibly dying, trapped in the scuttled freighter. That was their priority. They needed to get them out first, then they'd worry about everything else.

"Everyone armed?" she asked, and the crew nodded, Cabe and Torbon holding up their bolt pistols.

S'thlor shrugged, empty-handed, and Lina patted him on the back. "Don't worry, big guy, I don't have a gun either. We aren't going with them."

"Can't say I'm disappointed," he admitted. "Besides, you don't want a blind soldier bringing up the rear. Could get kind of messy in a firefight."

"Yeah, I'd prefer not to get shot in the back," Cabe said.

"Then stay behind Torbon," Lina joked, choking back a barking laugh.

"Hey!" Torbon huffed and shook his head. "I'm not *that* bad of a shot!"

"Your service records say otherwise," Lina replied.

"That's not true." Torbon snarled at her. "My record for stationary targets is exemplary."

"Knock it off. We don't have time," Taj told them.

Torbon grumbled but didn't argue.

"We need you two on the *Discordant*," Taj explained to Lina and S'thlor. "In case there are any surprises and we need to get out of here quickly."

"We've got you covered," Lina assured her. She turned back to the console beside the umbilical doorway and nodded her approval at what she saw. "Atmosphere is breathable inside the freighter. Systems are failing ship-wide, but the backups register as online and sufficiently powered for now. Won't be much more than emergency lighting in there, but life support and gravitational systems will hold out long enough for you to find our wayward survivor and raid the stores and get both back onto the *Discordant*."

"Can't ask for more than that," Taj said.

"Well, we can, but it's not like Rowl'll grace us with any luck," Torbon muttered. He cast a sheepish grin skyward, looking as if he regretted saying anything.

"Maybe not, but you keep tugging her tail, and she's gonna turn her eyes your way, Torbon," Cabe told him. "I don't want to be anywhere near you when she does."

"Me either," Taj agreed, "so let's get this over with." She drew in a deep breath and met Lina's eyes. "Keep an eye out for more pirates while we're gone, okay? Can't have them sneaking up on us."

"You sure you don't want more backup?" Lina asked in reply.

"No." Taj shook her head. "If something happens, I want to be sure you and the others are safe and can get away, have a chance at a new life, and not be stuck on that wreck like us." Taj cast a glance down the corridor, where a small cluster of their people gathered, keeping their distance as requested. "This goes south in any way, you run, you hear me? No questions, no hesitation. You run."

Lina paused a moment, saying nothing before she finally offered up a moist-eyed nod. "Be careful and get back here quickly."

"We will," Taj said with a soft smile for the engineer before turning to face Cabe. "Let's go."

Cabe nodded and opened the umbilical door, stepping inside with his weapon's business end facing into the science freighter. Torbon and Taj followed without a word, stomping down the tunnel until they reached the far end. Cabe peered through the opening to the freighter and waved them through a moment later, seeing that it was clear.

Even before they entered the ship, Taj could feel the difference in temperature between the *Discordant* and the science craft, its atmosphere leaking into the tube, a light coating of frost forming in the air.

While the backup systems aboard the freighter were still running, pumping breathable air into the ship and keeping them firmly attached to the floor once they'd entered, the ship's climate control was clearly malfunctioning. Wisps of fog spilled from her mouth as she exhaled. She hunched in on herself a bit to ward off the unexpected cold. The sparse, dimly lit hallway did nothing to ease the chill, an ominous quiet taking over. Even their footsteps seemed muffled aboard the damaged freighter.

"Someone forgot to turn the heat up this morning," Torbon mumbled, huffing out quick, sharp breaths so he could watch the steam billow.

"Not very welcoming," Cabe agreed. "Wonder if they have any nip onboard."

"You smell that?" Taj asked, breathing in short, sharp breaths to ward off the harsh scent that steeped the ship.

"It sure ain't nip," Cabe replied with a sigh. "Antiseptic maybe? Some sort of cleaning agent?"

Torbon shrugged. "Place reminds me of Gran Verren's office, all clinical and clean, like right after they mopped the place. You think the ship always smells like this?"

"I don't plan to spend enough time in here for that to matter," Taj answered. "We've got to find the last survivor."

"Hope that's not them I smell," Torbon grunted.

"So, where do we start?" Cabe asked.

Lina came across the comm, confirming she'd been listening in. "Scanners show me the lifeform should be somewhere to the left of your current position. Need to hurry, though. The signal is still decaying. It's getting weaker by the moment."

Taj growled low in her throat and started off without any further hesitation. She'd put her people at risk trying to save this unknown being, and she was *still* putting them at risk. Every second they spent on the listing alien ship meant more opportunity for something to go wrong.

"Come on," she called out, waving the others on behind her.

They moved down the hall at a fast clip, weapons out and at the ready. The clinical stink of the ship remained, but they slowly got used to it, the sting in Taj's nose seeming to ease as they moved along. It wasn't long, however, before the smell was replaced with another, far worse one.

"Oh, Rowl," Cabe muttered as he stumbled across the first of the science ship casualties.

A body lay on the floor in the corridor. She was lithe and short, maybe half the height of Taj, if that. Skin a purplish-blue, the woman's eyes were massive, taking up the majority of her face. They were a brilliant orange, even in death, and they stared at the ceiling without seeing, no pupils to distort the shine.

A tiny dot of a nose and a narrow slit of a mouth sat

below its eyes, scrunched into a pained rictus. Greenish blood pooled around her, gelatinous in the chill, having spilled from a large gash on the side of her head. There was way too much to imagine she'd survived the blow that felled her.

"Should I…uh, check to see if she's…" Torbon asked. He examined the body, clearly unsure of where to even start hunting for a pulse.

Taj shook her head. "She's clearly not the lifeform Lina detected. She looks like she's been dead for a little while now," she told him, reaching down and closing the woman's eyes, transparent eyelids doing little to mute the orange shine.

Like everything else in the ship, she was cold to the touch. Taj shivered. "We need to keep going."

Taj turned away from the body, her breath clinging to her lungs. She'd seen far more death in the last few months than she'd seen her entire life, and she was already sick of it.

Even though she didn't know this woman, had no clue as to her nature or who she was, Taj felt bad for this woman's unfortunate demise.

The crew made their way through the ship, casting glances here and there in chambers they passed, but there was little they recognized as having any value to them or.

And driven toward the source of the last remaining lifeform on the ship, there was little time to stop and properly search or determine what the strange items did. Besides, it being a science ship made Taj a bit more tentative than she might otherwise be.

Who knew what they might stumble across.

Taj snarled as she realized their little adventure was likely going to end in failure with regards to supplies. The only thing in abundance aboard the ship were dead bodies. They were nearly everywhere as they made their way down the quiet corridors.

Taj pushed the crew on, doing her best to not examine each and every one, wondering how long they'd lasted after the gacking pirates had struck. Fortunately, Lina's voice in her ear pushed her forward with a determined relentlessness, the engineer spewing a running dialogue of directions through the comm. Grateful for that, Taj pressed on, her grip growing tighter and tighter on her weapon.

That was when the unthinkable happened.

"Gack!" Lina swore, growling into the comm. "The signal died...er, I mean, went out."

"Where was it last?" Taj called back, unwilling to stop now. They hadn't come all this way for nothing.

"Ahead a little, to the right. That was where the last blip pinged from."

"Let's go," Taj called out and ran off, sliding on the slick flooring as she shifted directions and bolted into the room Lina had pointed out. The others followed right behind.

The room, as it turned out, appeared to be the mess hall. Row after row of tables were splayed out in haphazard fashion, attached benches running alongside. Trays and various bits and pieces of food littered the tabletops and were scattered across the floor, the pirate attack clearly having occurred during meal time.

Distracted momentarily by the trays and plates, Taj made a face and grunted.

"I'm guessing that stuff is what these people eat," Cabe muttered, glaring at the blobs of black and green goo splattered about, some of it dripping from the table edges with a muddy *splat*.

Taj scanned the rest of the tables and groaned. "Guess the hunt for food is over," she said, shaking her head. "No one's gonna want to eat that stuff, even if we can."

"It certainly doesn't look edible," Cabe agreed.

Torbon poked a finger into a pile and brought it to his nose. He hissed and flung the goop away, wiping his hand on the table to scrape the remainder away. "Oh Rowl, this gack reeks."

"Leave it," Taj told him, returning her attention to the bodies.

"Gladly," Torbon agreed finally peeling the goo off. "Now if only I can get rid of the smell." His face was scrunched, whiskers twitching.

Taj ignored him in her efforts to find the being who'd signaled them.

Dozens of the purple aliens filled the room, some hunched on the benches, locked in place by misshapen seats, but most were awkwardly sprawled across the floor, having come to rest where they'd landed.

Like the poor woman they'd first come across, there were obvious signs as to how most of the aliens had died. Open wounds covered their bodies as well as massive bruising, the result of the ship being tossed about during combat, the crew unprepared for such violence.

A few might have died of more natural causes, shock or physical ailments during the battle, but the mess hall looked like a battlefield, greenish blood coating the floor in a way that left little of the original flooring visible.

"Nothing but corpses here," Taj told Lina. "How many crew members do you think were onboard?"

"Struggling to connect to the ship's data logs, a lot of incompatibilities cropping up between the Wyyvan system and these guys, whatever they are, but it's looking like there might have been close to two hundred crew aboard if I'm reading this right."

"What the gack were the pirates looking for?" Cabe asked. "If there was something aboard the ship they wanted, it had to be sturdy or it would've ended up like the crew. They were merciless in the damage they inflicted, clearly not caring what happened to the beings in here."

"I think the ship might have decompressed at some point during the fight, too," Lina answered over the comm. "Exterior scans show some pretty serious damage to the hull and one good-sized hole near the bridge, in the neck of the craft." Taj heard Lina draw a surprised breath. "The big one looks like it's been repaired, though, albeit a bit haphazardly. There might be maintenance bots aboard somewhere seeing how recent the patch is, or maybe that was our last survivor, having finished up the job too late for it to make a difference."

"You think?" Taj asked.

"Your guess is as good as mine," Lina replied.

"Is the patched area nearby?" Taj let her gaze roam over the walls and ceiling, not seeing any obvious repairs attempted.

"No, it's all the way on the other side of the ship, so I'm guessing the bots were trying to cope with the damage, seeing how it's unlikely our signal lifeform could have made it so far in the short amount of time between the patch placement and the loss of signal," Lina replied.

"You're sure this is the place, though?" Taj asked, hoping to be sure. "It doesn't look like someone just keeled over in the last few minutes."

"Absolutely. The room you're in was the last place the signal showed up, though, so I'm guessing the source is somewhere among the bodies at this point since it's been quiet for a while now."

Taj grunted. She hated the idea that she'd wasted their time only for the being to die anyway. No food and no survivors put a checkmark in the failed column of this mission as Taj saw it.

Sucking in a chilly breath, she glanced around, surveying the room one last time and seeing what appeared to be the galley through a set of arched entryways on the other side of the room.

"Let's check the galley out and see if there's food we can actually eat stashed away somewhere," she ordered, motioning toward the ship's kitchen. "Maybe they had other beings aboard and there's something that doesn't smell or look like moldy tar."

"I'm guessing the odds of that are pretty slim," Cabe challenged. "All the bodies in here are the same species."

Taj agreed, though she wasn't ready to quit yet.

"Still worth a look," she pressed. "You never know."

That determined thought in mind, she marched off, going to look despite Cabe's objections. He grunted and started to follow, apparently not willing to let her adventure alone.

The lights flickered right then, and a deep, low hum resonated, vibrating the walls and floor. Then the lights died entirely, plunging the mess hall into darkness without warning.

"Bloody Rowl!" Torbon cursed, dropping to a crouch and turning in a quick circle, his weapon trailing around the room.

Taj did the same, her eyes adjusting to the darkness quickly. "What happened?" she asked Lina, spying Cabe hunkered down next to her and surveying the mess hall in search of threats.

"Ship's losing power a bit quicker than I'd anticipated. There was a sudden spike, like a system was triggered, and then the power plunged," the engineer replied. "The ship just coughed up its death rattle. Atmospherics are gonna drop off next, life support *and* gravity. Best get out of there before you end up as furry ice cubes. You're not exactly dressed for deep space exploration," Lina reminded them.

Taj spun about, nodding even though Lina couldn't see her. "Back to the *Discordant*," she called out to her crew. "Quick and orderly, but emphasis on *quick*."

Neither Cabe nor Torbon argued with her. Both hopped to their feet and started off, Taj at their heels. Cabe flew through the mess hall door, followed by Torbon, but a flicker out the corner of Taj's eye caught her attention.

She stumbled to a halt and spun about, wondering what she'd seen if everyone aboard the ship was dead and her crew were traipsing along in front of her. She unholstered her bolt pistol.

A shadow flickered near the galley, a deeper darkness

against the black. It swelled and shifted, moving in her direction, steadily forward.

"Uh, guys…" she muttered across the comm. "There's something in here." She raised her bolt pistol and backed toward the corridor where Cabe and Torbon had disappeared only a moment before. "What's in the room with me, Lina?"

"Nothing," the engineer came back right away. "The only lifeforms in the ship are you three."

"You sure?"

"As sure as I can be," Lina answered. "These are aliens we're talking about. How the gack do I know if all of them show up on scans? For that matter, I might be reading these scans all wrong to begin with," she admitted, and Taj heard S'thlor mumble something in the background. "Might be one of those maintenance bots, too. No way for me to tell, I'm afraid."

"Great," Taj muttered to herself, unable to draw her gaze from the shifting darkness of the room.

She backed into the hall and put as much distance between her and the room as possible. Cabe and Torbon came up behind her, their weapons ready, having heard the entire conversation across the communicators.

A muffled *clank* sounded in the mess hall, and Taj spied the shadow coming through the doorway, a figure slowly taking shape.

"There!" she shouted. "Do you see it?" she asked Cabe and Torbon.

Both nodded, readying their weapons.

"Still not showing anything," Lina said.

"Well, the scanners are clearly wrong," Taj spit back,

making sure she didn't let the shadowy shape escape her line of sight. "Whoever you are, *whatever* you are, stay right there!" she called out to the emerging shape. "I'll shoot if you keep advancing."

The figure ignored her warning, stumbling forward in the darkness, drawing closer and closer without pause.

Taj backed up further, her crew moving right along with her. Cabe circled around her on the left, placing himself between her and whatever it was coming toward them. He was letting Taj take the lead, but it was clear Cabe wasn't going to let her face this thing down on her own.

"Last chance!" Taj shouted.

Once more, the shadowy figure ignored her commands. It moved steadily down the hallway, and Taj's finger twitched against the trigger guard of her bolt pistol. She made ready to fire as the figure ambled toward them, unwilling to halt its advance despite her warnings.

Taj was ready to blow the figure away, the safety of her and the crew tantamount, but there was something about the way the being had emerged from the mess hall that kept her from squeezing the trigger.

"Hold on," she called out to her crew, raising her free hand and making a fist to give her a few more seconds to examine the newcomer without them opening fire.

With the figure out in the hallway, the gloom slightly less oppressive thanks to the blessing of her Furlorian heritage, the figure began to take a familiar shape.

It was humanoid, a male she believed, much the same as the other aliens they'd come across in the ship. Purplish-blue skin seemed to absorb the darkness, lending him the shadowy form Taj had been so caught off guard by originally.

The fact that the creature didn't show up on Lina's scanner readings, however, made the pit in Taj's stomach open up. That this person, this *thing*, could be up and about yet not trigger the scanners sent chills down Taj's spine, which had absolutely nothing to do with the frigid air.

She aimed her bolt pistol at its head, her finger tightening against the trigger, just below the required amount of pressure needed to fire the weapon. It looked as if she'd have to make good on her threat to shoot him.

Taj drew in a steadying breath and double-checked her aim.

Only the stranger's sudden reply saved him from an unfortunate end.

"He-lllp...me," the being muttered in a roughened voice, a ragged edge making the words raspy. "I-I...I neeeed—"

The being twitched and collapsed, crashing face-first into the floor with a mighty *thump*.

Taj hesitated only an instant before yanking her finger off the trigger and holstering her pistol. Decision made, she raced toward the fallen alien to examine him and offer what aid she could.

"Are you insane?" Cabe shouted at her, though he stayed glued to her side, his gun never wavering from the alien.

Torbon ran to remain alongside them. "You're only now asking that question?"

"Be quiet, you two," Taj growled at them. "He's hurt. We need to do something."

She knelt beside the fallen alien and touched a hand to

its throat where she hoped there'd be some indication of life, something to contradict the scanners readings. Maybe it had simply been too wounded to show up any longer.

Taj sighed when she felt nothing, not knowing whether that was because the alien's biology was different from hers or because it had truly died this time. Either way, she needed someone better equipped to deal with the situation than she was.

"Lina, get Gran Verren to meet us at the tube. We need a doctor, incoming alien wounded."

"On it," Lina called back.

"Wait, we're taking him to our ship?" Torbon asked, shaking his head. "Is that smart?"

Taj shrugged. "I don't know what I'd call this, right now, Torbon. Just help me." She grabbed the alien's legs, and Cabe scooped up the man's upper body, grimacing the entire time, straining to move him.

He was far heavier than she imagined he could be.

Torbon groaned and joined in, helping her carry the alien, clearly struggling, too. "I want it known I think this is a bad idea," he said. "The worst of bad ideas. The baddest of worst ideas."

"Noted," Taj replied, "now shut up and get moving."

"Are you su—" Cabe began, but Taj cut him off.

"If you ask me if I'm sure, I'll shoot your tail off," she told him. "Now is *not* the time."

Cabe went silent, cowed by her threat, and the crew raced toward the tube, carrying the limp alien in an awkward shuffle. By the time they reached the end of it and set him on the floor in the *Discordant*'s corridor, all three were sweaty and out of breath.

Lina and S'thlor met them at the umbilical control panel, worried expressions plastered across their faces. Lina stared at the alien, eyes wide.

S'thlor just stared in no particular direction.

"Rowl, this guy is heavy," Torbon muttered, wiping his forehead after they'd put the alien down. "Must be all that goo they eat."

Gran Verren and two other Furlorians arrived moments after they'd set the alien down. "Get him to the infirmary, now!" she called out, her wrinkled face squished into a grimace, and her assistants jumped to the task.

They huffed and puffed and scooted the alien onto the hover-gurney. Once he was settled, they triggered the gurney's anti-grav pads, and it rose into the air. Even still, it seemed to hum under the weight of the alien being.

That didn't stop them from rushing him off, though, the two clasping the edge at either end and directing the gurney.

But as soon as they started down the hallway, an alarm erupted, bathing the corridor in red and bringing everyone to a sudden halt.

"What's that?" Cabe shouted, trying to be heard over the blaring of the alarm. "All these alarms sound so different. I have no idea what any of them mean."

Neither did Taj, but she knew it couldn't be anything good.

"Proximity alert," S'thlor answered, his head tilted to the side, listening.

Jadie's voice came across the comm. "Incoming ships, starboard side," she informed them. "Three of them, flying tight and sharp. They look similar in make to the ones you blasted earlier, no identifying markers, and they're coming in fast. I suggest we hustle on a bit."

"Pirates," Taj spit out, snarling. She spun around and shoved Cabe down the hall ahead of her. "Get to the bridge and get us out of here!"

Cabe bolted, tail trailing behind him, stuck straight out. Lina sealed the umbilical and retracted it as quickly as she could, the machinery offering up a quiet buzz. Taj glared at the flashing red lights, urging both the engineer and Cabe on with urgent thoughts.

For a moment, she regretted stopping to help the strange alien, but she shook that thought away, knowing it was the right thing to do. Beaux and Mama would have agreed with her, she was certain. She had to trust that Cabe would get them moving quickly enough to get away from the pirates before they engaged.

The last ship's distress call had clearly gotten through.

Her thoughts spinning, she ran her hands through her long fur, feeling bits of ice and moisture from her jaunt on the alien craft. She shook it off with a grunt.

"Time to shoot the pirates," she muttered to herself, chasing off after Cabe and the others, leaving Lina to corral S'thlor and get him back to the bridge safely.

CHAPTER NINE

The *Discordant* shrieked through space.

The three pirate ships followed, slowly losing ground, the leech craft managing to increase the distance between them despite its heavy load.

Right then, she was glad Vort had convinced her to take the leech craft, though she'd never admit that out loud. Had they been in the *Paradigm*, they would have had zero chance at outpacing the pirates on their tail.

Taj sat on the bridge, watching the enemy ships in the view screen, teeth bared, hands clenched into painful fists, claws digging into her palms. She didn't want to run, but she knew she had to.

They'd caught the other two pirates off guard. The fight with these new ones wouldn't be anywhere near as easy, and she couldn't risk it.

"Can we go any faster?" she asked.

Cabe shook his head. "Probably pushing too hard as it is," he told her. "This ship is fast, but we're way overloaded with bodies. Engines are running a twitch below red, and it won't take much to throw it over. We're gonna need to find some way to slip the pirates before we burn something out and we end up floating lifeless in space."

Lina chuckled. "It's like we've traded up for the new *Thorn*, exchanging one beater for another."

"You're hurting my feelings," Cabe muttered, though Taj noticed him hiding a crooked smirk. "The *Thorn* went out on her shield like the good ship she was."

"Leave his baby alone, Lina," Taj told her. "It's bad enough that we had to wreck the windrider, you don't have to rub it in."

"We?" Cabe replied, shaking his head. "I don't remember any *we* in the decision."

Taj grinned. "I was simply sharing the success of our efforts."

"Sharing the blame, more like," Torbon said, joining the conversation.

"I'm generous like that." Taj joined Lina, a throaty chuckle rumbling loose from both of them.

Their amusement didn't last long, however.

A tinny *beep* sounded from Lina's console.

"What is that?" Taj asked her.

"I'm not entirely sure," the engineer answered, returning her focus to her station. She and S'thlor carried on a quick conversation, Lina's fingers flying over the console in a blur as they chatted back and forth. A moment later, her expression smoothed and her grin returned.

"Looks like there's a planet ahead," she said, then turned to S'thlor, explaining the technical imagery on the screen.

"Am I right thinking all this gibberish scrolling across the screen means it's inhabited?"

S'thlor nodded. "It most certainly is. The planet is known to my people. Kulora is its name. It's a tourist world, a kind of crossroads in this sector. A gateway between galaxies." The alien sat back in his seat, rubbing his chin. "It means, however, that we are drawing closer to Wyyvan space. I recognize where we are now."

"Great," Torbon muttered. "So, we've got pirates on our six and angry lizards waiting ahead."

"That's most likely true," S'thlor replied, "but Kulora is a very diverse planet, which doesn't observe any Wyyvan influence. The Wyyvans we'd find there will be the royal caste or business people, the wealthy elite. You're not going to find any of us grunts around them because we can't afford the amenities."

"Which means we'll stand out nicely in our *liberated* Wyyvan ship," Taj said, amused once more by their awful luck.

S'thlor shrugged. "Maybe, maybe not," he replied. "The types of Wyyvan who visit this world aren't overly concerned with the mundane, day-to-day aspects of the military. Yeah, they might wonder in passing why a leech ship is docked there, especially without its fleet complement in orbit above the planet, but things like that are generally below their notice. As long as Wyyvan soldiers aren't knocking on their doors, looking to arrest them, it's likely a non-issue."

"Likely?" Cabe asked. "Likely is not the same thing as definitely."

S'thlor grunted his disagreement, opening his mouth to

argue, but Taj didn't let the two get into it. "It doesn't matter," she told them, no time to listen to them go back and forth about what the Wyyvan elite may or may not notice. "We're not stopping on the planet anyway. It's too much of a risk. With the pirates on our tail, we can't afford to give them a chance to catch up and—"

"I beg you to change your mind," an unfamiliar voice said right after the hiss of the bridge door opening sounded.

Taj snapped her head about, eyes narrowing at seeing the strange, purplish-blue alien staring at her from the doorway. Kal stood beside him, pistol in his hand, towering over the alien. Gran Verren was there, as well, also looking rather large in comparison.

"Sorry, Taj," Kal said. "He insisted on seeing you, said it was urgent."

"Your skills as a guard are questionable," Torbon told Kal, shaking his head. "Every time a prisoner wants to be escorted to the bridge, you oblige them, which is kind of the opposite of how it should work.

"'Yes, murderous alien creature, I'd be happy to take you to the most sensitive part of the *Discordant* where you can slaughter the entire crew and fly the ship into the nearest quasar, laughing maniacally the entire way.'"

"He's not entirely wrong, Kal," Cabe agreed, "even if he is being a bit dramatic about it."

"I assure you, I intend you no harm," the alien said, spreading his arms and offering up a shallow bow, arms spread wide.

"That's what all the bad guys say right before they reveal their master plan and unleash chaos on the unsuspecting innocents who foolishly believed them." Torbon jabbed a claw in the alien's direction. "We're onto you, buddy. That's like Evil 101. Next up is the super-threatening monologue, then the world ends."

Taj drew in a deep breath and let it out slow, her gaze shifting back and forth between her crew, the alien, and Gran Verren. At last, she settled in on the Gran.

"Is he even healthy enough to be up and about?" she asked, pointing at the newcomer. "He was pretty much dead an hour ago."

"Yes," she answered, "and, well, no. Not exactly."

"Uh, there's a whole lot of words in that sentence that don't equal anything resembling reassurance," Cabe told her.

Gran Verren chuckled. "Well, *he* is not exactly a *he*, at least not beyond external appearances."

The alien straightened to its full height and turned to face the Gran. "I am most assuredly a *he*, as that is the identification I was assigned by my masters. They would not lie about that."

"Assigned?" Taj rubbed her temples, wondering what the gack the two were talking about. "Masters?"

"Yes, *assigned* by my masters," the alien replied. "It is who I am."

"I know that sometimes…okay, a lot of the time, I'm the last to understand what's going on, but am I the only one who's confused right now? It can't only be me, right?" Torbon questioned.

"No, it's not just you this time," Cabe answered. "I'm a bit lost myself."

Taj raised her hand. "Yeah, me too."

"What he means is," Gran Verren clarified, "he is a he because that's what gender he was assigned, what he was programmed to identify as."

"Programmed?" Torbon asked, clearly still confused.

"Wait! You're saying he's not...an alien?" Taj asked, finally making some sense of the conversation they were having.

Gran Verren shrugged. "Well, he was built by aliens, so technically he still kind of is, but again, not exactly."

"You're an android," Lina blurted out, apparently catching on. There was no hiding the mouse-eating grin on her face at her deduction.

"I prefer the term mechanoid, but yes, I am a synthetic being, an artificial intelligence core housed inside this—" He motioned to his body, the slightest of sneers creeping upon his narrow lips. "—*unfortunate* shell." He nodded to Gran Verren. "But thanks to your assistance, I was able to reboot my systems...mostly."

"Why unfortunate?" Lina asked, leaving her station and coming over for a closer look. She circled him, examining every inch of his body, getting caught up in the moment.

"Mistakes were made. Many, many mistakes, I'm afraid," he answered with a sigh. His head twitched right then, a spasmodic burst of motion that ended almost as quickly as it began. When his voice kicked back in, there was a rawness to it, a digital undertone of frustration that faded a few words in, becoming smooth again. "My creators, the Dandrinites, built me in their image originally. Tall and lithe, graceful yet strong and powerful, I was the finest example of their species in form, absolute perfection if I might show my bias."

"And then?" Torbon pressed, an eyebrow raised, clearly sensing more to the story seeing as how everyone could see the android was neither tall and lithe, nor graceful. The book was still out on whether he was strong or powerful. The only certainty was that he was *very* purple, Taj noted.

"And *then* my people were subjugated by a cruel, malevolent sub-species of meflu droppings, the Grung." Another twitch set the mechanoid to trembling, one leg tapping the floor a bunch of times before settling.

S'thlor grunted. "I've heard of them." His voice dripped of disgust, as if the Wyyvan disliked even the taste of the species' name. "They've raided a few of my people's holdings across the borders of our galaxy. Brutal little reprobates, if you ask me. Left nothing but wreckage and corpses in their wake. They're not anywhere near as sophisticated or dangerous as the Federation, but what they lack in function, they make up for in abject cruelty."

"So, what happened to you?" Lina asked the android. "Why weren't you destroyed as well?"

"Before my masters were completely overcome, they uploaded the whole of their knowledge, the very core of their existence, everything that made them who they were, into my mind." He reached up and tapped the side of his head, which set off another spasm, which took a moment to pass.

"Looks like they fried a few circuits doing it." Torbon chuckled.

The mechanoid nodded, but the motion looked more like he was thrashing his head to the sound of music no one else could hear. It took a few seconds before he settled and regained control of his movements, but one eye started blinking to a similarly fast-paced rhythm and didn't slow for several moments.

"Indeed," he answered, his voice once more trilling oddly. "My cranial server was filled to capacity, but it maintained its structural integrity well enough."

"You sure about that?" Cabe asked.

"It *was* sufficient… for a time, until my masters realized there was no chance the invading Grung would allow me to leave the planet unharmed in my Dandrinite form." The mechanoid shrugged and stood there, stiffening and doing nothing.

Several long and quiet moments later, Taj urged him to continue. "And?"

The mechanoid started, as if he'd been woken out of a deep sleep. "Oh, yes. So, in their infinite wisdom…"

Taj bit back a laugh, wondering how wise the android's people could be if they send this derelict wretch off into the world with the whole of their knowledge stashed in his busted skull. It was like trusting Torbon with the secrets of the universe. Or with cookies.

"…transferred my AI core into this form, a simulated Sperit, a race which happens to be a loose ally of the Grung. They provide the beasts with weapons and technology and the means to continue their rampages in exchange for peace, the Grung vowing to leave their people and settlements alone."

A smile brightened the mechanoid's face.

"My masters provided me with a cover story opportunity, imprisoning me before they fell to the Grung's cruelty, allowing me to play the role of a captured Sperit scientist. The Grung, hardly the intellectual giants of the universe..."

Taj swallowed her laugh, hiding it behind a quick wave for the android to go on.

"...believed the tale I told them and had me shipped to Speritu, the Sperit home world, believing they were appeasing their *friends*, hoping for a reward, of course."

"And they didn't notice your...uh, differences?"

A twitch preceded the answer. "I wasn't yet so...poodle."

Taj blinked, her mind struggling to process what he'd said. She glanced at the rest of the crew, and each returned a similar confused expression.

"Poodle?"

"Fragmented, yes, exactly that," the mechanoid answered. "This Sperit form was crafted quickly, using substandard parts my masters had on hand, easily accessed, but it remained completely convincing until a short time after I arrived upon Speritu.

"By then, I had blended into their society and had become one of them, so they overlooked my more obvious flaws. Which was fortunate, as I needed their assistance to complete the mission laid out by my masters."

"And that mission is?" Taj asked.

"To carry the genetic material and complete history and wisdom of the Dandrinites to a suitable planet and plant the seed where they might start anew." The mechanoid straightened, his chest jutting out in what was an obvious show of pride. "It is my duty to shepherd their return."

"So, let me get this straight. An entire race of beings is depending on your success to be reborn?" Torbon asked.

"Pomegranate," the mechanoid answered, nodding.

"Well, good luck with whatever that is," Torbon told him, barely managing to hold back his laughter, his hand cupped over his mouth.

"Thank you," the android replied, smiling. One side of his lips wiggled like a hooked worm, clearly oblivious to having misspoken.

"Ooookay then," Cabe said, letting out an amused *whew*.

Rather than ask about the random word insertions, clearly an artifact of the rushed effort to transfer the mechanoid's brain to the new body or the damage ensued afterward, Taj waved Torbon to be quiet and gave Cabe a dirty look to keep him from egging Torbon on. There was an opportunity here, and Taj didn't want the crew's teasing to ruin it.

She had no idea if the android had legitimate emotions or feelings, and she didn't want to upset it if it did.

"You originally suggested we should visit Kulora instead of avoiding it," she said, circling back around to the topic of conversation they were having when the android first interrupted them. "Why is that? What's there?"

The mechanoid spun in a tight circle. "That is where I was headed when the Sperit science ship was intercepted by the Terants."

"The *who*?" Lina asked.

"The Terants, or the pirates as you referred to them when I arrived on your bridge," the mechanoid answered. "They learned of my...*cargo* somehow and tracked me to Speritu, forcing me to abandon my secretive life there and set off on my mission earlier than my masters had intended."

"So, the pirates on our six are there because of you?" Cabe asked.

"They *were*," the android replied, a lopsided grin appearing on his twitching lips, which looked like worms crawling across his face. "I suspect your destroying two of their vessels might have impacted their reasoning somewhat. Now, I believe they have two goals in mind: to capture me *and* to murder you."

The whole crew groaned, including Kal, Jadie, and Gran Verren. "Thanks, Taj," they all muttered in unison.

Taj went over and flopped into her seat, shaking her head at the unified mutiny. She spun the chair about so she faced the mechanoid again. Her whiskers eased back against her cheeks, and she blew out a huffed breath.

"You still haven't answered my question, though. Why should we go to Kulora?" Taj cleared her throat. "No offense, but with pirates chasing us down, whoever's fault it is," she emphasized, "it makes more sense to avoid the planet altogether and lose them in space. The first place they'll check is Kulora, given its proximity to our current location."

"Indeed they will. They would be stupid not to," the mechanoid answered, a broad grin appearing. "However, I am not without my resources to make it worth your while." He tapped the side of his head again, setting it to wobbling a bit. "My masters, reasoning I might face diversity in my journey, gave me access codes to all the Dandrinite reserves, which means I have near-limitless finances to bring to bear in my pursuit of reawakening the Dandrinite people."

"*Now* you have our attention," Torbon told the mechanoid, earning him a threatening glare from Taj.

"If you would be so kind as to assist me in my quest to reach my contact on Kulora, I am authorized to be quite generous in return."

Taj slumped back in her seat, staring at the mechanoid. After a moment, she glanced around the bridge, taking in the expressions of her crew, and even the blind S'thlor. All of them had a look that spoke of uncertainty, a hint of concern even, but buried beneath that, barely peeking out, was the appearance of hope. She imagined she had the exact same expression on her own face.

If the strange mechanoid was being truthful, and she didn't see why he wouldn't be given that he needed their assistance, he might well be the answer to their problems.

By agreeing to take him to Kulora, Taj could refuel the *Discordant* and supply her people with enough food for them to find a new home, a permanent place where they could settle in and be safe. Someplace they could take their time researching, learning about it without having to settle for wherever they ended up because they ran out of food or fuel, which was likely where they were headed currently.

She grunted, realizing her decision wasn't really much of a decision after all despite the threat of the pirates.

"We could use some help resupplying and preparing for our own journey if we do this," Taj told the android. "We also need some information regarding an organization called the Federation in exchange for our help."

"The Federation?" the mechanoid asked. "Bethany Anne's organization, from Earth?"

Taj stiffened in her seat, excited to stumble across someone who had some knowledge she could use. "Yes, that's them. Do you know where we might find them, an outpost or base or anything, somehow we can contact them?"

He nodded. "My databases have several references to the queen. I can—"

"I thought she was an empress?" Torbon asked, shaking his head. "I'm confused. Are we talking about the same woman?"

"A common presumption," the mechanoid replied. "She was once empress and is now queen, a voluntary re-titling I'm told, though I am not privy to the specifics of said adjustment. The ways of humans are quite...odd. They do what they will, it seems."

"No argument here," S'thlor muttered from his seat.

"We'll have to take your word for it," Taj said, but she started up again, not giving the android a chance to reply, preferring to pin their deal down before his...*quirks* distracted him. "So, to be clear, you're willing to help us with supplies and fuel and finding the Federation if we agree to take you to Kulora?"

"Indeed," he answered. "I am a mechanoid of my word."

Taj grinned, glad to have found the means to her people's safety. *Thank Rowl,* she thought.

"So, what do we call you besides mechanoid? You got a name?"

"My friends call me Dent."

"Well, Dent—"

The mechanoid raised a finger and waggled it in the air like a school teacher scolding a child. "I said, my *friends* call me Dent," he corrected. "If we're completely honest, I'm not entirely certain we're friends as of yet. Such distinctions are not so easily earned." He placed his stubby little hands on his hips and lifted the dot of his purplish chin her direction. "I'm sure you understand."

"Really?" Taj raised an eyebrow, her tail twitching with annoyance. She stared at the android, the tiniest flicker of regret rearing up at her idea to rescue the little mechanoid. She let his snark pass unchallenged, though, realizing it was in the best interest of her people to not anger the android and miss out on his timely offer. "I imagine taking you to Kulora is how we go about earning your friendship?"

Dent grinned. "It would most certainly be a wonderful start to one, don't you think?"

Taj snorted. "That being the case then, *Dent*, we're gonna be the best of friends real soon."

The mechanoid grinned and offered an enthusiastic thumbs-up. "Coconut!"

CHAPTER TEN

The Terant pirates had fallen back while the Furlorans questioned the android, and Taj ordered the crew to bring the *Discordant* onto a course for Kulora.

As a tourist planet, security was light and fairly casual, which was both good and bad as far as Taj was concerned. As easy as it was to gain access to the planet as an unknown ship with shaky credentials, she had to assume it would be almost as easy, if not easier, for the pirates to do the same.

That meant they'd be along soon after the *Discordant* set down, which wouldn't be long given the lack of security delay. The crew would have to hurry.

Their stolen ship passed a cursory scan with S'thlor helping guide them in past the security protocols, telling Cabe how to respond and showing him how to interpret the parking beacons. Cabe, having never piloted a ship through metropolitan traffic, sat rigid in his seat the entire time.

Taj could see the nervousness playing over his features. His ears were pinned to the side of his head, his whiskers peeled back, little spastic wiggles making them dance across his cheeks. He *meowed* low under his breath, lips curled into an unconscious sneer, teeth bared.

She grinned the entire time while watching him. It reminded her of when they'd first started their training under Beaux.

Those had been happy times, and Taj was determined to get them back.

S'thlor stood beside Cabe, hand on his shoulder, repeating the procedures the entire time and doing his best to keep him calm.

Kal hovered in the background, weapon held casually in his hand, the barrel tapping against his leg as he kept watch on the mechanoid. Dent simply stood rigid, watching the landing play out, one side of his face smiling while the other drooped in a foreboding frown. It was an expression Taj couldn't imagine fooled anyone into thinking he was a flesh and blood creature.

It was quite unnatural.

Jadie had escorted Gran Verren back to the infirmary as the *Discordant* followed the prescribed flight lines over the massive planet of Kulora, headed toward its parking designation outside the sprawling city on the horizon.

The whole time, Taj stared at the view screen, amazed at what she saw.

Raised on Krawlas, and having never traveled anywhere beyond the planet's orbit, Kulora was a marvel. Once through the atmosphere, a great ocean splayed out beneath them, meeting the hazy horizon as far as she could see. It glowed crystalline, and Taj was both fascinated and terrified by it.

Not that Krawlas was without its bodies of water, but none of them remotely compared to the vastness that loomed below. Taj had never held any fear of water, unlike most Furlorians, having swum in ponds and even a small lake once, reveling in the experience.

And even though she knew creatures lurked beneath the surface, flitting back and forth around her, she'd never once given it a serious thought. Nothing in those bodies were a threat to her.

Now, staring at the cerulean majesty that colored the view screen, she couldn't help but feel an ominous twinge creeping up on her. There was simply so much water that she couldn't comfortably imagine herself submerged in it. Too much room for something monstrous to lurk under the surface...until it was too late.

"Keep us in the air, Cabe," she called out. "There's no gacking way I'm up for swimming in that."

"Majestic, is it not?" Dent asked from behind her. He'd crept up so close that Taj started, biting back a hiss. She hadn't even noticed him.

She spun in her chair, heart rumbling like thunder, but Kal's steady presence a pace behind the mechanoid eased the tension of his unexpected approach.

She met Dent's gaze and grumbled. "Best not to sneak up on a girl like that, Dent," she told him. "I've an itchy trigger finger. You might just get some part of you blown off."

"As long as you don't shoot me in the head, you'd likely be doing me a favor," he answered with a smirk.

"No one should be a Sperit this long, not even an actual Sperit."

Taj grinned. Short as the mechanoid was, she had a hard time picturing him as a physical threat, despite knowing he was an android, not flesh and blood.

He moved so gracelessly it was impossible to see him as anything but an awkward alien out of his element. Even in her seat, she had to hunker down to look him in the face. His huge eyes were animal-like, soft and vulnerable. There'd be no missing them in combat.

Still, there was a coldness that lurked behind them, a sense of what he truly was deep down: a robot with a mental capacity that dwarfed them all.

In theory, at least, she thought, grinning as she watched the little quirks and tics that defined the mechanoid. Though, she wondered if it was all an act.

"It is quite amazing," she admitted finally, turning back around and trusting Kal to warn of anything untoward. "I'm just not interested in diving in, thank you very much."

Dent leaned over the back of her seat and pointed at the view screen. His finger wobbled, hand shaking, but he didn't seem to notice. "Fear not, for that is not where we are headed," he told her. "There, a bit beyond the ocean, do you see that growing splash of green?"

Taj had to narrow her eyes and stare hard, the mechanoid's vision clearly better than hers, but after a moment, a splotch of foliage became clear on the horizon. Its very presence sent a ray of warmth through her bones, chasing away the chill the view of the ocean had left behind.

A great, glimmering mass of silver shone beyond the

welcome foliage, and the sight of its brilliant sheen froze Taj's breath in her lungs. Hulking buildings rose high into the air, reaching for the clouds. Sunlight reflected off their steel frames. Taj stared in awe as they flew closer, seeing the city spread out before their eyes.

It was even more beautiful than the landscape had been.

"Oh...wow," Lina muttered from her station. "That's incredible."

"That is where we are headed," Dent told them, waving toward the city growing quickly in the distance. "Kulora's capital city, Ovrun. My contact will be found there, in the Waring District."

"We're coming in fast," Cabe announced, the beacon drawing them in. "Looks like the port is on the far side of the city and we're being directed to circle around rather than fly directly over it."

"Flight lanes," Dent replied without being asked. "All traffic will be routed in that direction to avoid collisions with smaller craft allowed to fly within Ovrun's borders."

"Allows us to keep an eye on the arrivals," Lina said. "Means we'll be able to see the pirates coming in before they land as they'll have to follow the same route."

"Good. That'll give us some time to prepare a welcome, if we need to. I'm hoping we can find Dent's contact and be done and gone before the pirates even reach orbit," Taj told them before turning her attention on Cabe. "Can you land us somewhere out of sight, somewhere far from the main berths, a place we can defend better?"

He shook his head. "Sorry, but our spot is already assigned, J-17 according to the system broadcast. If we deviate from our course, we risk drawing attention or being considered a threat, which they've reminded me about a thousand times since we started our approach." He tapped the console, asking S'thlor to bring up the scanner readings. The alien did, and Cabe pointed to the two tiny blips appearing a short distance behind them. "See those?" he asked. "Those are security fighters tailing us. If they get nervous about anything we do, we get shot down."

"Yeah, that'd be bad," Torbon replied. "Let's not do that."

"I agree," Taj said with a sigh. It wasn't the ideal situation, but it would have to do. "Get us on the ground then, and we'll figure things out from there."

"Coming in now." Cabe turned his focus to his instruments and guided the ship around the city's perimeter, following the beacon's signal until it became a steady buzz.

"Would be nice if they had an automated system, but I guess they can't be bothered. Gonna have to do this manually." He maneuvered the *Discordant* into the open space between a pair of pleasure ships moored in massive, raised berths and started to ease the ship toward the ground.

Taj stared at the opulence of the hulking ships, grateful when they disappeared from the view screen as Cabe landed and the bridge fell into silence, the screen going black. "We're here."

"Then let's get this show on the road," Torbon shouted behind them. "I wonder what kind of food they have here."

"We finish the mission first, then maybe we eat," Taj said, waving a finger in his direction before triggering her comm. "Jadie, round some folks up to guard the ship, then meet with Kal on the bridge to coordinate while we get Dent to his contact." She glanced at the mechanoid, who nodded in her direction. A crooked smile wiggled on his lips. It was disconcerting to watch, so she looked away. "If the pirates come looking for us, reach out to us on the comm and give us a heads up, but don't engage them unless you absolutely have to. I don't want anyone getting hurt, understood?"

Both Jadie and Kal replied affirmatively, though they didn't look happy about it, and Taj had to hope the warning was enough because it was all she had to offer. She needed to get Dent to his contact as quickly as possible and get back to the ship before the pirates found them and caused a kind of trouble they couldn't get out of.

It wasn't likely to work out that easily, but she could always hope.

"Oh, and keep an eye on Vort and Dard," she followed up. "The last thing we need is for those two to get out of their hole and let their people know we're here."

"I'll watch them personally," Jadie replied, and that satisfied Taj. She knew that, unlike Kal of the loose prison morals, the queen would shoot first and worry about what the captain and commander were doing later. She grinned at the thought, but it was short-lived. They had to get moving.

"Come on," she told the others. "We need to hurry." She patted S'thlor on the shoulders as she started off the bridge. "We'll be back soon. Try not to miss us."

The alien nodded. "I will endeavor not to."

Taj grinned and the crew headed off, Dent in tow, random twitches making him look as if he might break into a dance routine at any moment even though there wasn't any music to be heard.

Outside the ship, Taj let Dent come up front and lead the way. Cabe, Torbon, and Lina stuck close to Taj's side, each one with a hand rested on their pistol grips, doing their best to be subtle.

They weren't doing a good job of it.

There was no doubt they looked like scared children or nervous criminals, but Taj was okay with that.

She would rather they be mistaken for idiots than be caught off guard in a foreign city on an unknown planet. At least most of the traffic utilized the automated cab systems Dent had told them about. That kept the visitors in the air and above the notice of such things as Furlorians stomping across the tarmac.

She watched them glide overhead, clusters shooting back and forth across the landing area, but she soon found herself staring ahead, getting caught up in the wonder that was Ovrun.

In opposition to the relative quiet of where they set down, people of all sorts appeared as soon as the crew left the landing area behind and entered the city prime. The auto-cabs dropped off group after group of people, then jetted back into the sky for more.

It was immediate culture shock.

Taj had planned to keep her head down and march her way to Dent's contact in a hurry, but not more than a few minutes after starting down the walk, she found herself examining everyone who passed, blatantly gawking.

From aliens with tentacles for hair to sentient blobs that oozed down the street, to creatures made from pure energy, their physical manifestations held together by barely visible containment suits, to walking, talking trees whose branches rustled as they spoke, the richness and diversity of the planet caused Taj's breath to hitch in her lungs. There was simply too much to take in all at once.

They even passed a pair of creatures with fur and sharpened teeth, somewhat similar in build to the Furlorians. The first sneered and growled at them, the second breaking into a ragged bark, posturing, her chest puffed out, before the crew crossed the street to avoid a confrontation. Torbon hissed back, and the crew hurried on until the creatures were out of sight. Taj watched as Torbon's tail slowly receded to normal poof.

"What kind of animals are those?"

"Caninites," Dent answered in a serious tone. "I'd be careful around them. They can be such dogs, I'm afraid."

After their encounter, the journey was largely uneventful. Jadie checked in twice, saying everything was okay, and that pacified Taj's nerves a little. Dent telling them they were close to their destination helped even more.

Dent led them down the street a little farther, then slipped into a narrow alley between two smaller buildings. Unlike the main part of Ovrun, the area they'd landed in and traveled through was more subdued, less glamorous than what they'd viewed flying in.

That shining wonder towered in the distance, looming over everything.

It hadn't been so obvious that the city had a darker side when they'd first arrived, but it didn't take long for the seedier aspects of Ovrun to appear.

All the silvery beauty she had glimpsed faded into a

murky gray that seemed to choke the excitement out of the crew. The farther they went, the more apparent it became that they were not traveling in a nice part of town.

That set the hair on Taj's nape to standing on end.

The sidewalks were cracked and scuffed, and the buildings looked worn and weathered, a sharp counterpoint to the gleaming brilliance that first greeted their entry into the atmosphere.

No wonder security was so lax.

Taj found herself tightening her grip on her pistol and glancing about furtively, her head on a swivel. Dent seemed oblivious to her concern, chattering on like a tourist guide and pointing out things he felt were interesting about the city, even if they really weren't.

And once more, Taj wondered how damaged his brain was as there seemed to be far more artificial to the android than there was apparent intelligence.

"Here," he called out a short while later. "This is the place."

"Finally," Taj muttered under her breath. The thrill of the trip had faded a while back.

"Looks...questionable," Cabe told the mechanoid, glancing back at the rest of the crew, a displeased look pinning his whiskers back.

"Well, it's not as if a being who deals in secretive information can exactly advertise his business and set up shop in the Art or Trade districts," Dent clarified, "hence the less than sparkling location we find ourselves in now."

He started off toward a door hidden in gloom at the end of the alley. The crew slowed, putting a little space between the android and them.

"I'm quite sure this is what we need to do right now. We need supplies and money if we're gonna have a chance at finding a new home, not that I need to tell anyone that." Then she pointed at Dent, who walked on ahead, seemingly oblivious to their conversation, the android still spitting out travel details alongside the occasional inappropriate word. "Right now, he's our only hope."

"Which tells you how gacked we really are," Lina said, and the crew nodded their agreement.

"Enough! Let's get this over with," Taj told them. "We can brandish I told you sos later."

"You're taking all the fun out of my self-satisfaction," the engineer told her. "I was already warming up an I told you so, wrapping it around my tongue for ease of access."

"It's what I do," Taj replied, glancing up to see Dent waving at them from the door, which was now cracked open.

"Come on," he called out.

Taj shrugged and hurried toward him. The others followed her closely, but she kept her eyes locked forward. That was where their future was, and the last thing she wanted was miss out on an opportunity to see her people to safety.

Dent disappeared inside, and Taj ran up behind him to keep from losing the android, her eyes adjusting to the dimness of the small hallway they'd entered. Dent didn't seem bothered by the darkness, Taj presuming his eyes were better attuned than the species he pretended to be.

He marched on, leading the way down the hall until it turned to the right. Then he came to a halt a moment later, a door appearing out of the gloom at the end of the second hall.

The whole place smelled of mold and dust. Taj snorted to keep from sneezing.

"This the place?" Torbon asked.

"It is indeed," Dent answered, knocking on the door in a clearly prepared series of rhythmic *thumps* that sounded juvenile in its simplicity.

"Oh cool, a secret knock," Cabe muttered, shaking his head. "This is like every bad holo I've ever watched."

Silence followed the knock for what seemed like a long time afterward, and Taj found herself glancing over her shoulder to watch the corridor behind them while she waited.

Though she couldn't hear anything out of place in her surroundings, and the musky scent of the building didn't trigger her sense of alarm, she stayed ready regardless, hand on her pistol.

The crew grew tense as they waited, and Taj just wanted to get it over with.

When she was ready to kick the door down and storm inside, she heard latches unbolting on the other side, then the door was eased open. A pair of bright emerald eyes stared out at them, their brilliance catching her off guard.

They shined like emeralds in the dim lighting.

"*Zi vall ra,*" the alien said, and Taj realized the translators didn't even attempt to make sense of the words.

"*Ra tora bal,*" Dent answered, and the alien hiding behind the door offered a dour grin and opened the portal wide, waving for them to enter. The translator ignored Dent's comment, too.

"Come in, come in, Dent," the contact said, breaking into a wide grin. "I've been waiting for you."

"Thank you, Pandu," Dent answered, replying with his own grin, however twitchy it might be. Pandu didn't seem to notice or care.

That was when Taj got a clear look at the welcoming alien.

Like Dent's Sperit form, the alien contact was short compared to her and her crew. However, quite unlike Dent, Pandu was nearly wider around than he was tall. He had short, stubby legs that didn't look as if they'd be able to hold him up let alone allow him to move. She couldn't see anything resembling knees on the man.

Taj immediately pictured him dropping onto his side and rolling wherever he needed to go.

She bit back a laugh, disguising it behind a loud cough, and followed the rotund alien inside. Pandu's shirt barely managed to contain his bulk, looking more like a blanket draped over him, and she could swear she heard the material screaming as he waddled away. Tiny arms, thick as tree roots, swung back and forth stiffly as he walked, as if they were engaged in the movement solely to keep him from toppling over sideways.

Torbon wasn't so restrained, and Taj heard him chuckling behind her. Lina hissed at him under her breath, telling him to shut up, but he ignored her.

"I wasn't sure you'd ever arrive," Pandu told Dent as he led the way through the small foyer toward a thick metal door at the rear of the room. "I'd begun to worry after receiving your frantic message."

"I was uncertain myself," Dent answered as Pandu

pressed his squat hand upon a sensor plate set low on the wall beside the door. "The Terant arrival had me concerned, I'll admit. I had not expected them to track me down so quickly."

Pandu nodded as the door *clicked* and swung open their way, the alien clasping its edge, pulling it toward him. "I can understand your concern. I had plenty of my own once I learned you had escaped the Terants and were making your way here with utmost haste." Pandu shuffled to the side of the hall, basically moving behind the door itself as if he moved too slow to get out of its way.

Dent stiffened then, freezing in place. "Wait! How did you know I escaped? I hadn't sent you any—"

The wafting scent of leather oil and alcohol struck Taj right then, and she realized why Pandu had taken cover and Dent had stalled in his apparent accusation.

She bared her teeth and hissed.

"Bloody Rowl, we are *so* gacked."

CHAPTER ELEVEN

"The mechanoid is all yours, Doran," the wide alien mumbled from his safe spot behind the door. Only the shuffle of feet answered him from within the other room. "Remember our deal," the round alien whined. "I have your word."

Taj reached for her weapon, realization sinking in fast, only to hear a gruff voice warn her away from it.

"I wouldn't do that if I were you, Furlorian," the voice said, a shadowy figure strolling out the doorway, followed by a dozen others, all dressed similarly in black leather pants and loose, frilly shirts.

Their auburn skin stood out in stark contrast to the paleness of their shirts. The men had narrow, crimson-colored eyes, and each wore their bluish-black hair long, some of the men tying it back with strips of colorful cloth, which stood out in sharp contrast. Their features were long and thin, almost hawk-like, completely the opposite of Pandu, their chins coming to triple, bony points. Several hid the growths behind scraggly wisps of blue-black beards.

Each of the men held a blaster pistol. All the weapons were pointed in the crew's direction, blackened eyes of death staring them down.

"You did good reaching out to us, Pandu." The first man out the door patted the little alien on his head, as if he were a pet. "The boss will be proud. And fear not, we'll hold true to our promise, as we always do."

Taj groaned when she realized who the men were. "Pirates," she muttered, easing her hand away from her gun as she'd been told, all under the harsh scrutiny of the pirates.

"We prefer to be called mercenaries, if you don't mind," the lead pirate, apparently the one Pandu had called Doran, told her, waving his gun in her direction. "We're businessmen, out to make a deal wherever we can, that's all. Nothing so cutthroat as what one would associate with pirates, I assure you, or we wouldn't be having this conversation, now would we?" he asked. "Now, all of you, ease your weapons out of their holsters and hand them over like good little cats. Your guns are making me a mite nervous, and that's never a good thing for a sensitive fellow such as myself. I wouldn't want to mistake your hesitance for defiance. That wouldn't end well."

Taj growled at the man, and he simply grinned back, no hint that he was remotely threatened.

"You can do as I ask, cat, or we can end this right here and now and I have my men shoot you," Doran said, shrugging, clearly happy with either option. "The boss has no interest in you or your crew, if we're being completely honest here. He only wants him." He pointed at Dent, his grin widening. "Hand the `droid over without a fight and you can go on about your business. I'll even have the boss call off the men currently encircling your ship at the port, landing pad J-17 I recall it being." He turned to the man standing at his left-hand side. "That's the right one, yes, Gully?"

"It is indeed," Gully responded, nodding. "Plenty more cats on board the ship there, a Wyyvan one, unless I'm mistaken."

Taj grunted as she realized she'd walked her people straight into a trap, but she still felt she had some wiggle room to defy the man, hoping to call what she believed was his bluff. "There's no way your ships have arrived already, and my crew are keeping tabs on us through our comm." She tapped the side of her head. "If you had men approaching the ship, I'd know. We'd have seen your ships land."

The pirate leader chuckled. "What, you think all the men we have available are in the ships following you? Come now, don't be so naïve, child."

He shook his head as if he pitied her, and Taj hated the man even more then than she had moments before when he'd gotten the drop on her.

He was reaching max Vort dislike right about then.

"We've an army on Kulora, and more beyond, and those three ships are only a tiny part of it. They're still in space, in fact, making sure your own ship doesn't leave without my say-so. And, if I ask them nicely, they'll blow your ship up from orbit just to make me happy. Shred it right there on the tarmac."

"You're lying," Taj told the pirate.

"Am I?" he replied. "Care to test my resolve, Furlorian? You wouldn't be the first to try it, for sure." He winked at her. "Sometimes, people need to learn the hard way. Are you one of those people, cat? Do you need to suffer to learn your lessons?"

She glared at him a moment, but no matter how much she didn't want to believe the man, there was a malevolence behind his eyes that told her he wasn't one to play games. Unfortunately, she couldn't reach out to Jadie or Kal to confirm anything without alerting the man to what she was doing.

They were on their own.

"So, am I to take your silence as acquiescence to our terms?" he asked. "They're quite generous, if I say so myself, but I'd rather not have to repeat them. Saying them out loud again might make me feel as if I'm being *overly* generous, if you know what I mean. The boss always says I'm too nice. Might need to prove him wrong here soon if we can't come to an accord."

Taj glared a moment longer, feeling the tension in her crew growing as they awaited her decision, and then she gave in, knowing it was the best move to walk away right then. She eased her bolt pistol from its holster and handed it over by the barrel to one of the pirates who stepped up to collect it.

"There we go," Doran told her, offering a pleasant grin as if he'd politely asked her to dinner and she'd accepted.

It made her regret handing the weapon over.

However, as much as she needed Dent and his resources, she wasn't willing to sacrifice her crews' lives on a desperate, half-gacked attempt at resistance. This was not the hill she chose to die on.

"The rest of you, too," the man said, waving his pistol at the crew, a hint of impatience in the gesture.

There was a weighty moment as the crew hesitated, but Dent's voice cut through it all, reinforcing the pirate's demands before things spiraled out of control.

"Do as they ask," the mechanoid said. "I will not see you hurt only to prove a point as to who can be the most chair. Please, pass over your weapons while you still can. I will go willing with these...men. There is no need for violence."

Doran grinned. "That right there is a smart `droid," he noted with a wry chuckle. "I'd do what he says. Well, most of it, at least, minus that *chair* part, whatever that was about. Is that some kind of secret code you've worked out?"

"I wish," Taj muttered, motioning for her people to comply.

The crew mumbled and complained but did exactly as ordered, passing their weapons to the man standing before them. He collected them without a word and moved back behind the rest of the pirates.

"There, that wasn't so difficult, was it?" Doran asked, not giving them a chance to reply. "Now, if you don't mind, clear a path so we can go show our friend here his new digs and introduce him to the boss."

A handful of weapons waved at the crew, black barrels pointing ominously, and Taj and the others were forced to step aside.

"Pleasure doing business with you, cat," Doran told Taj as he and his men strolled past. Guns stayed trained on them the entire time, but Doran didn't waste so much as a backward glance.

Dent did, though. He stared back at the crew, looking as forlorn as his Sperit features allowed, as long as he could before he was led down the hallway and out of sight. Taj felt her stomach knot into a ball, the last image of the mechanoid's face burned into her memory.

Artificial or not, there was no hiding the sorrow she saw in his expression. He'd failed in his mission, and who knew what the pirates had planned for him.

"Gacking Rowl!" she shouted, spinning around to face Pandu, ready to beat the round off him.

He wasn't there anymore.

The alien had scurried through the doorway, faster than Taj would ever imagine he could move, and the last she saw of him was his smirking face as he pulled the heavy door shut with a metallic *thud*. The rest of the crew jumped at the sound.

"Aaaaaaaaaaaah!" Taj kicked the door and felt a sharp stab of pain reverberate up her leg. There was no way they'd get that door open, not without any weapons on hand. "Rowl's bloody gack!"

Unable to question Pandu to find out where the pirates were taking Dent, she spun around again and bolted off down the hall after Doran and his crew. She couldn't let them get out of sight.

"Taj," Cabe called out as he chased after. "What are you doing?"

"I need to see where they're taking him," she answered, not bothering to slow her pace.

The rest of the crew followed her, weaving through the

hallways until they hit the streets again. There, only a short distance ahead, was Doran and his men, the group clearly not in any kind of rush to ditch the Furlorians. Dent muddled along in the middle of the group, several guns blatantly trained on him to keep him from trying to escape.

Cabe clasped Taj's arm, dragging her to a halt as she tried to take off after them. "Are you insane?"

She hissed, batting at his hand. "We can't let him get away," she told him. "He's our only chance at making a real go of settling somewhere. Besides, he's counting on us." She shook Cabe loose, but he grabbed her again, this time harder, desperate to hold on.

"Maybe that's true, but we can't go running off after them like this," he implored. "We're unarmed, outnumbered, and we don't have a clue as to what we're getting involved in."

"You mean like when we were on Krawlas?" Torbon asked, an eyebrow raised in Cabe's direction. "Seems we did all right there."

"Not the same thing, and you know it, Torbon," Cabe hissed at his friend. "We need to be smart about this. This..." he motioned to Taj trying to chase down the pirates, "isn't what I'd call smart."

"What do you suggest?" Taj asked, fighting to get the words out past her rage. The last thing she wanted to do was waste time arguing while Dent—her people's future— was hauled away, never to be seen again.

"We need weapons and a plan," he said. "We don't have either."

"We don't have time for all that," Taj nearly shouted.

"Then we make time." Cabe stepped around her so he

was in her face, not letting her go. "I'll follow them, sneak behind and see where they're going." He tapped the side of his head. "I'll keep in touch via the comm so you know what's going on. You three return to the *Discordant* and get some weapons and people to help us out, and then come find me. We can work something out then, when we have our own army at our back."

"What if they've already gotten what they need from Dent and have destroyed him by then?" Taj asked.

"Then we're no worse off than we are now, but I won't let that happen." He grabbed her again and pulled her in close, planting an insistent kiss on her lips, stunning her into silence. "Go, now!" he told her as soon as he broke free, shoving her back toward the crew.

She stood there, staring, a finger trailing her lips.

An instant later, he was gone, racing off after the pirates, who'd disappeared around a distant corner. She struggled to catch her breath, only realizing too late that he'd pulled the same trick on her that she'd done to him.

"Gack!" she muttered a moment after he was gone, torn between racing after Cabe and doing what he suggested.

It was Lina who shattered her indecision.

"There might be another option if Cabe can't keep up with the pirates," she told Taj. "Gran Verren ran scans on Dent while he was in sickbay, before she realized he was a mechanoid and rebooted him. "She'll have his lifeform signal in the database still. We can use the *Discordant*'s systems to dial in on it and help pinpoint his location."

"He's a damn mechanoid, Lina," Taj argued. "We couldn't pick him up in the wreckage of his ship, so what makes you think we can pick him up on the scanners now?"

Lina grinned. "Because we weren't looking for synthetic lifeforms, which is why he disappeared even though we first picked him up. We narrowed the search too much, which caused us to lose the signal. With S'thlor's help, I can modify the waveform and establish a reasonable link." She waved her arms, encompassing the whole of Ovrun. "The system might struggle with the size of the city, but if we do it quickly enough, we can triangulate a general location and zero in on him."

Taj grunted, splitting a frustrated stare between Lina and the place where Cabe vanished.

"We gotta do it now, Taj," the engineer warned.

"Then let's do it." She nudged Torbon toward the ship, and the three of them shot off, running as fast as they could, dodging pedestrian traffic or plowing through it. Whatever got them there faster.

Right then, she didn't give a gack what anyone thought.

"Be safe, Cabe," she said through the comm once she'd settled into her run.

A whispered, "I will," was the response she got, and hearing his voice was enough to reinforce her determination. They were going to make this work.

She'd return to the *Discordant* and grab every weapon and Furlorian she could, then hunt down the pirates and make them pay for stealing Dent and their chance at a future.

At least that was the idea...until they returned to find a squad of Wyyvan soldiers gathered in front of the leech ship, weapons aimed at the hatchway.

CHAPTER TWELVE

"Uh, that's not good," Torbon muttered, scrambling to an awkward halt and seeking cover behind a nearby ship's landing gear.

"What the gack are they doing here so soon?" Taj asked no one in particular. She huddled up alongside Torbon, Lina right there with them, and glared out at the dozen aliens standing about the *Discordant.* "How the gack did they find us? They couldn't have known where we went after traveling through the gate."

"I'd say the current circumstances suggest otherwise," Torbon said, motioning toward the soldiers. "Those are Wyyvan soldiers standing there, blocking the way to our ship. Well, their ship, but you know what I mean."

Taj reached for her weapon and sighed as her fingers hit the empty holster, scraping leather. She'd forgotten that the pirates had taken it in her rush to get back to the ship. "Rowl," she muttered under her breath. "Can nothing go right today?"

Lina hissed. "Don't tempt fate *or* Rowl," she warned. "We don't need any more challenges."

Taj nodded her agreement. They sure didn't.

What they had splayed out before them was more than enough already, but Taj knew they couldn't let all the gack stop them.

And then, like a sparkstorm roiling in her brain, she remembered why she'd returned to the *Discordant* in the first place. Just inside was an army of Furlorians and enough weapons to arm a good percentage of them.

Taj chuckled. "Gack these lizards."

She tapped the comm and called Kal and Jadie.

Only static answered.

She did it again to the same response: nothing.

"What's going on?" Taj asked Lina. "I'm not getting through."

Lina tried her own comm and groaned, clearly not getting a better result than Taj had. "They're blocking the signal," she replied, waving toward the Wyyvan soldiers, their black armor absorbing the sunlight. "That's why we haven't heard anything from Jadie or Kal. They've been cut off."

"Still, they have to know these guys are out here, milling about," Taj reasoned.

"Probably, but why didn't they engage them while we're gone? That's the quickest way to bring Ovrun security forces down on them, leaving us stranded and them locked up...or worse."

Taj growled. She hadn't thought of that.

Even now, with her and the crew there, to start a battle

on the tarmac would only cause them all more grief. That left her with only one option, which was the very last one she wanted to enact.

But given the circumstances, there wasn't anything else she could do if she hoped to clear the soldiers from the ship without alerting local authorities and muddying the waters.

At least Doran really was bluffing about the men surrounding the Discordant, she thought as she glanced about, seeing nothing but the day-to-day traffic of the port and the mass of Wyyvan soldiers. *That would have mucked things up nicely if he hadn't been.*

She pulled her crew back into the shadows of the landing gear a little further and turned them to face her. "Here's what we're gonna do," she said, meeting each of their eyes in turn. "You two are gonna sneak around over there," she told them, pointing to a small refueling station where they'd be out of sight of the Wyyvan soldiers. "Once you're behind cover, I'm gonna draw the soldiers off. Then—"

"What do you mean *you're* gonna draw them off?" Lina asked. "Alone? Like you snapped at Cabe for doing?"

"I'm allowed to be hypocritical sometimes," Taj told her. "Anyway, I need you two to get onto the ship and prepare the crew once the soldiers are out of the way," she said. "I'll lead the Wyyvans through the city and circle back toward the landing pad, then you guys can get the drop on them and—"

"Blast the green off their scaly lizard hides," Torbon finished, smashing his fist into his palm.

Taj shook her head. "No, we can't do that unless we absolutely have to," she told him.

"What do you mean?" he argued. "Isn't that your plan?"

"It can't be," she replied. "We start shooting people here on the tarmac or in the city proper and there'll be an army of security forces doing the same to us a few seconds later, just like Lina said earlier," she explained, trying to get through to Torbon like Lina had her earlier. "That's not something we're prepared to deal with. Not until we have Dent and Cabe back, and we're ready to get off this rock."

Torbon grunted, throwing his hands in the air. "Then what do we do?" His tail *fwapped* back and forth, slapping his legs. "You two are confusing me. It's like the spirits of Mama and Beaux are right here with us, squashing all the fun."

Taj chuckled despite herself.

"We take the Wyyvans hostage, tie them up, and stash them aboard the *Discordant* until we're ready to leave. Then we dump them and run and let Ovrun security sort it all out once we're off planet."

"So, we're gonna capture a bunch of hostile aliens and add them to the collection we already have, in a ship that can barely fit the people in it now?"

Taj sighed. It was never good when Torbon was the voice of reason.

Still, with Cabe running who knew where after the pirates and all the weapons and reinforcements on the *Discordant*, this was the best plan Taj could come up with.

They were running out of time, and they needed to act.

"Just do it, Torbon," she told him, forcing the last out as

a growl, making sure he understood it was an order not a request. "There's nothing else we can—"

Her sentence was cut short by the mechanical hiss of the leech ship's gangplank swinging down. It landed with a muffled *thump*.

Taj stiffened, her gaze snapping to the ship. "What the gack are they doing?" *No, stay in the ship!* she screamed inside her head as the ship's door opened. She started toward the craft, then froze as a familiar voice struck her, catching her completely off guard.

"Gentlemen, it's clear there's been some form of mistake here," Captain Vort said as he strolled down the gangplank toward the mass of Wyyvan soldiers as calmly as though he were out for a stroll.

They stiffened like Taj had, staring up at the Wyyvan captain through their darkened visors, heads tilted. If Taj could see their faces, she knew their expressions would be ones of serious *what the gack?*

"Captain Vort sir?" one of the soldiers managed to ask. "Uh, why are you here?"

"I was wondering the exact same thing," Taj mumbled from their hiding spot, glaring at the unexpected arrival of the captain. "Kal and I are gonna have to have a talk about appropriate prisoner behavior and boundaries."

"As opposed to being blown to tiny pieces on the surface of Krawlas, you mean?" Vort asked, shaking his head and letting out a weary sigh. "I know the decision wasn't yours, of course, that being well above your pay grade, but I still find myself disconcerted that my own people would rather see me dead among the local rodents than to send a rescue team down to the surface. How difficult would that have been?" He raised a finger, demanding silence. "I'll answer that for you. Not remotely difficult at all. A tiny concession on behalf of Grand Admiral Galforin and a few moments of a shuttle crew's time and we wouldn't be in the current situation we find ourselves in, now would we?"

"Uh, sir, I don't know what you're talking about," the soldier told Vort. "My orders are to follow the tra—"

"Of course it is, and of course you don't," he replied, cutting the soldier off before he could finish whatever he was saying. "We must all do what we must do, such is our lot in life. As such..." he waved behind him, "I truly hope you understand that this is what I *must* do."

Vort stepped off the side of the gangplank, clearing the way to the *Discordant*'s door. Commander Dard appeared from the gloom, carrying a massive-barreled weapon Taj had never seen before. He aimed it at the cluster of soldiers and pulled the trigger without even a hint of hesitation.

A great, burst of electricity shot forth, searing a blinding streak across Taj's retinas. It ripped through the cluster of surprised soldiers. The men stiffened as their armor lit up, glowing white against the blackness. Bolts of lightning shot between the men, current tearing through one Wyyvan only to do the same to next.

Not more than a split-second later, all of the soldiers were caught in what looked like a ferion spider web of licking blue-white current. They thrashed in place, the current leading the dance.

Backlit by the electricity, Taj could see the faces of the Wyyvans beneath their visors, agony distorting them as their skin charred and smoked. The scent of char grew thick in the air.

A moment later, it was all over.

The squad of Wyyvan soldiers collapsed without a shout or a pistol drawn, armor smoldering in the creases as Dard eased his finger from the trigger. The commander grinned, holding the weapon aloft.

The Wyyvan soldiers dead, Taj shot off toward the commander. She only had a moment before he or Vort spied her and the rest of the crew outside.

Then she didn't even have that.

Dard turned toward her, a sly grin on his face. He shifted the barrel in her direction.

"Not a chance, lizard," Kal said with a growl, appearing from inside the *Discordant* and pressing his bolt pistol to the back of the commander's head. "Put it down slowly, like we agreed."

Dard sighed and lowered the weapon. Jadie came up behind him and snatched it away, sneering the entire time. A half-dozen more Furlorians spilled from the doorway, each carrying a pistol aimed at the two captive Wyyvan.

"Valiant effort, Commander," Vort told him with a shrug. "Perhaps next time." He chuckled, shifting his gaze to Taj. "It might be easier to say thank you if you closed your jaw."

Taj snapped her mouth shut and glared up at Kal. "Are you crazy?" she asked. "Letting these monsters have a weapon?" She turned her attention to the cannon-like gun Jadie now clutched to her chest. "What the gack is that thing, anyway? Where did it come from?"

"It's a charge rifle," Vort answered, "and it, along with

many other weapons, are stored aboard the leech craft." His grin grew wider. It was clear the alien loved an audience. "And had you listened to me during our little chat in the closet you so kindly stuffed Dard and I into, you would have realized I truly *do* know far more than you do. About pretty much everything, if we're being honest. It's embarrassing, really."

Taj growled and started toward the captain, baring her teeth.

"An example of such," he said, ignoring her threatening advance, "you might want to clean up the mess before the locals spy a bunch of dead soldiers littering their tarmac. The charge rifle won't trigger their security protocols, seeing how its discharge is so very much like a ship testing its shields according to their automated scanners." He chuckled. "Such a lazy system here. However, while they might not sense the weapon, a pile of corpses can't be explained away should it be seen by someone." Vort shrugged. "Of course, you could leave them there if your plan is to be captured and held until Wyyvan Command is contacted and you are delivered to them for murder and piracy of a leech craft. I certainly wouldn't be offended if that were your choice."

Taj glared at Captain Vort a moment, finally managing to bring her temper under control. Still, her ears were warm, pinned against her head, as she waved to Kal.

"Get these bodies inside and keep the weapons and armor away from Vort and Dard," she said, offering the pair a dirty look in turn. "And I want them in their cell until *I* say otherwise, is that clear, Kal?"

Kal's shoulders slumped, and he nodded, knowing he'd crossed a line even though it had saved them all.

He motioned for the other Furlorians to do as they were told, and Taj's people raced down the gangplank, quickly scooping up limp Wyyvan soldiers and hauling them into the bowels of the *Discordant*. A few moments later, there was no evidence anything had happened on the tarmac save for a few scorched spots, for which Taj was grateful.

Not grateful enough, however, to forget how furious she was with Vort. She spun on him, jabbing a finger in his face. "How did your people find us so quickly, Vort?"

The captain didn't so much as blink. "I have no idea, Furlorian," he answered, shrugging, "but I'd be worried there are more coming soon after. I can hardly see Grand Admiral Galforin only sending one pathetic little squad after the *Discordant* and the unfortunate souls who stole it." He cast a glance toward each of the crew in turn before turning his focus back to Taj. His smile brightened. "Were I you, I'd pack up and run before anyone notices the empty Wyyvan craft and its missing crew. It won't be long before they do, I assure you."

Taj growled, realizing he was right. How long would it take before someone noticed a Wyyvan ship parked unattended in port and called the authorities? Or had the soldiers already been there on planet when Taj and her people had arrived? Were there more of them waiting for the first group to check in?

There was no way to know if Vort was telling the truth or feeding her misinformation in order to take advantage of the situation. Either was likely because both stood to confuse her, and both benefited him.

"Bloody Rowl," she muttered. "Get these two out of my face before I—"

A raspy voice cut through the reinstated comm right then, cutting her off. Though it was clear the message had been whispered, the words barely audible above all the noise on the tarmac, Taj knew immediately who it was: *Cabe!*

"Uh...bit of a problem," he said. "Help!"

CHAPTER THIRTEEN

Taj and Torbon raced to where Cabe last contacted them from, having left Lina behind to work with S'thlor and Gran Verren to better coordinate Dent's location should they not be able to find either of them.

Kal and Jadie came with Taj, as well as about twenty of the younger Furlorians. Each of them carried bolt pistols or stolen Wyyvan blasters hidden beneath their clothing to keep from looking conspicuous, though Taj didn't figure it mattered much now.

Torbon carried the charge rifle they'd taken from Captain Vort, and there was no way to hide its bulk. He held it out in the open, grinning at it the entire time they walked.

"Where is he?" Taj asked, breathless, slipping down an alley in a huff. She surveyed the area, eyes darting back and forth. "Where is he? I don't see him."

"He's not here, Taj," Torbon answered, catching up to

her and leaning against the wall to relax, the heavy rifle hanging loosely in his hands.

"No gack, Torbon," she growled. "I can see that. We need to find him." She tapped her comm hard, sending a ringing thrum through her skull. "Lina, can you pinpoint Cabe?"

"Uh, I wasn't looking," she answered. "He's not where he told you he would be?"

"No," Taj replied, only barely managing not to bite the engineer's head off. "He's not here."

"Been focused on Dent," Lina said, deflecting Taj's anger. "I can maybe target Cabe's comm and see if he's nearby..." There was a pause, and Taj read the question in Lina's voice. She was asking if that's what Taj wanted her to focus on rather than tracking down the mechanoid.

"Gack it," she moaned. "No, stick to confirming where Dent is. We'll find Cabe if they aren't together."

She stomped down the alley and peeked around the corner at the other end. Her heart sputtered at what she saw, and she darted back behind the cover of the wall. She had a bad feeling she knew exactly where Cabe was.

"What is it?" Jadie asked, coming up alongside Taj.

"We're in the right place," she replied, nodding toward the corner.

Jadie eased forward and snuck a glance. She hissed and pulled back, much like Taj had. "You think he's in there?"

"What are you talking about?" Torbon asked, leaning on the charge rifle, unable to get around Taj and Jadie to take a look.

"The pirates," Jadie answered. "They're guarding a building across the street. Quite a few of them."

Lina came across the comm. "Looks like Dent is right near you," she said. "I'd say less than twenty meters by my determination."

"That puts him right behind our army of pirates," Taj said with a grunt. While she was glad of confirmation as to his whereabouts, the small army of men outside the location wasn't exactly reassuring.

Torbon chuckled and patted the weapon in his hands. "I can take care of them if you want."

Taj waved him off. "Not yet. We need to be sure where Cabe is before we go indiscriminately blasting people and making a whole bunch of noise. If our pirate friends have captured him, they could hurt Cabe if we start killing them. We can't have that."

"So, you're saying I get to blast people, just not yet?" he asked, looking for confirmation.

She nodded.

"Then how about now?"

Taj sighed. "Wait a minute, gack it."

"How about now?" he asked, waving the rifle about. "Now a good time? I'm ready."

"I'm gonna shoot you first," she told him, spitting the words out between gnashing teeth.

"Always so hostile," he told her, shaking his head and letting out a disappointed sigh. "I bet you would let Cabe do it if I were in there."

"Let Cabe do what?" Cabe asked as he strode up to them, having come from the far end of the alleyway.

Taj snarled at his sudden appearance and threw herself at him, wrapping him up in a tight hug. His eyes went wide, his tail waggling hard behind him.

Torbon's voice echoed across the comm. "We found our wayward kitty, Lina. Call off the hounds," he said, letting loose with a chuckle he muffled against his hand. "Get it?"

Lina sighed. Everyone else ignored him.

"Ack...can't breathe," Cabe choked out, arms flailing. His whiskers fluttered as he gasped, finally managing to get his hands wedged between him and Taj's arms, peeling her off. "What's wrong?"

Taj took a quick step back. "What's wrong? What do you mean what's *wrong*? You called for help," she said, her voice rising at the last. "Then we couldn't find you. I thought you were in trouble."

"Well," he replied, raising his hands to ward her off, "I kinda was for a minute there. Doran spotted me at one point. He sent some men after me, but I managed to lose them and sneak back around in time to catch the pirates delivering Dent here, to that building across the street. I was circling back when you showed up."

Taj grunted, fighting back her frustration with the happiness that Cabe was okay and that nothing had happened to him. She sucked in a deep breath to keep her words from coming out like flying knives. "You couldn't have let us know you were okay? We were worried about you."

"And by *we*, she means *her*," Torbon clarified with a crooked grin. "I wasn't worried. I had this to comfort me." He lifted the charge rifle, winking at it.

Jadie raised her hand tentatively. "I was a *little* worried."

"Really?" Torbon asked with a huff. "It's always Cabe this, Cabe that. Oh, Rowl, Cabe's gonna die, what will we ever do without him?" He pushed out an exaggerated sigh.

"Well, I am prettier than you," Cabe replied, chuckling.

"How do you figure? I've got—"

"You 've got to stop wasting our time, is what you've got," Taj said, cutting him off. She sneered at Torbon and turned away to face Cabe. "You have any idea why they took Dent? Why they brought him here?"

Cabe shook his head. "No, they didn't say, but I did hear them mention they were waiting for the boss to show up."

"The same one Doran mentioned back at Pandu's?"

Cabe shrugged. "I guess, but it's not like anyone's mentioned a name. They only called him the boss. Seems likely it's the same person, though." He waved in the general direction of the building with all the pirates out front. "Probably not a good idea to be here when he arrives, so if we're gonna get Dent out of there, I suggest we do it now. There's over twenty men inside, plus all those guarding the front. Who knows how many the boss will bring with him. It's gonna get a bit hairy if we try to take them head on."

Taj nodded. They needed to rescue Dent, but if they went after him now, they would have to fight their way through a bunch of pirates to reach him, which was bad enough. But if the boss showed up while they were inside, the crew would be caught between the two forces and would likely end up losing.

Losing meant dying, she was sure.

Doran had only let them go the first time because they hadn't caused him any grief. He had no personal stake in their fates. She couldn't imagine him feeling the same way if they went busting into the building and killing a bunch of his men in their efforts to free Dent.

But what other options were there?

Taj peeked around the corner once more, watching as the pirates moseyed back and forth in front of the building. They were loose and relaxed, but their hands hovered near their weapons in a casual way that made Taj think it really wasn't all *that* casual. They were ready for anything.

She thought about sneaking around back and surveying the building, but she dismissed the idea, doubting it would provide her with additional opportunities to get inside. As prepared as the men were, she had to assume there were more around back or there simply wasn't any way to get inside from there at all.

Besides, if she sent someone, or even went herself, there was no way they could do it alone if there was an opening. That left her people short up front, putting them at even more risk than they were already.

She growled and looked about, letting her eyes take in everything around her. It took a long moment, her brain processing every little detail of the scene but, at last, she noticed something she hadn't seen before.

She spun around to speak with Cabe. "Where were you when you were losing the pirates?"

"Uh, only a little bit that way," he answered, motioning off toward the left side of the building they were surveilling. "Down that narrow street over there."

"What's there?" she asked.

"What do you mean?" He scratched at his fur. "There's nothing there, really. There's an alley that leads out to the street, a kind of bottleneck, then the city opens up in every direction after a short distance. That's how I lost them, veering off into the normal, day-to-day street traffic once I made it past the enclosed area."

"Did you happen to go past there?" She pointed at the alley on the right side of the pirate building, where a high fence blocked the opening of the alley.

He nodded. "I did, but it's blocked off on the other side, too, pretty congested. It's like a delivery area. Tons of boxes and trash litter the entire thing, making it almost impossible for anyone to traverse it from one side to the other without having to move a bunch of junk."

Taj grinned, her teeth reflecting the dim light of the alley. "Good. That's just what I wanted to hear."

"Wait," Cabe started. "Why is that a good thing?"

She ignored him and turned to Torbon. "You and Jadie stay here and wait for my signal. The rest of you, come with me."

"Hey!" Torbon called out before she started off. "What are we supposed to do while we're waiting on you, sit around and fluff our fur?"

"You wanted to blast people, right?"

He nodded. "Well, yeah."

"Then sit tight, stay quiet and out of sight, and you'll get your chance."

It looked as if he wanted to ask another question, but a quick glance at the charge rifle in his hands seemed to pacify him.

"Keep an eye on him," Taj told Jadie, who replied with a nod. "Don't let him start anything until I give the order." Torbon sneered his disappointment at Taj, but Jadie brought him into check with a smack on his shoulder. He grunted and conceded to his aunt.

After that was settled, Taj waved the rest of her people on, backtracking through the alley the way they'd first come in. The crew circled the nearest building and headed toward the area Cabe had described. He sidled up alongside her. "Care to let me know what you're planning?"

"Nope."

Cabe raised a questioning eyebrow. "Might help if we knew what the gack we were supposed to be doing."

"Probably would," she agreed, "but that would mean *I* needed to know what I was doing first."

Cabe stumbled for a second, slowing and falling behind, then raced to catch back up to Taj. "So, what you're saying is, we're winging it?"

"We're winging it."

"Great," he replied with a sigh as they ran on. "That never goes wrong."

In actuality, Taj knew exactly what she intended. She didn't think Cabe or the others would approve, however, but this was what leadership was all about. Making the hard choices when other people couldn't or wouldn't.

Or making the foolish choices.

Taj mentally shrugged, thinking about her decision.

This one could go either way, but she'd weighed the options, and her course of action was the best.

CHAPTER FOURTEEN

After the crew made their way to an alley a short distance from the building where the pirates were holed up with Dent, Taj brought the group to a halt. They spread out around her, getting ready for whatever she had in mind.

The location looked onto a street with no foot traffic. It was a rundown neighborhood under a blanket of gloom that kept everyone on the main street from veering off into it. Only the occasional chirp of a bird echoed between the buildings to let Taj know the place was real.

She stared at the nearby crossroads, counting off steps in her head and wondering how quickly she could reach each corner.

"Uh, care to let us know why we're here now?" Cabe asked. His impatience showed in the frantic twitch of his tail. She understood his worries, but the last thing she needed was him trying to talk her out of what she planned.

And he would try, but it had to happen.

She ignored him, continuing to survey the area, ears cocked to listen.

Cabe had apparently had enough and wrapped a hand around her arm. He spun her around to face him. "Seriously, Taj. What are we doing here?"

She met his stare for a moment until she realized he wasn't going to back down. At last, she snorted and shook her arm free. "I don't see any other way for us to get everything we need without putting all our people at risk. This idea of mine eliminates some of that."

"Only if you let us in on it, Taj," he told her, gesturing to the gathering of Furlorians that surrounded them. "Leaving us in the dark only compounds the risk we're taking, our people are taking. You can't expect them to just go along with whatever—"

"I'm gonna kidnap the boss," she said, cutting his admonishment off mid-sentence.

He stiffened, eyes going wide. "Say what?" Cabe shook his head, as if trying to make sense of her words. "Are you crazy?"

Taj shrugged. The thought had crossed her mind once or twice while she envisioned her plan. "Maybe, but I think it's the best chance we have of getting what we need and not putting Dent, or us, in any more danger than necessary."

"So, your idea is to kidnap the boss of a bunch of pirates and you think that's not gonna put us in more danger than...say, walking away and finding another way to get supplies and directions?"

Taj hissed, shushing him to keep the rest of the Furlorians from overhearing them. "Tell me what other options we have, Cabe," she said, crossing her arms over her chest. "I'll wait."

"I just told you one. Walking away," he answered, slamming his fists into his hips and standing defiant. "This is stupid."

"Not arguing that it isn't," she replied, "but it's also an unexpected move and provides us with leverage to get everything we need."

"Or to get everyone killed."

Taj growled. "We're already close to that," she told him, inching closer. "We've no money, no food, and no way to contact the Federation, if they can help us or even want to. What's left to do, Cabe?"

"We can ask around about the Federation here on Kulora," he suggested. "Someone has to know about them and how to find them."

"Sure, we can do that. Then what happens if the Federation is the enemy here?" She waved her hands around, encompassing the city. "Wyyvans land here freely, pirates, too, and who knows who else. All of these people operate freely, out in the open. They're not skulking around in the dark," she explained.

"That likely means the Federation isn't nearby or this place would be way less peaceful, one side or the other pressing the issue and drawing the planet into a war. The fact that there isn't a battle raging over our heads right now likely means that everyone here is in league with the Wyyvans, or at least tolerate them. It also stands to reason they don't have any love for the Federation."

Taj turned and paced in a tight circle, letting the heat of

the moment burn off. She hated being mad at Cabe, but she felt he was being obstinate.

Maybe she was, too, but she knew it in her gut that her plan was the best move they could make given their circumstances. She just had to make him see that.

A few seconds later, she stopped and met Cabe's eyes again.

"You think Wyyvan Command isn't gonna notice the crew missing that they sent after us? You think they won't send more soldiers?" she asked, picturing a flood of Wyyvans coming after them after they'd murdered an entire ship's crew. "Even if we ditch the *Discordant*, they'll know we're on the planet. We might as well surrender to them if that's the plan, Cabe."

He groaned, turning away. Still, Taj saw what she needed to in his eyes before he did. She'd gotten through to him, made him see the sense in her argument. Only, he wasn't ready to admit it yet.

Fortunately, he didn't have to. Circumstances forced the issue.

One of the other Furlorians tapped her on the shoulder. "Someone's coming," she whispered, pointing around the corner where they'd hunkered down to watch the traffic beyond.

Taj nodded and resumed her place at the corner, peering around it. Her stomach tightened at what she saw.

In a good way.

She grinned. While she and the crew hadn't had much in the way of luck of late, it was clear fate was working in their favor at the moment.

The pirate boss—as that was the only person he could

be—strolled down the street with confidence in his stride, his auburn skin marking his affiliation even better than the leather pants and frilled shirt he wore in common with his underlings.

It might as well be a uniform, Taj thought. *Sad.*

The boss stood tall and lithe, a subtle grace—or more likely a natural arrogance—setting him apart from the other pirates Taj had encountered, barring his second in command, Doran.

Alongside him walked only a handful of men, and Taj thanked Rowl for her unexpected generosity to their cause. For once, the persnickety cat goddess had offered her blessing.

The men seemed nearly as aloof as their boss, unprepared for violence, as if they couldn't imagine anyone daring to challenge their supremacy here in their very own den.

Taj bit back a chuckle and turned to her people. She whispered, "We need the tall one alive, but the rest have to go. Understand?"

The Furlorians nodded and hoisted their weapons, making ready to leap out at Taj's command.

Taj nodded and waved her people forward, glad to have Cabe at her side. She couldn't imagine doing this without him there.

"Hit them hard and fast and, most of all, be safe," she ordered.

Then she was around the corner, racing straight toward the boss and his men.

"Hey!" one of the pirates shouted, only going for his weapon when the twenty or so other Furlorians spilled out of the alley behind her, giving him a pretty good idea as to what they intended.

Violence.

"Get down, boss," the same pirate screamed.

As it turned out, those were his last words.

Taj pulled the trigger and blasted a smoking crater in his chest. He hit the ground an instant later, clutching at his wound, wide eyes staring blankly at the gray sky.

Bolt pistols and stolen Wyyvan blasters sounded all around her, a torrent of noise, and Taj watched as the rest of the boss's guards were hit. Each stumbled and fell under the barrage of gunfire, only one getting off a shot in return. That blast streaked into the alley behind them, striking nowhere near any of the advancing Furlorians.

Within seconds, the pirate boss stood alone in the street, his men scattered dead at his feet. Calmly, he glanced from his appraisal of the corpses to Taj as she approached.

"You're making a grave mistake," he said, his voice like a handful of stones being ground together. "There will be consequences for your actions, you can be sure of that."

Taj grinned and plucked the man's pistol from its holster. He hadn't even tried to draw it. "I'm counting on it actually." She passed the confiscated weapon to another Furlorian and waved them forward. "Search this man, then bind his hands and hobble his thighs. Not too tight, though. I want him to be able to walk a bit, just not run." As Cabe and three of the Furlorians went to follow her orders, she motioned to the others. "Let's get these bodies out of sight. Stash them in the alley. We can't have anyone stumbling across them until we're long gone."

Her people jumped to the task and dragged the bodies away. Taj settled in alongside the pirate boss as they worked, grabbing him by the arm to help hold him in place, not that he resisted. Once he was secured, and his guards were hidden away as best they could be, she marched him down the alleyway, heading back toward the first building they'd come across.

"What do we call you?" Taj asked the boss.

"I'll be your executioner soon," he answered, "but my parents named me Rath, if it makes any difference."

Taj shrugged. "Just being polite," she answered. "We're gonna be spending a little while together, so figured it'd be best if I knew your name so I can call you something other than pirate boss. Mine is Taj, and that's Cabe over there, the guy giving you the dirty look. He was against all this, for the record."

"Then he's the smartest of the lot," Rath told her, quite certain in his assessment. "This is a mistake.

Cabe gestured to Rath with his eyes, an I told you so aimed at Taj unspoken in his glare.

She let him have his quiet jab. "Funny, Cabe said the exact same thing a little while ago."

"Then you should have heeded his warning, girl," he said. "My men will—"

"Your men will regret their part in all of this in a moment," she replied, yanking him hard against the wall as they neared the first alley where they'd tracked down Cabe and Dent earlier. She pressed her gun against the boss's ribs, eliciting a satisfying *oomph* from him, and triggered her comm. "You're on, Torbon," she said. "Hit them."

Around the corner, not more than a second later, there

was a sudden burst of electrical energy, and Taj moved the pirate boss out where both of them could see what was going on.

The pirates stationed outside the building where Dent was being held shrieked in sudden agony. Torbon emerged from the alleyway, grinning, the charge rifle aimed at the pirates. Current surged from its barrel and engulfed the guards. They danced awkwardly under the electrical burst, smoke billowing from their eyes and mouths. Then, not more than a few seconds later, Torbon released the trigger and the men collapsed in charred heaps.

Taj waved Torbon back out of sight, Jadie along with him, and Taj moved toward the door of the building, the rest of her people alongside her, weapons out and ready. Cabe positioned himself beside her, inching forward enough to defend her should he need to.

She grinned at his protectiveness.

"Shouldn't be long now," Taj said, hunched down behind the boss, turning him into a shield to help reinforce her position and allow her to leverage the man against his people.

Right on cue, the door to the building was flung open, and a dozen pirates stormed out, guns in hand and fierce snarls aplenty. They froze when they saw their boss standing among the Furlorians, bound, a gun pressed unkindly to his head. They stiffened and came to a halt, clearly unsure how to react.

Taj made it simple for them.

"Unless you want your boss's brains decorating the street, I suggest you drop your weapons and stand down," she called out. They didn't need to know she was bluffing.

There was no way she could kill Rath in cold blood, tied up as he was, unable to resist, but all that mattered was that his men believed it.

The pirates hesitated a moment, and Taj *thumped* the gun against their boss's skull loud enough for everyone to hear. The sound echoed between the buildings.

Rath grunted at the impact, and that got his men's attention. The clatter of guns hitting the street followed.

"Excellent choice," she told the pirates. "Collect those," Taj directed her people, watching and waiting until they'd completed the task of rounding up the weapons.

When they were finished, she spoke to the pirates again. "Now, move over there and put your noses to the wall," she said. Again, they hesitated but another *thump* of her pistol against their boss' skull had them scrambling.

Once they were there, she ordered them onto their knees. "Everyone but you," she said, pointing to the man nearest the door. "You get to go inside and bring out the mechanoid." She motioned for five of her people to go with the pirate. "Do anything stupid, alert your friends, try to hurt mine, and I guarantee your boss will be nothing more than a gooey stain on the street. You understand?"

He nodded, let the Furlorians gather around him, and then led them inside the building without a word of protest. Once they were gone, Taj glanced over at the pirates huddled against the wall. She knew she needed to do something about them, but she couldn't find it in herself to simply kill them, no matter how much of a threat they were.

Still, if the one they sent inside managed to bring out reinforcements, the last thing she needed was a bunch of angry pirates sitting nearby. Their presence could turn the tides on what had been a surprisingly successful plan.

She moved over to the first in line and smashed her pistol grip into the back of the man's skull. He grunted and slumped unconscious. Taj returned her gun to the boss's ribs, calling out to her people. "Knock the rest of them out."

Her people did as they were told with no hint of dissatisfaction. They clearly enjoyed the opportunity, and Taj couldn't blame them one bit.

Within a few moments, all the disarmed pirates were unconscious on the ground.

Not a minute after that, the pirate Taj had sent inside returned with his entourage in tow, Dent following along behind the group. His mechanoid eyes widened even further than possible when he saw Taj and the other Furlorians standing there, the pirate boss subdued.

"Interesting outcome," he said, nodding in what Taj believed was approval. "I-I had not expected...this." He twitched in time to his words, one eye fluttering and growing dimmer than the other.

It was clear he'd been through an ordeal in the time since they'd lost him to the pirates. He ambled slowly, even more awkwardly than before, swaying as if he struggled to keep his balance. His shoulders were slumped, and he appeared to have developed a hunched back, as if his servos were incapable of holding him upright.

"Neither did I," Cabe replied before smacking the last standing pirate in the head with his gun. The man crumpled to the ground. "We should get going," he told Taj. "I doubt the Ovrun security forces have much traction in these parts, but you never know."

"I couldn't agree more," she told him, tearing her eyes from Dent's battered appearance.

She then waved her people back toward the *Discordant*. They started off in a shuffle, surrounding Rath to keep it from being so obvious they were dragging along a bound man.

They might well get away with roaming the streets with weapons brandished, but there was no way someone wouldn't report the hostage in their midst if he was spotted.

It was even more likely if the man were recognized.

Dent matched his pace to Taj's, walking alongside her. He stared at the pirate boss as if analyzing the man. The boss stared back without blinking, appearing even more mechanical and cold than Dent ever could.

"All this fuss over you?" Rath asked, shaking his head. "It's a shame you dragged these innocent souls down with you. They're going to suffer for helping you, mechanoid."

Dent seemed genuinely concerned by the threat, his alien features narrowing into a look of uncertainty. "I did not mean to involve them," he said, "but be certain, I will do everything I can to ensure their bisque."

Rath stared at Dent a moment, then burst into laughter. Sharp, slicing laughter.

Dent appeared offended.

"I'd heard you were a bit...damaged, but I hadn't realized the extent, mechanoid. You should really surrender and let me free that information from your skull before it erodes to the point of being useless to everyone," the pirate boss told Dent. "You're no good to your people if your data is all muddled. In fact, you're a threat to their survival. You could be the very reason they no longer exist. Do you want that burden on your mechanical shoulders?"

Dent stumbled at Rath's words, his face pinched with distress. Taj slowed to stay right there with him. She wished she had a free hand to comfort him with. He looked like he could use it.

"Don't listen to him. He's only trying to get into your head, Dent," she told the mechanoid.

"Quite literally," Rath replied with a chortle. He looked about, casting his gaze over his shoulder to Taj. "You are truly in this deep, and you don't even know it." He shook his head, sighing like a disappointed parent. "What this `droid carries in his skull is worth more than the lives of all of your people combined, and my associates won't hesitate to kill you to get their hands on it."

"No one asked you, Rath," Taj said with a growl. "Keep your mouth shut or I'll have you gagged."

He shrugged. "Gag me, shoot me, whatever. It won't change anything. I'm only good as leverage for a short time, and then everything changes, and there's nothing you or anyone else can do about it."

"Then I best take advantage of the time I have, right?" She smacked him upside the head with her gun, drawing a pained grunt from the pirate boss. He glared at her, but she ignored him, not wanting to be drawn further in. "Let's go, people, we're on the clock. Back to the ship."

She didn't know exactly how honest Rath was being with his threats, but she didn't like the idea that there might be more to the kidnapping of Dent than she understood. Not that she understood much more than there was money to be made by controlling Dent.

Rath had said *associates* in his tirade, which didn't make her think he meant his men, the cluster of pirates he surrounded himself with. Given the haughty way he carried himself, she couldn't see him considering his soldiers as anything near equal.

That meant someone else was out there searching for Dent and Rath was only a pawn in that. It also meant that target would land square on her crew's back if they were still around when that someone came looking.

She growled, wondering how much more trouble she'd gotten her people into, all the while wondering how she was going to get them out of it.

CHAPTER FIFTEEN

Moments before they reached the *Discordant*, Cabe, who was leading the way, spun around and grabbed Taj. He yanked her and the pirate boss back into the shadows of a nearby pleasure craft and slapped his hand over Rath's mouth to keep the man quiet.

A quick-witted Furlorian tore a thick strip off his shirt and handed it to Cabe, who then gagged the pirate boss. To his credit, Rath grinned through it all as best he could, not appearing to show any signs of discomfort or frustration.

The coldness of his stare was unnerving, so she peeled her eyes away, looking to Cabe

"What is it?" Taj asked him.

Cabe passed control of the boss to the Furlorian who'd offered up his shirt, and he waved Taj over, leading her to the base of the pleasure ship's raised landing berth. Taj glanced around the corner and bit back a snarl. Torbon joined them a moment later.

Taj heard him muffle a gasp behind them.

"You have got to be yanking my tail," Taj groaned.

Much like how they'd found the mass of Wyyvans earlier, a milling group of pirates stood near the *Discordant*. A quick count told her there were almost thirty of them, all armed and clearly waiting for them, ready for action.

"How did they know what we did so quickly?" Taj asked, racking her brain, and then it hit her. "Bloody Rowl," she cursed. She thought back and growled low in her throat. "Doran," she said. "He wasn't among the pirates we lured out of the building. He must have slipped away in the chaos."

She spun around and called over the group of Furlorians who'd gone inside. "Was there anyone else inside the building where you retrieved the mechanoid?"

They all shook their heads, and Taj raised her face to the sky, snarling. "Rowl giveth and Rowl taketh," she muttered.

"Mostly taketh," Torbon replied with a shrug.

"Doran must have realized things weren't working out in his favor and fled, letting the rest of his men know what was going on once he was clear." She gestured toward the mass of pirates around the *Discordant*. "They're making it so we can't get to our ship. They know we have their boss."

"Why can't we use him to push past?" Cabe asked. "I'm sure he'd make a good shield. Isn't that what you wanted him for anyway?"

"There's too many of them," Taj replied. "Plus, we don't have any idea if that's all of them. There could be more hidden about where we can't see. If we march in there, there's a good chance we can't control all of them, and they'll end up getting their boss back. If that happens, we're dead."

Cabe nodded his acceptance of her reasoning, though it was clear he didn't quite agree. Taj understood. They were too close to getting off planet, and now they were stuck once again, facing off with a large, dangerous force that had settled in beneath their ship to wait them out.

Worse still, the pirates were smarter than the Wyyvan soldiers who'd come calling. They didn't mass at the end of the gangplank, waiting to be shot by emerging forces. No, they surrounded the craft and stayed out of easy fire lines. If anyone came out of the ship, it would be them in danger, not the pirates.

These men were well-trained.

"So, what do we do?" Cabe asked. "It's not like we can sit around here waiting. The longer we do that, the more likely more pirates will show up and pin us between them, then we're truly gacked."

Taj agreed and tapped her comm, not remotely surprised to find the signal blocked again. She stared at the ship, wondering if her people inside had any clue of what was going on outside.

She hoped not, since she didn't want to put any of them at risk, but she knew better. Lina had been tracking Dent, and she was sure the engineer was still doing it. She'd know he was outside.

Then it clicked in Taj's head that Lina wouldn't necessarily know the pirates were out there, too, only that Dent was. Now that he'd stopped moving, Lina might question why and come out looking for them.

Taj glared at the *Discordant*'s entryway and willed Lina

to be smart and not reckless. The last thing they needed was her or any of the others coming outside and exposing themselves to being captured or killed. That'd seriously gack all the effort that went into the capture of Rath.

"We need to move," she told the crew, shaking her head all the while. "Need to draw these pirates out, give our people a chance to react." This wasn't what she wanted to do, putting them all at risk, again, but she had to hope that making a commotion would ensure things played out in a way that Taj could control, at least to some small degree.

She growled and stepped around the landing berth, ready to call out to the pirates and draw their ire. Then she froze, the words clinging to her tongue.

Torbon bumped into her from behind. "What the gack, Taj?" Then he too stiffened in place, and Cabe glanced over their shoulders to see what had so stunned the pair.

"You have got to be gacking me," he mumbled, pushing past them so he was stationed in front of them.

Taj continued to stare.

The pirates, suddenly aware something was going on, gathered and moved across the tarmac with purpose, weapons leveled.

Fortunately for Taj, that particular purpose didn't involve her or her people.

There, on the far side of the *Discordant*, two squads of Wyyvan soldiers marched forward, headed directly toward the stolen leech craft and the mass of pirates surrounding it.

"Seriously, which one of you pissed Rowl off?" Torbon whispered.

Taj wondered the same thing.

It was one thing to have to face down an army of pirates, but now they had another army of Wyyvans to contend with at the same time. This was about as difficult a circumstance as Taj could imagine right then.

"Gack me," Taj muttered and turned around, running her hand through her fur in hopes of spurring some sort of plan...*any* sort of plan.

Rath grinned at her through his gag, his amusement gleaming in his eyes. He was loving every moment of her frustration, even if he didn't know exactly what was going on.

She wanted to give him a taste of the same violence she'd visited upon Vort. Her fist clenched in response to her fury.

Taj looked away, unwilling to face the pirate boss. Smashing her fist into his face wouldn't do anything to help them no matter how good it would make her feel.

Dent wandered over to her side and peeked around the corner, apparently needing to see what the commotion was all about.

"That looks qu-quite unfortunate," he said. "It seems my quest is doooooooomed."

Taj sneered at the mechanoid. "Is that all you care about?" she asked. "Your quest?" Taj shook her head. "Your people are already dead, Dent. Dead and gone. Yet my people, those who risked their lives to save you, are in danger. They're still alive, but they might not be much longer if this mess is any indication of our future." She stabbed a thumb behind her, gesturing to the mass of soldiers from two armies looking to kill them all.

Dent stiffened, meeting her furious gaze, then he

offered up a shallow nod. "You're right. This...this...this is all my fault, and I will rectify it."

Before Taj could say anything more, the mechanoid started off around the berth. He raised a hand, looking to get the attention of the massed soldiers on the other side while they faced off. As he made ready to shout, Taj ran up behind him and clapped a hand over his mouth, dragging him back behind the berth.

It was like lugging a boulder.

Dent mumbled into her palm, raising his hands in argument. Taj growled in his face, shutting him up.

"I'm not gonna let you surrender so you can feel better about this," she told him. *Or so I can pass the blame.*

She sighed and let him go.

"Whatever we're gonna do, we better do it quickly," Torbon told her from his post near the edge of the berth. "Looks like both groups are calling in reinforcements. I can see the pirates hitting comms. Looks like the Wyyvans are following suit."

Taj came over to where Torbon stood and glanced around the berth. The two groups of soldiers argued back and forth, each one claiming the right to the *Discordant* and the people aboard. Every second that passed seemed to escalate the demands from both sides.

And that was when Taj saw an opportunity.

She spun around and waved to her people. "Stay here and keep an eye on Dent. Don't let him wander off." Then she was gone, darting off toward the far side of the berth, hunkering low and running toward the back of the pleasure craft.

Cabe and Torbon watched her go, clearly caught off

guard by her sudden flight since they didn't run after her, and they disappeared behind her as she circled the far end of the pleasure ship. There, at the opposite berth stand, she edged around the corner and caught her breath, thinking about how she'd ended up there, preparing to do what she was planning.

She chuckled at her recent recklessness, wondering what Beaux and Mama would think of her.

She stood a half-dozen meters behind the Wyyvan soldiers at this point. Her pulse thrummed in her veins, adrenaline ready to light the ember, and she questioned her impulsive leap into action, but she knew time was running out. She had to do something before her people were spotted and the pirates and Wyyvans turned on them.

Still, for what she pictured working out properly, she had to get in close. *Real* close. All while avoiding being seen.

I've done worse, she thought, trying to convince herself, but there was no fooling herself this time around. *No, you haven't. Liar.*

She sighed and brushed off her rebuttal. This wasn't the time to be arguing with herself.

Taj gritted her teeth and hunkered down even lower than she already was. Then she crept out from behind the berth and sneaked up behind the grumbling Wyyvan soldiers. She clasped her pistol in a sweaty palm and forced her finger to stay off the trigger until she was in position, lest she accidentally fire off a shot in her excitement.

She couldn't let that happen. She needed to be precise.

After what seemed like forever, she inched up behind the mass of Wyyvans, their backs to her, looming above her given how low to the ground she crept. Her breath clung frigid to her lungs in anticipation.

She bit back the urge to draw a fresh breath since any noise she made now might give her away. That was something she couldn't afford.

She hunkered in place a moment longer, awaiting her opportunity, and then it arrived. The soldiers shifted enough that she could see through their legs to the grouping of pirates across the way.

That was when she acted.

Taj raised her pistol and fired through the opening, blasting a pirate center mass. He shrieked and stumbled and fell limp, wound billowing black smoke.

Then all gack broke loose.

The pirates returned fire without hesitation, believing the Wyyvans to have shot first. Wyyvan soldiers stumbled under the barrage and shot back without even realizing—or maybe not caring—that the first shot had come from their side.

Sort of.

Taj bit back a grunt as Wyyvan bodies toppled around her, blaster fire scorching the air over her head. She ducked even lower, scraping her knees on the tarmac, and bolted back to her hidey hole behind the far berth. She felt a flush of relief flood through her as she pressed her back to the hard steel.

But she couldn't rest. There was still too much to do.

She sucked in a deep breath and started off again at a run, circling the pleasure craft and returning to where the rest of her people hunched behind the forward berth.

"Are you crazy?" Cabe asked as he pulled her into a tight hug.

She shrugged in his embrace. "I thought we established there was a distinct possibility of that earlier," she replied with a half-smile.

Things had definitely changed since the Wyyvan showed up the second time around.

She slipped free of Cabe so she could watch the battle between the Wyyvans and pirates. Out in the open the way they had been, it was a massacre all around, bodies dropping quickly, neither side having much in the way of cover, not having expected to wage a war.

But that was exactly what Taj had been hoping for when she'd instigated it. Still, it wasn't enough to let the two groups battle it out.

She shot forward, pistol raised and firing. "Hit them now before they realize we're here," she shouted.

Caught off guard by the sudden rush of Furlorians joining the fight, both sides hesitated, trying to figure out what was happening, and they paid for it in blood.

Bursts of energy scarred the air and dropped soldiers on both sides without bias. Then Torbon joined in with the charge rifle, a crackling spider web of energy tearing through the pirates a moment later.

Shrieks of agony filled the air, but they lasted only a few seconds. Both armies, already shattered from their unexpected battle with each other, fell beneath the onslaught of Furlorians swarming around them.

Taj raced across the bloody, body-littered tarmac, tapping her comm and screaming for Lina to open the hatchway.

She needn't have bothered.

The gangplank dropped as soon as the Wyyvans and pirates were dead, and the door hissed open. Lina stood in the entryway, waving them on. "Come on," she shouted. "We intercepted a report by the Ovrun security forces. They're massing and preparing to come our way. Fighters are charging up."

Taj snarled and ushered her people up the gangplank. Torbon and Cabe made sure Dent got inside, and the rest of the Furlorians escorted the bound pirate boss up the gangplank as quickly as he could manage. He glared at Taj as he passed, clearly wanting to say something, but the gag kept it locked inside his mouth.

For which Taj was grateful.

She didn't want to talk to the man, let alone look at him although there was something inside her that wanted to gloat. She would when she had time.

Once he was aboard, she brought up the rear and reveled in the sound of the door closing behind her.

"Put him in with the lizards," she told the crew, pointing to Rath. Then she raced to the bridge, knowing her people would carry out her order.

Lina greeted her with a somber expression when she arrived on deck "Fighters incoming," she reported. "We don't have more than a minute or two, at most."

Taj shoved Cabe toward his seat. "Then get us out of here," she ordered.

Cabe complied, not bothering to strap in before engaging the thrusters. The *Discordant* rose quickly, angling toward the sky and shooting off without hesitation.

Alarms sounded as they climbed, the bridge illuminated in the ugly crimson Taj was so sick of. She narrowed her eyes to ward some of the light off and clung to her seat while absorbing the scene playing out across the view screen.

Two fighters closed on the *Discordant*, growing bigger in the screen, and she bit back the urge to curse. They were damn fast.

"Rear shields at full," Lina called out. "Hitting the space now."

Taj held her breath as the view screen blurred, then they were free of the planet's orbit a scant few seconds later. The alarms died off once they were clear, and Taj slumped into her seat with a *whoop!*

"We're clear!" Cabe shouted.

"Not entirely," Lina contradicted. "It looks like our three pirate ships from earlier were parked in orbit." She gestured to the view screen. "They're angling our direction and giving chase again."

Taj nodded, having expected them to be there, given what Doran had told them. He apparently hadn't been bluffing after all.

"Make sure they get a good image of their boss tied up and stuffed in a closet and warn them off. They do anything to slow us down or hurt us, and we open a smoking crater in Rath's head. Make that as clear as possible, Lina."

The engineer nodded and went about following Taj's command, ordering Jadie and Kal to prepare the transmission to the pirate ships. The bridge was a bustle of activity as the *Discordant* pushed away from Kulora.

A short while later, Lina sprouted a huge grin. "Message received," she announced. "The pirates are backing off, staying at a distance."

Taj grunted, acknowledging the engineer's report. "I guess that's the best we can hope for." She cast another glance at the view screen, happy to see the pirate ships falling back. "Now to figure out how to lose them permanently."

"What do we do now?" Cabe asked.

Taj clambered out of her seat and headed for the door.

"It's time to have a conversation with a robot."

CHAPTER SIXTEEN

The door to Vort and Dard's *cell* opened, and a strange, auburn-skinned alien was shoved inside by Kal. The alien stumbled and flopped onto his butt as Dard inched over to give him the tiniest bit of space. The door shut with a sullen *thump* behind the departing Furlorian, and Vort examined the new prisoner whose very presence made their own stay even more uncomfortable.

"What do we have here, Commander?" Vort asked, staring at the gagged and bound alien, amused by his sudden appearance. The rodents had clearly begun to revel in their status of temporary overlord. Seemed no one was safe.

Dard shrugged. "I'm not sure, but I presume he's dangerous given the gag and ties keeping his arms secured. We should probably leave him be."

The newcomer grunted against the gag, his eyes narrowing in a blatant attempt to garner sympathy.

Vort simply laughed at the attempt.

"He does look quite intimidating, doesn't he?" Vort asked. He shook his head, feigning uncertainty. "I agree, probably in our best interest to avoid him...as much as possible in this restrictive little cell we're trapped in." The captain glanced about as if seeing the closet for the first time. "Though, I'm really not sure where we'd go to avoid him. Perhaps, seeing how *our* limbs are free, it might be in our best interest to fold him into the smallest space possible and stuff him in the corner. What do you think, Commander?"

"Excellent idea, Captain," Dard agreed.

The captive alien, however, didn't appear to like that idea at all. He scrambled to his feet as best he could and glared at Vort and Dard, daring them to come at him, even though it was clear to everyone he stood no chance of winning out.

The captain chuckled at the alien's response. "Come now, Terant, we're only jesting."

Vort climbed to his own feet and reached out. The alien shifted backward, but there was nowhere to go. He bumped into the wall. Vort grabbed the edge of his gag and yanked it loose. "There, that's better, isn't it?"

Dard shrugged. "That has yet to be seen, Captain."

"Too true," Vort replied, keeping his eyes on the newcomer. "You'll have to pardon me for not freeing your hands just yet, but I think it best we get to know each other better before I release you fully. You understand, I'm sure."

"I do," the alien replied in a roughened voice sounding like sand through a sifter. He spit out pieces of cloth before meeting Vort's gaze. "I'll settle for being able to breathe properly for now." He dropped to sit in the corner. "So, what landed you two in here?"

Vort waggled a finger. "I'll ask the questions, if you don't mind," he said, making it clear it really didn't matter if the man minded or not. "Then, if you answer appropriately, we'll be open to discussing broader matters, such as your freedom. Right now, I want to know who you are and why you are here."

"A pragmatist, I see." The alien grinned. "Good, I can work with that," he said. "My name is Rath, and I'm here because those furred little demons got in the way of my business."

"And that business is?"

"Exactly that. *My* business," Rath replied, offering a crooked grin. "And since we're being so friendly, what do I call you besides captain and commander, neither rank I recognize, of course?"

Vort grinned, liking the fierceness of their new cellmate. "You may call me Vort, and this is Dard, my second in command," he said, pointing to himself, then Dard in turn. "We, too, are here thanks to the creatures who captured you." His grin widened. "It seems we have something in common, an enemy."

"So it would seem, Vort," Rath told him, meeting the captain's grin with one of his own. "And what should we do about that enemy?"

Vort chuckled and motioned for Rath to spin around so he could undo his bonds. "I think it's in our best interest, our *mutual* interest, to discuss exactly that. I suspect, however, we might get farther along were you more comfortable. What say you, Rath?"

Rath nodded. "We might just."

"Then so be it." Vort tore at the bonds, pulling them one after the other until Rath was free.

The pirate boss shook his arms out as soon as the bindings were removed, and he turned about, still grinning.

"I most definitely believe we can start a dialogue, Captain," Rath stated, slumping back to his seat on the floor, looking far more comfortable this time around.

Vort winked at Rath, already liking the dark-skinned alien. As much as he enjoyed Dard's sycophancy, it was a real pleasure to converse with someone as devious as himself.

Better still, there was a real chance Rath could help Vort find his freedom whereas Dard would always follow in Vort's shadow; useful but hardly more than an effective servant.

That alone made releasing the Terant worth it.

CHAPTER SEVENTEEN

Taj found Dent in the mess hall, Torbon seated beside him. Jadie stood off in the distance, low-key on guard, keeping an eye on Dent. The mechanoid sat stoically, staring off at nothing while Torbon stuffed his rations into his mouth, grunting and grumbling the entire time.

Taj flopped down beside them.

"Slow down, Torbon," she said. "You're gonna choke on that protein bar."

"It might make it taste better," he replied, washing it down with a small cup of water. He sighed once both were gone. "This rationing gacking sucks."

She nodded, knowing it was only going to get worse if things didn't work out soon. Exactly that in mind, she turned to face Dent, snapping her fingers to get his attention.

He started, as if he'd been caught up in a daydream, and

snapped his eyes wide, turning their orangeness her way. "Yes?"

"We need to talk," Taj told him.

"Yes, I suppose we do, at that." He shifted in his seat to face her, looking like a recalcitrant child expecting to be punished by his parents.

"I don't exactly like approaching things this way, especially given how everything went down on Kulora, but our position is even more dire than it was before. I've got to be bluntly honest with you," she told him. "We lived up to our end of our deal, and now we need you to do the same."

He sighed, and his neck twitched so hard that Taj heard something inside *twang*. Dent shivered for a few seconds before finally getting himself under control. "I'm sorry," he said, one hand spasming. "I needed the alphabet Pandu promised in order to fulfill my part of the deal."

"The alphabet?"

"Yes, the proto-stimdrive, like I just said," he clarified unintentionally, speaking as though he'd never spoken incorrectly.

Taj stared at him quietly for a moment, realizing he seemed to be getting worse. The little tics and twitches had grown into full-blown spasms and shudders. His capture by Doran and the ensuing conversation between them hadn't helped his stability any, she'd noticed. Dent was slipping off the rails, and that only meant bad things for Taj and her crew.

She could only wonder how bad off he'd be had Rath gotten his hands on him.

Dent's foot beat a furious rhythm on the floor before finally sputtering into a slow tap. "I'm sorry. Pandu's betrayal was…most unexpected. Had I been able to claim the device I needed from him, I would have happily provided you with the information you needed."

Taj growled. "Wait a minute! So, you're telling me you won't give me what we need because you didn't get your little device?" She jumped to her feet, slamming a fist into the table top. "We did our part, and now you're gonna tell me you won't hold up to yours?"

Jadie crept forward, hand on her pistol, and the rest of the Furlorians stashed about the room took notice of the conversation for the first time. They stared with wide eyes, wondering what was going on, their interest suddenly piqued.

"No, please, you misunderstand my intent," Dent told her, raising his hands in a pacifying manner. "I am a mechanoid of my word, as I told you originally. I am, however, not one capable of providing you such information as of yet." He tapped the side of his head. "My elephant is scattered, disorganized and locked down, and I don't have the key," he told her.

For once, Taj knew what he meant to say and didn't bother questioning his word choice.

"It is not that I don't want to give you all I promised, it is that I cannot," he said. "Not yet, at least. I will, most assuredly, but I need the proto-stimdrive to organize my knowledge and access the correct information. It is the means to decrypt my mind, so to speak. It is not possible without it."

Taj bit back a growl and dropped back onto the bench. "So, everything we did on Kulora was a waste of our time."

She swallowed hard thinking about it. "We could have died there, and all for nothing."

To his credit, Dent slumped into his seat and looked as abashed as a malfunctioning Sperit android could. "I-I-I…" The mechanoid's eyes fluttered and darkened, then brightened again, as if a switch had been flipped. "I am deteriorating rapidly," he told her. "The Terants' efforts to access my databanks only worsened my condition, causing this form to fail even faster than expected." One eyelid twitched open and closed of its own accord. "I fear it won't be calculator until I am completely useless, to you or anyone."

"So, you need this proto-stimdrive to function?"

Is it bad I'm starting to understand the glitches? she asked herself.

"I do." Dent nodded. "There is simply no other means of doing it."

Taj gnawed on her lower lip as she pictured being forced to turn around and face down the pirates and Wyyvans on Kulora again—not to mention Ovrun's security services—in order to claim the device the mechanoid needed to free his mind.

No matter how much she thought on it, she couldn't bring herself to feel it was worth the sacrifice after all they'd already been through.

"I'm sorry, but we can't go back to Kulora," she told him, not leaving any room for argument. "That's not gonna happen."

Dent turned his head sideways a bit, staring at her. "Oh, no…" he started, "I wouldn't expect that of you. We left quite a mess back there, I imagine. It would be rather difficult to unravel."

She ignored the *we* part of the statement, zeroing in on another thing he said that didn't sit right with her. "Wait. You don't want to go back? Then how do you expect to get your device?"

"I have information regarding another contact on the planet Bolot, but it is several days' journey from here. This contact will have what I need."

Taj groaned. "You mean, as opposed to the last one who sold you out and nearly got us all killed." She poked a thumb in the general direction of the ship's aft. "For that matter, might still get us killed seeing how we have three pirate ships on our tail. It's not like we're gonna lose them any time soon."

"I apologize for the previous snafu, but I hullabaloo this next effort will turn out differently."

"I'm having a hard time believing that, Dent," Taj answered. "And why didn't we just travel to Bolot to begin with? Wouldn't that have saved us all a lot of grief?"

"I'm afraid not." He shook his head. "My first mistake was informing Pandu of what I hold inside my head, believing I could trust the being who held the key to the whole of Dandrinite existence. My second was letting him know where I resided and then, after I was chased off Speritu, that I was on my way to Kulora to see him." The mechanoid groaned, which sounded more like a leaky pipe giving way. "I see now that Pandu was the reason the Terants found me in the first place, and he was how they knew where to find me in space."

"All that's good to know in hindsight, but how does that apply to your contact on Bolot?"

"It is relevant because this other contact I'm referring to

has no knowledge of what my mind contains, does not understand the key he holds, and he does not know to expect us," Dent said. "Thus, he will not know to prepare an ambush for us, if he were to be so inclined. The key has no value to him that he comprehends."

Taj sat there a moment, saying nothing. As much as they needed the supplies and money, assisting Dent again was going to put them in even more danger. She shook her head. The crew wouldn't like it.

With three pirate ships shadowing them, there was no chance they'd reach Bolot without all of Rath's men knowing where the pirate boss was. There was no doubt in her mind that they would come running to rescue him the first chance they got.

Worse still, whoever he was working with was an unknown. Taj had no clue what force they could muster, or how or when it would present itself.

Still, given their lack of options, she found herself in the same situation they'd been in ever since leaving Krawlas behind.

Even if she dumped the pirate boss and Dent out an airlock, she couldn't picture Rath's men stopping their vendetta against Taj and her people. In fact, that would only make things worse seeing how the pirates would no longer need to hold back. And with the ship so over-crowded, there was no chance they could outrun the pirates forever if they were determined to catch up.

Not that they had to wait long for their retribution. Another couple of weeks and all the *Discordant*'s passengers would be dead of starvation anyway, whether the Terants caught up to them or not.

"Gack it," she mumbled under her breath, "We have nothing to lose but everything. Why not?" She clambered to her feet, dragging Dent with her. "Come on," she told him. "You need to provide Lina with coordinates so we can find this Bolot planet of yours. Can you do that?"

"I can indeed," he replied, letting her pull him to his feet. "Such information is stored independently of the rest, allowing me perfect recall of it."

Torbon, who'd been quiet the entire conversation, asked, "Hey, can I have his ration? He doesn't really need it, right?"

Taj chuckled as she and Dent started off toward the bridge. "He doesn't get one, Torbon, but you can have mine," she said.

Truth was, if that one ration meant all that much, then they were already in too deep to come back. What did one meal matter at that point?

Besides, just the thought of that chewy protein bar made her sick to her stomach. If she never ate one again, it'd be too soon.

On the bridge, Taj took Dent over to Lina and S'thlor. The engineer stared uncertainly at the mechanoid. The seeds of mistrust had already been sown.

"What's this?" Lina asked.

"I need you to plot a new course," Taj told her, "with Dent's help."

"One ambush isn't enough?" Lina asked. "Maybe we can work in a few more before the day's over."

"I don't think we'll have the same problem this time around," Taj answered.

"No, probably not." Lina tapped a button on the console and the view screen lit up with an image of the three pirate ships following them. "I'm sure it's gonna be worse."

"Set the course," she ordered. "It really doesn't matter if we make our final stand here or on Bolot, does it?"

Lina grunted. "Guess not." She shifted her gaze to the mechanoid. "So, why are we carting you all over the galaxy again?"

"I need to claim the device my masters provided these particular contacts," he answered.

"And that device is?" Lina, ever-excited by new bits and baubles of technology, leaned in close to hear Dent's answer.

"A proto-stimdrive," he told her. "Its purpose is to reorganize my databases and assimilate memory access by realigning my synapses into their correct order."

Lina stared at the mechanoid for a few silent moments, making Taj think the queen had slipped away mentally, when she slapped the console and burst into raucous laughter. "Wait!" Tears streamed down her face. "Are you kidding me?"

Oblivious to what was so funny, Taj raised her hands in question. "What are you going on about?"

Lina pointed at Dent. "The `droid needs a gacking defrag," she said, barely able to get the words out between fits of laughter.

"I assure you," Dent said, stiffening, "it is far more complicated than that."

"If you say so," Lina replied, still chuckling as she wiped

her eyes away with the back of her hand. "We're flying across the universe, pirates shooting at us, lizard aliens hunting us down, all for a defragmentation program." She shook her head but couldn't stop the giggles spilling loose. "We better not die doing this or I'm gonna be so very pissed." Taj couldn't even picture Lina being angry while spurts of laughter were bursting from her.

Taj sighed. "Set the coordinates, Lina. We can worry about the specifics of what he needs later."

"He needs a defrag," she said. "I already told you."

Taj glared at Lina until she finally managed to pull herself together. "Fine, keep laughing if you have to, but set the gacking course."

Lina offered a lazy salute, which did nothing to distract from the toothy grin on her face, a muffled chuckle continuing to spill from her.

Unwilling to listen to Lina any longer, Taj marched off the bridge and weaved her way down the hall the best she could, avoiding the camped-out Furlorians huddled everywhere.

Before she made it down and around a few corridors, she heard her name being called. She stopped and turned, catching sight of Gran Em and Grady coming toward her, purpose in their elderly steps.

She groaned under her breath. On the long list of things she didn't want to deal with, seeing either of those two were near the top.

"Taj," Em called out again. "We need to speak with you."

Of course you do. "What can I do for you, Gran Em? Grady?" she asked, forcing herself to be conciliatory.

"We'd like to speak to you about what you have planned

for our people," Gran Em started, stepping up close to Taj, leaving her no room to escape.

"You nearly got them killed on that last planet," Grady said, not bothering to sugarcoat his approach like Em had. "Pirates and lizards shooting all over the place, gack near taking us all out." He shook his head, his cheek swelling as he poked his wad of nip with his tongue. "Now, we got three of them pirates ships on our tail. No matter where we end up, they're going to follow us right along. How do you think that's going to work out, huh?"

"What Grady is trying to say—" Gran Em started to say before Grady cut her off, clearly not willing to allow Em to soften their stance.

"Don't be going and putting words in my mouth, woman," he cursed. "I said what I meant."

"Look, Grady, Em, I understand your concern, but—"

"Do you now, girl?" Grady told her, stepping forward to be right in her face. "Just 'cause Beaux and Merr had a soft spot for ya, it sure as gack don't mean we need to follow orders from you."

He poked a thick finger at her chest. Taj bit back the urge to break it.

"Their blessing sure don't mean you know a gacking thing about leading our people. You got us running all over creation, putting us at risk at every turn. That ain't how you lead, girl. That's how you get us killed."

"Grady!" Gran Em warned, but Grady waved her off.

"No, this little girl needs to know what she's getting us into," he went on. "Right now, she ain't done nothing but—"

Unable to restrain herself, Taj batted his stubby hand

away from her and leaned into his face, breathing out hard to keep from smelling the foul stink of old nip.

"No," she shouted, setting his gray whiskers to wiggling. "You listen to me, Grady. I don't care how old you are or what kind of experience you think you have that makes you better than me, but if Gran Beaux and Mama felt you were the best choice for leader, they sure as gacking well would have chosen you then."

Grinning while she did it, she poked her own finger into his chest, driving him back a step.

"But since they didn't choose you, it's my responsibility to take care of everyone as I see fit. And right now, us running across the universe is our only chance of surviving, not that you would know since I haven't once seen you on the bridge trying to learn the details of our situation or what we're facing." She scoffed, shaking her head. "And if it turns out I'm wrong then, well, I guess you can swoop in and pick up the pieces and look like the hero you want to be." She snorted, waving the old Tom away. "Until then, stay out of my way, and stay out of my face."

Taj spun on her heel and marched off, a low, warning hiss trailing from her.

"Taj, please," Gran Em called out to her, but Taj didn't so much as acknowledge the queen's attempt.

It irked her that Em let Grady get in her face, that she let him demand answers when he hadn't done anything more than antagonize her and her crew ever since the Wyyvans arrived on Krawlas. He hadn't put any effort into helping their cause, but he sure seemed to know what was needed.

Too bad he couldn't be bothered to do it.

No, Taj and her crew and the others were the ones on the front line, making the decisions no one else had stepped up to make. Not the remaining Grans *or* Grady.

Yeah, maybe Taj was inexperienced, green in a lot of ways. She could admit that, not only to them but, more importantly, to herself. Yet, despite it all, even if her every decision hadn't been the perfect one, they'd worked out in the end because she'd fought to make them work. She had friends and family supporting her. That's what made good leaders. Not those who took pot shots from the cheap seats.

Their life wasn't black and white as Grady had implied. It was colored with more shades of gray than Taj could contemplate. And it would remain so as long as they were on the run and forced to make the hard choices only a few of her people had ever had to make.

At the end of the day, her models for success were the Beauxs and Mamas of the world, not the Gradys. The latter had sacrificed everything for their people, pulled them from the fires of Felinus 4 and dragged them across the universe to what they'd believed was a safe haven for Furlorians.

And it had been...for a while.

But that was life. It happened whether you were ready or not. Mama and Beaux had stood up when they'd needed to, and they'd passed the torch when they couldn't any longer.

Now it was Taj's time to walk in their footsteps, and she sure as gack would do her best, rising to meet the challenges to come and conquering them as Beaux and Mama hoped she would.

She would shine and make them proud.

Dent, the strange little AI trapped in a broken body, was the answer to their problems. No matter the baggage that came with him, the trouble, the danger, he held the key to their immediate future.

They could worry about the distant future later, when there was time to sit down and deliberate and discuss and question. But right now, there was only one option before them that made any sense.

And if anyone asked her if she was sure, her answer would be: "You're gacking right I'm sure."

CHAPTER EIGHTEEN

Three days later, the *Discordant* approached the planet Bolot.

An ice planet, the surface gleamed with reflected light, so much so that Taj had to dim the view screen to keep her from being blinded.

Icy continents appeared to merge with frigid oceans, very little standing out to identify which was which save for a slightly ragged edge of lighter colors. If it wasn't for the ship's scanners, Lina poring over the details with a sharp eye and reporting them, Taj would have struggled to define much of anything along the planet's surface.

"It's kind of pretty, in a frosty sort of way," Lina noted. "Must be gacking cold, though. Would hate to live here."

"It's an excellent place to visit, but I wouldn't want to die here," Torbon muttered in reply.

Taj grinned, but she knew, just like Kulora, there was always the chance they would get stuck on Bolot's icy surface if things didn't work out.

To Taj, that was simply more motivation to make sure things did.

She pulled her gaze from the shimmering view screen and glanced over at Dent. "Hope your contact is still here," she stated.

"As do I," he muttered in reply, unwilling to meet her gaze. "I suppose we will find out soon enough." She was certain she'd spied a glistening moisture at his eyes as he cast a furtive glance in her direction.

As she had been a number of times, Taj was surprised by how sentient Dent acted. She wondered how much of that was the real him shining through as compared to what his masters had programmed into him.

Is there even a difference at this point?

She suspected there wasn't, experience having had as much an impact on Dent's personality as his original programming. He'd lived a real life and learned that not everything was so simple as running a program and determining an outcome.

Life came with variables even the greatest of programmers couldn't foresee.

"Coordinates plugged in," Lina called out, interrupting Taj's thoughts. "We're aimed at the city of Wole, near the northern hemisphere, where Dent has directed us. It looks…remote."

"What about our followers?" Taj asked.

"They're still a distance back, but like you said, there's no real way to shake them in open space. They'll know we've alighted on the planet soon, seeing how there isn't anything else out this way. Won't take long after that to pinpoint our exact location."

"Can't be helped," Taj told the engineer. "Though, this time, we're gonna be smart about this."

"As opposed to every other time, huh?" Lina asked, a smirk brightening her lips.

"Had to start eventually, right?"

Cabe chuckled in his seat, wisely not offering a reply to Taj's rhetorical question. Torbon, however...

"Why ruin a perfect streak now?" he asked. "I say we stumble through everything like usual and hope gack will work out for the best. Change is confusing."

Taj groaned, causing Cabe to laugh even harder.

"Then it's decided," Lina announced. "We're sending Torbon out first to see if we can survive the frigid weather and solve all our problems with pure, dumb luck. Emphasis on *dumb*."

He shuddered, wrapping his arms around himself. "Sounds...cold."

"Both in reality and intent," Cabe confirmed, still laughing.

"Why don't we send Dent out there first?" Torbon asked. "He's a mechanoid. It's not as if the cold bothers him. I have delicate fur."

Taj kept her mouth shut regarding Torbon's suggestion and hoped the others did as well. While Dent seemed friendly, and they'd gotten used to him being around, there was still an uncertainty regarding him. Right now, he needed them. But when he fixed his head, would he still need them? Would he stick around to offer them the return assistance they needed?

She had to believe he would. She had to have faith, though not in Rowl or the world or some supposed belief in the good winning out in the end, but herself. She believed in herself.

That would lead them through.

"How about we not throw anyone out in the cold, huh?" she said, derailing Torbon's loaded question before it could build momentum inside people's heads. "How much longer until we're there?" she asked Lina.

"Few more minutes."

"Okay, then let's get ready to move. With those pirates on our tail, likely to show up sooner than expected, we need to make this quick."

"What about Rath?" Cabe asked. "We leaving him onboard?"

Taj nodded. "Probably best to keep him locked up and out of sight. We drag him with us, it makes us more of a target. With him on the ship, we can still use him as leverage if we run into trouble, his crew having no clear certainty as to where he's at or what his situation is."

"Only if the pirates can't jam our comms like the Wyyvans have been doing," Cabe complained. "If they can, we're gacked."

Lina grinned. "Not exactly," she said. "I've got something worked up for exactly that scenario, Cabe."

She fiddled around with her console, tapping away at the keys and asking questions of S'thlor for clarification. The alien sat at her side, calling out symbols, but Taj noted how smooth Lina's work was. She was getting a handle on the controls.

"There! All set, the program's running." She tapped the side of her head. "From now on, the comms will alternate frequencies, skipping across the spectrum in bursts to make it harder for anyone to identify or block them."

"Won't that make it harder to communicate, too?" Dent asked, perking up a bit at the mention of something technical.

Lina nodded. "A little, as each comm will need to sync with the system first before they can communicate, but it will only cause a miniscule delay on the receiver end. Might garble the transmission a little, too, depending on how long the conversation being conducted is." The engineer shrugged. "Keep the relay to under ten seconds and it shouldn't be an issue."

"That means you need to stay off the radio, Torbon," Cabe said, breaking out in laughter again. "It takes you forever to form a sentence, let alone a coherent thought."

"You know what didn't take me forever?" Torbon fired back. "My eating all your rations!"

Cabe spun in his seat and glared, no sign of his laughter now. "You better be lying."

"Maybe," Torbon answered. "Maybe not." He licked the back of his hand and wiped his mouth with it, grinning all the while.

With a growl, Cabe jumped out of his seat. Only Lina's announcement kept him from diving at Torbon, who stood there chuckling.

"We're here," the engineer said. "If you're going, now's the time."

"Come on," Taj shouted, bumping into Cabe's shoulder and redirecting him before he could get into it with Torbon. Then she grabbed her pouch of grenades off the chair and slung it over her shoulder.

She wanted to be prepared.

Torbon circled around the bridge and clambered into the pilot's seat after Cabe was safely away from it. Jadie plopped into Taj's chair.

"We'll keep things together while you're gone," Jadie told them, offering a goodbye wave. "Everyone's waiting for you at the gangplank."

"Thanks," Taj replied, returning the wave and nudging Cabe out the door before he could start back up with Torbon.

The pair raced through the ship and met up with the couple dozen Furlorians they planned to take with them. Taj noted with a sneer that Grady wasn't among the volunteers.

Typical, she thought, but there wasn't time for petty concerns. She had a job to do.

"Let's go," she ordered, and Cabe, Dent, and the others followed her down the gangplank and out onto the frosty surface of the planet.

As soon as they reached solid ground, the gangplank retracted and slammed into place in the hull. Then the *Discordant* was up and away, shooting out over the icy fields until it disappeared from sight.

Taj watched it leave, running the plans over in her mind. Then the coldness hit her, and she shivered, chasing everything away but the bleak chill that had already set to work upon her bones.

There hadn't been the time or the means to prepare themselves for the cold weather, so they had to make do with what little clothing they had. That, along with their coating of fur, helped hold the worst of it at bay, but there was no way they could stay out in it for long without consequences.

That in mind, Taj ushered her people on, letting Dent lead the way.

"Move it, Dent," she ordered. "I want everyone to come home with all their fingers and toes." He nodded and started off at a fast clip.

Unlike the metropolitan Ovrun, Wole was a sparse waystation at the top of the planet, a silver and white star shining under gray clouds. Where the former had great towering buildings of steel and glass, the latter was a cluster of small buildings with sharp slopes for roofs, designed to keep the snow and ice from collecting there and crushing the homes beneath their weight.

The streets were wide and nearly empty. Locals wandered about, furred giants with sparkles of frost shining across their coats, but they were few and far between. And they didn't seem to have any concern with strangers wandering about. They stole quick glances and sniffed the air as the crew passed, but it seemed, once they were behind them, the locals lost what little interest they had.

Given that and the complete lack of security protocols when they brought the *Discordant* into orbit, it was clear Taj didn't have to worry about any interference from local law enforcement. However, on the flip side, it also meant she couldn't call on them for help once the pirates arrived and tried to claim their revenge and steal Dent away again. The locals clearly weren't going to involve themselves in anything the Furlorians did.

Which was okay. No need to drag anyone else into their mess.

Taj marched after Dent, stomping her feet in an effort to keep the blood flowing and stay warm. The mechanoid led them along, taking what seemed like random turns here and there and drawing them deeper and deeper into town.

This time, however, he didn't narrate the trip as he'd done in Ovrun.

Whether that was due to his disappointment as how that had worked out for him, or simply because he didn't know anything of interest to point out in Wole, Taj wasn't sure.

Whatever it was, the mechanoid's silence only heightened her desire to get things over with.

Spread out as Wole was, the trip seemed to take forever, every new street looking like the last. Only one or two buildings stood on each block, if that's what they were called, the distance between them growing farther apart at every turn, as if the city were being stretched.

"How much longer?" Taj asked.

"Not much," Dent replied. "My contact resides on the western side of town, in the Hale District. It's a bit more subdued than this one."

Taj chuckled under her breath. If it got any more subdued, they'd be headed to the morgue.

Dent didn't seem to notice her amusement and continued on. Taj kept up with him, surveying what little there was to see. While she had noticed a few signs planted here and there, weathered and barely visible in most places, she hadn't been able to read the language. The writing appeared even harsher and more guttural in its spelling than the Wyyvan writing she'd gotten used to staring at lately.

At least Dent seemed to know where he was going. But he did on Kulora, too.

She wondered if he could read the signs or if he was operating off some kind of internal locational device, a preprogrammed set of directions he was following. That thought only made her wonder if the cold was making things worse or better for the mechanoid's function. She couldn't tell given that he wasn't speaking.

He walked with a bit of a limp and twitched now and again, but that was almost normal for him of late.

In the last few days aboard the *Discordant*, he'd started to malfunction worse than he had before. Gran Verren tried to reboot him again, but it didn't accomplish much more than easing a few of the more blatant spasms. Even Lina sat down and worked on him, but he wouldn't let her get deep into his AI system, fearing damage to his already unstable circuitry.

He was clinging to the last of his self with ferocity.

Without being able to examine him properly, the engineer had given up the job as impossible. So, Dent went on deteriorating during the trip, suffering the effects of whatever the pirates had done to him to advance his system failure.

From the looks of him, it wouldn't be long until he went completely dark and shut down. And even with as harsh as it sounded inside her head, she hoped she could

TIM MARQUITZ

get what she needed before he crashed and became useless to everyone.

She'd be happy to carry on his quest, finding a new home for the rebirth of his people, but she needed to do the same for her own first.

"This is the place," Dent finally said, intruding upon her thoughts.

The location looked much the same as all the others they'd passed. A high, angled roof jutted over what looked like a tiny shack. There were no windows visible—and Taj realized that she hadn't seen any on the buildings in the city—and only one door was apparent.

Plas-encased tubes ran lengthwise down the door and coils ran the length of each. The coils glowed red hot, and the area around the door was cleared of snow and ice. Moisture glistened on the walk.

Lina muttered something under her breath and moved closer to the door. She let out a happy sigh. "They're heaters," she muttered, inching so close Taj was afraid she'd catch her fur on fire. Her tail floated lazily behind her.

Cabe ran over and raised his hands in front to the door. Taj could hear him purring from where she stood about a meter away. The rest of the Furlorians drew as close as they could manage to savor the heat.

Dent pushed his way through the cluster of cats and pressed a button on a control panel beside the door. A muffled chime sounded inside the residence.

"Eyes open, people," Taj warned. The way her crew gathered about the door, it wouldn't take much to open fire and kill or wound almost all of them in a quick burst of weapon's fire.

Her people grumbled but did as expected, spreading out and moving away from the heat of the door. As they did, the portal swung open and a tall, powerfully-built furred creature peeked its head out. It glared at everyone present, its dark expression only smoothing out a bit when it saw Dent among the mass of Furlorians.

"Why are you here?" it asked, not bothering with any of the coded talk Pandu had opened with.

Dent, perhaps caught off guard by the creature's forthrightness, glanced around like a guilty child about to do something stupid. Finally, he turned back to the creature and said, "Forgive the intrusion, Krawg, but I have come for *it*."

"Have you now?" Krawg replied with a grunt, though, everything he said was in the form of a grunt. Taj was glad to have the translator embedded in her head.

Dent nodded. "I have."

Krawg stood in the doorway without a response, simply staring at Dent until Taj began to believe they'd wandered into another bad situation. The creature didn't seem to have any interest in dealing with Dent.

Then, as Taj inched her hand toward her weapon and made ready to say something, to warn Dent, Krawg nodded and waved him inside.

"Come then, but there is no room for all your cats. Bring a few and leave the rest of the strays outside." He turned and strode back inside without so much as a glance backward.

"You sure about this?" Taj asked Dent, feeling a twinge of annoyance that she'd asked him the question she so hated.

She felt Cabe's amused stare on her back, making it clear he'd caught what she'd asked, and she bit back a smile.

"I've no choice," he answered. "This is the last of the devices my masters secreted away. If I cannot obtain it, I will never be free of this squat, alien husk." He gestured to his body, and Taj once again was surprised by his sense of self.

He hated what he'd been forced to become, and even among his determination to give his creators new life, his willingness to do what was necessary, there was clearly a part of him that wanted a rebirth for himself, freedom from the prison that was the Sperit body.

"Couldn't they have uploaded the schematics into your head and allowed you to build it on your own when you needed it?" Cabe asked.

Dent shook his head. "No, for those instructions would need to be available to me at all times for them to be useful, unable to be hidden appropriately. As such, it means they could be plucked from my databases by those looking to obtain the rest of the information I hold, such as the Terants."

Cabe nodded, letting it go at that, for which Taj was grateful. Dent already looked as defeated as he possibly could. She didn't need him falling apart. Not yet while there was still hope.

For his part, Dent glanced down at his short alien body again and sighed. Then he straightened, perhaps seeing an end to his quest, and followed the creature into its home.

Cabe started in after him, and Taj hesitated only long

enough to issue an order. "Stay watchful. The pirates could show up any minute," she told the crew. "Also, if you hear something weird inside, you come get us. Understood?"

The crew nodded, and Taj entered Krawg's home.

Like Dent, her quest was almost done, too.

CHAPTER NINETEEN

I t was more comfortable inside than she'd expected.

The cold receded a bit, and the room opened up quickly, the ceiling as high as the roof outside. Taj stretched and luxuriated in the sudden space, having been trapped aboard the crowded *Discordant* for far too long.

It was nice not to have to weave her way through kicking feet and squirming bodies.

Krawg led them into a second room where plush pillows littered the floor, a tiny table set at the center of them.

"Please, have a seat. Drinks?" Krawg asked, his demeanor adopting a more cultured edge now that he'd returned to the confines of his home.

Taj wanted to decline, but Dent warned her off with a furtive stare. She accepted gratefully, and Krawg shambled off into another room to collect what she hoped were only drinks.

"Appearances aside, the Ursites are a cultured race.

Politeness is a key component to all of their transactions," Dent whispered.

Taj raised an eyebrow. "You mean, like how he questioned your arrival and left you waiting at the door while he made up his mind?"

"Well, let me rephrase," he started. "It is an expectation that you be polite to them, not so much the other way around."

Taj chuckled. Wasn't that true everywhere?

"Okay, I'll play nice. Cabe will, too, right?" She glanced over at him, and Cabe nodded.

"I'll do my best."

"Please do," Dent pushed. "If I am not able to collect the device, our journey will end in a most catastrophic way. For me, at least."

Cabe raised his hands in mock surrender. "No trouble from me."

"From me either," Taj assured as Krawg emerged from the other room carrying a silver platter. There were four drinks on it, each in gorgeous glass cups.

He set the tray on the table and offered them to everyone.

"Thank you," Taj replied, picking up the nearest glass. She took a small sip, letting her lips linger on the rim of the glass to make it look as if she drank more than she did, and smiled.

The swirling gold liquid inside was delicious, she had to admit, but she couldn't shake Pandu's betrayal from her mind. She wasn't quite ready to trust the hulking Ursite yet, but she also didn't want to offend him and ruin any chance they had of accomplishing their mission.

It was a fine line they were being made to walk.

"This is fantastic!" Cabe offered as he set the glass down, but Taj noticed he, too, barely sipped at the drink.

Dent had no such compunctions, draining half the glass in one gulp, much to the delight of Krawg. Of course, his mechanized systems would be unaffected by poisons, so he had nothing to worry about.

"You're appreciative of the Quilix, as your masters were," he said, clapping Dent on the back. "You honor me."

Dent offered a conciliatory smile. "No, it is you who honor us by sharing the Quilix with us."

If Krawg's face hadn't been completely covered in fur, Taj could have sworn she'd seen him blush. He grinned, showing off great, shining teeth, brilliantly white against his dark fur, and settled in across from Dent.

He sat with a grace that belied his size, and even seated, he towered over everyone in the room. His yellow eyes gleamed as he stared across at Dent.

"So, it is time for your masters to return, is it?"

Dent nodded. "It is, though the timetable has been advanced due to unforeseen Terant interference." He sighed, his gaze drifting to the ceiling. "In fact, in all openness, there are three of their ships headed this way as we speak, Krawg. They will be here soon, and I fear for your peace and safety should they arrive before we have concluded our business."

"Fear not, my mechanical friend," Krawg told Dent, "I expected no less when I accepted your masters' secrets. I knew this day would come." He rose to his feet and shuffled off into a different room than the one where he'd collected the drinks.

Krawg returned a short moment later with a pouch. From within it, he pulled a small, dark box that seemed to be constructed out of the vastness of black space. It shimmered and appeared to undulate, tiny white stars bursting to life across its face only to fade away to be reborn again instants later.

Dent gasped, raising a hand to his mouth. His Sperit eyes grew even wider than Taj thought possible. She could see the flutter of his pretend heart in the veins at his neck.

"It's beautiful," Dent said, barely managing to get the words out.

"Can you connect it and restore your systems?" Cabe asked, leaning over the table to get a better look at the device.

"Sadly, it is not that simple, and I cannot. Not yet, at least," Dent answered. "The process takes time, and I must be fully in stasis mode for it to work or it will struggle to properly assess and realign my systems. There is no time for that now."

"Then you must return to your ship immediately," Krawg told him. "Begin the process and restore your masters to their greatness before the Terants, or others, cast deeper shadows across their future."

Right then, as if Krawg's words had been prophetic, a burst of static strafed the comm. Taj bit back a curse as the sound set her skull to ringing. Then a voice came through, loud and clear. "The pirates are here," the voice of one of the Furlorians outside shouted. "Contact. They're coming at us fast, Taj."

Taj leapt to her feet, snarling. "The pirates are here and our people are about to be attacked."

"All three ships have landed in a nearby ice field," Lina confirmed, having been monitoring the comm. "They'll be on our people in seconds."

The first Furlorian muttered something else Taj couldn't understand, and then there was a scream that carried across the comm and her ears at the same time. It was the sound of someone dying, blaster fire drowning it out an instant after. "They're all over us!"

A blaster bolt tearing through the house and shrieking over their heads made his announcement redundant. Taj hissed and ducked low, and Cabe grabbed Dent, shielding him and moving him toward the next room as he yanked his bolt pistol free of its holster.

Krawg snarled, the sound vibrating Taj's bones and setting her nape standing on edge. He pushed her toward the same room Cabe had taken Dent. "Go!" he shouted, stuffing the strange device back into his pouch and slinging the strap over his shoulder. "There is an exit hidden two rooms back."

Once in the room, Krawg slammed the door and took the lead, pushing past Cabe and Dent, leading the way. He opened the door to a large storage room and ushered them inside, closing the door behind them. Then he grabbed the sides of a crate and yanked it aside. The crate creaked and warped under its weight and the stress the Ursite was inflicting upon it, but Krawg clearly didn't care about its condition.

A trapdoor appeared where the crate had sat moments ago, and Krawg hooked a clawed finger in its metal clasp and pulled it open. "In here," he shouted.

Taj went first, gun up and ready, and Cabe pushed Dent

in behind her. They clambered down the steep set of stairs and into a dank, gloomy tunnel that smelled of mildew. Cabe stomped down behind them, and Krawg came right after, closing the trapdoor above, engaging a stout lock attached to its face.

"Straight down, it's not far," Krawg ordered. "There is only one way out, you can't miss it." The Ursite shooed them down the hall, staying right behind them.

True to his word, the corridor ended a short distance later, another set of steps leading up to a massive steel door, with a circular locking mechanism set dead center. Taj didn't hesitate, reaching up and spinning the wheel. It turned easily, clearly having been well-maintained.

A hard push, and the door swung on pistoned hinges, making it easier for Taj to open. The cold hit her hard then, but worse still was the smell.

Blaster fire scarred the air, and she could smell charred flesh wafting to her from the battle she could now hear directly rather than filtered across the comm. She bit back a groan and forced herself to climb out of the secret exit.

She regretted her choice instantly.

Her people were being slaughtered.

In front of Krawg's house, where there was little in the way of cover, her people stood their ground, firing and dying in equal measure. She turned her glance to the pirates and realized they'd brought an army of men to collect the mechanoid and kill those who'd stolen him from them.

They were doing a cruelly fantastic job of it, too.

She raised her pistol, and her finger grazed the trigger

as she thought to join the fight, but Cabe stopped her, yanking her weapon aside.

"That will only destroy everything we're trying to accomplish here," he told her, tears in his eyes. He hadn't made his decision lightly, she noticed. "We have to go if we hope to save the rest of our people."

Logic and reason warred with the need for revenge inside Taj, and she knew what side she wanted to win. Still, Cabe was right. Her crew here was essentially dead, an army of pirates bearing down and murdering them right before her eyes.

She'd seen similar on Krawlas, when Vort had executed her people to lure the rest out of hiding. It sickened and made her stomach roil then, and it did no less now. Cabe pawed at her arm and started to drag her off. Taj allowed him to…but only for a moment.

"No," she shouted, shaking free of his grasp. "Our people deserve better than this, better than to be sacrificed without some kind of retribution."

"You can't help them," Cabe argued, desperately trying to get her to flee with him and the others. "They're dead, Taj."

She nodded. "Maybe, but we're not."

Taj tapped her comm, triggering a line to Lina. The engineer answered breathlessly, and Taj conveyed her orders in sharp, crisp terms.

"Do it now," she said in closing, then she went to silence the comm to mute the voices of her people who were dying before her only to stop herself. She pulled her hand away, letting a growl build up inside her.

They deserved her notice, her attention, especially then.

Cabe posted himself in front of her, doing his best to block her view of the carnage. "Now will you come with me?"

She moved him aside and shook her head. "Not yet," she answered. "Not until this is done."

"It already is, Taj!" Cabe hissed and went to grab her again, but Krawg stopped him, easing the enraged cat aside with a gentle paw.

"Let her have this moment of closure," he told Cabe, patting him on the back. "While it is true nothing can be done to save your people, there is much that can be done to save your friend's spirit. She needs this more than you can know."

Cabe glared at the furry giant, looking as if he might argue, or even take a swing at the Ursite, but Krawg's patient stare seemed to wear Cabe down even more than the massive paw at his chest.

"Bloody Rowl," he shouted. "This is stupid."

"It is," Dent confirmed, "but Krawg is correct." He gestured to Taj, who stood there with her hands clenched and teeth bared. "She needs this."

And they were right.

Taj howled as the last of her people crumpled to the ground, never to rise again. Wisps of smoke curled from their bent and broken bodies, and the auburn-skinned pirates who brought such death and destruction walked among them, smiles on their faces and laughter in their hearts.

And then all that went away.

A great peel of thunder echoed through the gray sky, drawing the eyes of the pirates to the heavens.

It was then that judgment rained down on them.

The *Discordant* broke free of the clouds and swooped toward the mass of pirates. The ship's weapons barked viciously, and a fiery burst of death hurtled toward the ground.

The Terants screamed and ran under the assault, but neither did them any good. The *Discordant*'s weapons railed on nonstop, tearing great troughs in the frozen ground and pirates both. Burst after burst streaked loose, and Taj watched as each bolt tore through a handful of pirates, casting their lifeless bodies into the air like leaves falling from a shattered tree.

The leech craft hovered in place, turning only to get a better angle to fire upon the fleeing mass of pirates below. There was nowhere to go, however. Pirates shrieked and died as the *Discordant*'s guns, manned by Lina, methodically worked their way through the Terants until there were none of the pirates left.

Only then did the roar of the ship's guns cease.

The absence left a ringing void in Taj's ears and a knot in her gut.

She stumbled toward the *Discordant* as the ship eased toward an area where there were no bodies, friend or foe, so it could land and collect the survivors.

Of whom there were few.

Taj stared as the leech ship's landing gear creaked against the frozen soil. Cabe came up behind her and wrapped his arms around her, doing his best to comfort her.

To his surprise, she shrugged him off. "I'm okay," she said, her voice raw from her howls, but there was a steely undercurrent to it. "I'm okay," she repeated, more to herself than him.

And she was, though she knew she shouldn't be.

Taj glanced across the field of bodies—the bodies of her people—and she felt a familiar rage building inside her, an ember of heat flaring to life. Where she'd expected to feel sorrow, there was nothing but a burgeoning anger at the cost to her people of a random event—the Wyyvan ship crash-landing on her planet.

They hadn't asked for any of this. *She* hadn't asked for any of it either. Yet this was what it was, and there was no changing it now.

All her decisions had led to this point. Taj now had a choice. She could wallow in consequences and the loss, or she could rise above it for the survivors, stand up for those who could still benefit from all they'd worked for.

She knew gacking well what Beaux and Mama would do, and while she'd held herself to their standards since long before she'd been handed the reins to her people's futures, she knew then why they'd been seen as such rebels.

They didn't do what was expected of them, they did what was right, what was necessary. They were in it until the end, always ready to fight, to win or die, but always striving to make a difference, to ensure the survival of their race.

And that's what Taj would do.

Cabe leaned over her shoulder, a questioning look in his eyes. "What do you want to do now?"

She drew in a deep breath and met his gaze. "First thing is we need to gather our people and bury the dead," she told him. "Lina can use the *Discordant*'s weapons to dig a hole in the ice."

Maybe this was what leadership was about, becoming so cold you couldn't feel any longer, becoming numb.

No, that wasn't it, she told herself, though it might be some small piece of the whole. Beaux and Mama had never become harsh, and they'd always had a greater burden on their shoulders than Taj was carrying now. She'd never seen anything but love and compassion from the pair, even when they were angry or disappointed. Still, they did what needed to be done.

She would have to do the same.

Taj triggered her comm. "Lina, send some people to the Terant ships to kill any remaining pirates and raid them of supplies," she ordered. "And when they're done, have them blow all three of them to smoking gack."

"And then?" the engineer asked.

"Then we plug Dent into his device and get on our way to our new home."

It was a simple plan, but it was all Taj could muster right then.

It'd have to do.

CHAPTER TWENTY

"You hear that, Rath?" Vort asked, leaning his head closer to the wall of their makeshift cell. "That's the sound of this ship obliterating your forces, lest I'm mistaken."

While the captain wasn't completely sure what was happening, it only made sense. He'd heard Kal talking outside the door about how Taj and the other Furlorians had gone to meet someone on planet. Then he'd been privy to Kal's emotional outburst regarding his people dying, and then the *Discordant* was on the move.

The fact that they were still alive told Vort that it was Rath's men who paid the price.

Rath leapt to his feet, cursing and stomping about, his fury making his skin even redder than normal. "Those fools! They're underestimating these cats. I should be there, leading them to victory."

"And you can be," Vort told him, stopping Rath mid-step.

"What do you mean?" he nearly shrieked. "We're trapped in here. There's nothing we can do."

"Is there not?"

Rath growled and leaned into Vort, putting them face to face. "If you know something I don't, now would be the time to share."

Vort grinned, letting the little pirate vent and feel dominant without retribution. "I do indeed. Now, if you would be so kind as to step aside and follow my lead, we can be free of this place and you can have your vengeance, as it seems you will be too late to turn the tide."

"Just do it," Rath howled.

Vort shrugged and went to the door, knocking on it. "Kal!" he shouted, his voice shifting from cold and calculated to raw and emotional. "I need to warn your captain."

"Quiet, Vort," Kal shouted back. "Now is not the time. You've gotten me in enough gack already."

"Now is exactly the time, my friend. This wrathful scum has spilled a horrible plot to murder the entirety of your people," he told Kal, winking at Rath as the Terant stared. "I've subdued him, but we need Taj to get the truth from him before his devious designs are seen through. They're already set into motion, I'm afraid. You'd be a hero to her if you'd only listen."

"He can't do anything from in there," Kal shot back, but Vort could hear a hint of uncertainty in his voice now, the rodent questioning himself and his decision. "He's locked up, remember?"

"He is indeed, but his minions are not." Vort let a long second drag out before he went on. "There are more of them out there, waiting for your people to let their guard down," he said. "Death is coming for you soon. You must let me speak with Taj so I might warn her."

Vort heard Kal mutter something, and he could see the shadow of the Furlorian's feet as they paced back and forth in front of the door. Then he heard the subtle scrape of metal against leather, and he grinned. Kal had unholstered his weapon.

"Make ready," he whispered to Rath and Dard.

Dard held his ground in the back of the closet, but Rath grinned, a maniacal sheen coloring his face.

The was a sullen thump as the door lock was undone, followed by a second, then the door swung open and Kal filled the entryway, his gun out and pointing at them.

Vort pushed forward, hands raised. "Please, there is little time before we are all dead. You must take me to Taj." He squeezed into the doorway, forcing Kal to back up. For an instant, he blocked the Furlorian's line of sight.

Then he stepped out into the corridor. That was when Rath struck Kal. A brutal punch slammed into Kal's jaw and sent the young Furlorian crashing into the door. His weapon wavered in a shaking hand, but Rath gave him no time to recover. A second punch sent Kal crumpling to the floor, his head bouncing off the steel with a *thud*. His bolt pistol clattered beside him.

The pirate boss snatched up the gun and pointed it at Kal's unconscious head. Vort knocked it aside before he could pull the trigger.

"No time for petty assassination, Rath," the captain told him. "We've bigger cats to fry."

Without waiting for Rath to the respond, he tugged him onward, Commander Dard closing in behind, making sure the Terant could only move forward. Rath nodded and gave in.

"You're right, Vort," he replied, grinning all the while. "Lead the way."

Oh, I shall, pirate. I shall.

And Vort did, marching them toward the gangplank and the hope of freedom that lay beyond.

CHAPTER TWENTY-ONE

Taj watched as a group of her people marched across the snowy terrain toward the pirate ships. There likely wouldn't be much to be had, the ships were not designed for overly long journeys, but any additional supplies they could scrounge would extend the Furlorians' survival a little longer.

And now that they had their hands on the device Dent needed to reorganize his scrambled brains, they could find their way to the Federation and start fresh.

Although it hadn't been that long since they'd fled Krawlas, it felt like it to Taj. It was a whole lifetime ago, given all that had happened in between, and it'd been a nonstop flight since that fateful day.

Now, they were ready to embark on the real journey, the one that would find them a sanctuary to build, where they could mourn their losses and raise litters and grow old and forgetful like all the Furlorians before them.

She glanced over at Cabe and a smile brightened her

lips despite her defiance. He helped organize the burial, Dent and Krawg assisting him while he called out orders, but he didn't avoid the work himself.

Taj felt blessed right then, despite it all, because she still had Cabe with her, still had Lina and Torbon and Jadie and Kal and all the others. She'd made new friends in Dent, and even Krawg, and they had a future now, one that had been nothing more than a dream only days before.

And even with all the blood on her hands, the bodies splayed out before her, Taj saw a chance at happiness for her people.

Then cruel fate intervened.

A flutter of movement out of the corner of her eye drew her attention. Her head snapped about, and one of the Terant bodies sat upright, rising from the pile of its dead companions. A vile grin was plastered across his face, and he held a blaster in his hand.

Taj recognized him instantly, despite the blood that marred his features. Doran.

Without hesitation, he fired into the crowd of Furlorians, blasting anyone that didn't dodge away.

Taj screamed her rage as two more of her people fell beneath the onslaught, and then Doran was shot in the head. The pirate appeared stunned for a second, eyes going wide and mouth falling open, as if he couldn't believe what had happened, and then he slumped to the side, dead.

Torbon stood behind him, the barrel of his gun smoking.

Taj screamed, "Check them all! Make sure they're all dead!"

Cabe and Krawg and Dent raced to do as she said, the previously quiet ice field suddenly exploding with motion.

She spun around to check her surroundings, paranoia in high gear, and that was when she saw Captain Vort emerge from the *Discordant* at a trot. Her stomach sunk, a tight knot of stones.

Rath emerged behind Vort, and she saw the gun in his hand.

"No!" she shouted, clawing at her holster to draw her own pistol. She was too slow.

Rath grinned and raised the gun, took aim, and fired.

As if the bolt traveled in slow motion, Taj watched it sear its way through the air toward its target. Her eyes flew wide at seeing where it was aimed, and her pulse threatened to shred her veins. She gathered the energy to scream, but the sound simply wouldn't come.

The bolt shrieked toward the gathering of Cabe, Krawg, and Dent, and Taj flung herself that way, as if she could hurl herself in the path of fire.

She'd barely taken a step when the bolt slammed into Dent and sent his mechanoid body flying.

"Noooo," she screamed again, scrambling to keep her balance as the rest of the group scattered, only now noticing the threat that had snuck up on them. Taj slipped and hit the icy ground hard, frosty shards whirling around her in a gleaming mist.

She stared up at Rath, his grin broad and malevolent as he made ready to fire again.

Then, to her surprise, she heard Vort cry out. "No! What are you doing?"

Rath hesitated an instant, turning to stare at Vort, and

that was when the captain lashed out with his tail. He spun about, whipping the appendage around with a force she hadn't known he could muster. It struck Rath in the chest and slammed him hard into the gangplank. The gun fell from his hand.

Commander Dard raced up behind Rath and kicked him in the side, knocking him from the ramp. The pirate boss toppled to the ice and landed with a bone-shattering *thud*.

That was the least of his worries, however.

Vort snatched up the dropped weapon and pointed it at Rath. Then he fired, burning a hole through the back of the pirate boss's head.

Taj scrambled to her knees, staring at the unexpected scene playing out before her, and only then did it really click in her head that Vort was now armed. She started to cry out, to warn the others, but Vort tossed the weapon over the side of the gangplank as quickly as he'd grabbed it, where it landed with a *crunch* beside the dead pirate boss.

Vort raised his hands. "Neither I nor Commander Dard had anything to do with this," he announced. "This was all Rath's idea, though it clearly didn't end the way he intended."

Taj shrieked for someone to put Vort and Dard back in their cage, and she only took her eyes off them once a handful of Furlorians stormed the gangplank. Once the two lizards were secured, she spun about to look for Dent, remembering that he'd been shot.

Her stomach sank as she spied Krawg carrying the limp mechanoid in his large arms, cradling him to his chest. "Is he...?"

"He still functions," the furred giant responded, "but I fear not for long. He is shutting down rapidly."

Taj saw the great charred hole in the side of Dent's head and groaned. "Get him inside," she ordered, then tapped her comm. "Lina! I need you and Gran Verren to sickbay now! Dent is down."

Taj shot up the gangplank, leading the way for Krawg to follow. He was forced to duck low to clear the ceilings, but he didn't complain. The giant ran behind Taj until she reached sickbay and darted inside. He followed her in and set Dent on the table Lina pointed out. The giant Ursite backed away, shuffling to the far corner of the room to give the crew space to work.

"Here," she shouted, ripping aside the faux flesh that hid the mechanism inside. She whistled when she saw the damage, shaking her head.

"Can you repair him before he shuts down?" Taj asked.

"I don't know, but I'll try." She turned her gaze on Krawg. "The device, do you have it still?"

He nodded and dug the cube out of his pouch, handing it over without question.

"Do you know exactly how long it takes to reorganize his system?"

Krawg shook his head. "I know only that his body likely does not have enough time left to accomplish the process." He motioned to the alien form twitching on the medical cot.

"Do what you have to," Taj told the engineer, and Lina leaned over Dent, examining his wound closer, the cube dancing in her trembling hand.

Dent reached up and clasped her arm. "Save...the m-memories," he whispered, his jaw creaking open and closed of its own volition, slurring his words.

"I will do my best," Lina told him.

"Avocado," Dent replied with a subtle nod, then went still.

CHAPTER TWENTY-TWO

"Why did you do that?" Commander Dard asked as soon as they were alone in their makeshift cell. "Betray the Terant like that?"

Vort took a seat and looked up at his second-in-command. "We had no chance of escaping then, and given the mood of the crew, their people murdered before their eyes, it would have been a fool's gambit to hide somewhere in the ship and hope for another opportunity to present itself. The rodents would have been wrathful, and we'd have paid for it eventually."

"But still, you killed Rath," Dard argued. "I thought you wanted his help."

The captain chuckled. "But he did help us, Commander. He killed the mechanoid the Furlorians have pinned their hope on to help them find the Federation. Now, that dream is dead, and we have more time before they find their way to them, extending our lives." He grinned, patting Dard on the shoulder.

"He also likely earned us a bit of good will with regards to the rodents, seeing how we stopped Rath before he could do more harm. And better still…" he stated, pulling a bolt pistol out from behind him and grinning, "his death provided cover so I could procure this."

Dard stared at the weapon, wide-eyed. "Where did you—"

"I pulled it off one of the Furlorians escorting us back to our cell," he answered, returning the gun to its hiding place. "Now, we are not quite so helpless when our next opportunity to escape presents itself."

"And that's likely to be soon, seeing how the Furlorians have yet to realize there's a tracker on board."

"Precisely, Commander. Now, we sit and wait while the rodents flail and whine and try to find their way to safety without the android's assistance." He chuckled and leaned his back against the wall, attempting to get comfortable. "It's only a matter of time now."

Vort sighed. "Maybe I can even leverage our good deed for better accommodations."

CHAPTER TWENTY-THREE

Taj paced the bridge, her footsteps echoing loudly. Cabe piloted the ship while Jadie took over Lina's position, S'thlor helping her as he'd done for the engineer.

The flight wasn't as smooth as it had been with Lina behind the console, but Jadie made it work well enough, leaving the bulk of the decisions to Cabe.

They flew aimlessly, having no idea which direction they needed to go. With Lina and Gran Verren doing their best to repair Dent before he shut down, they were lost. All the information they needed was trapped inside the mechanoid's damaged skull. And if they couldn't release it...

Taj groaned, not wanting to go down that path.

At least raiding the pirate ships had provided the crew with a few more weeks' worth of food and general supplies, but who knew how long that would last given they had no destination in mind. It might well have only delayed the inevitable, a bandage on a severed limb. Eventually, the blood would leak out and spill everywhere.

Taj cursed herself for her disturbing analogies and kept pacing. She refused to fall for the siren's call of despair.

They would succeed. They had to.

"You're gonna wear a groove in the floor," Cabe muttered from his station.

She shrugged in reply, not wanting to engage. Getting sucked into a conversation would only heighten her anxiety and anger, giving her an outlet to explode. She didn't want to do that to him.

So, she paced on and on and on, hours stretching into eternity.

At last, when she could barely drag her feet around for another pass, the bridge door hissed open. Lina stood there, covered in synthetic blood, as if she'd been dipped in a vat of it. The engineer stumbled inside, smothering a yawn with the back of her bloody hand.

"Well?" Taj shouted, racing over to stand before the engineer. Cabe came over and joined her, hovering close.

Lina drew in a long, deep breath and let it out slow. Her expression was stoic, neutral, and that worried Taj. "We couldn't save Dent's body," she reported. "It was simply too damaged, too broken down already. The gun blast fried what was left of its systems."

Taj stiffened, feeling a pang of sorrow start to wash over, but then she remembered Dent wasn't flesh and blood, he was a construct. His body meant nothing in the greater scheme of things. "And his mind?"

"We weren't able to connect the device to his body. It

was simply too involved a process, and there was no way he would have remained alive long enough to complete it."

"So, he's…dead?" Cabe asked.

Taj snarled. Had Rath still been alive, she'd have marched off and killed him.

Lina hesitated a moment, drawing the moment out longer. Taj stared at the engineer, who seemed reluctant to speak.

"Is he dead, Lina?" she asked, repeating Cabe's question, frustration rising at the lack of answers.

Lina sighed, then she broke into a grin. "Not in the traditional sense."

Taj stiffened, her upper lip peeling back into a disgusted sneer. "What?"

"What she means is," a familiar voice sounded around her, "you're going to wish I'd died on Gran Verren's dirty med cot."

Taj stumbled, her head on a swivel, looking every-where, trying to pinpoint where Dent's voice was coming from. She couldn't find the mechanoid anywhere.

"I-I don't…understand," Taj muttered. Cabe echoed her movements, surveying the room. He even peeked under the consoles.

"I'm right here," Dent replied. "Let me clarify, I'm *every-where!*" The last came out in an ominous boom that resounded across the bridge, and Taj caught the telltale metallic hum of the comm. Her heart thundered with real-ization.

"Wait! You're in the ship?" Taj asked, staring at the ceiling.

"No wonder you're in charge, Taj," Dent replied. "Brilliant deduction."

Taj stiffened and glared at Lina. "You did not put him in the ship's systems. Tell me you didn't do that."

Lina raised her hands in mock surrender. "I didn't put him into the ship's systems," she answered, "but I'm lying. I put him in the ship. Dent is the *Discordant* now, one and the same."

"Oh," Taj muttered and stumbled over to her chair, dropping into it heavily.

The view screen flickered and turned on. A giant smiley face stared at Taj.

"Think of it this way, Taj. Now I can lead you to a Federation planet and you don't need a blind Wyyvan to translate anymore."

"Great!" S'thlor groaned. "You're in the ship for two seconds and I lose my job." He slumped in his chair. "Guess it's back to the Toradium-42 mines for me," he said with a smirk.

Taj chuckled, staring at the view screen as a thought struck her. "Wait, didn't Lina say she didn't have time to connect you to your device?"

Lina chuckled.

"She did indeed, only she misled you," Dent confirmed. "She said she didn't have time to plug me in while my body was dying. She did, however, have time to plug me in after she'd transferred my synthetic consciousness to the *Discordant*—horrible name for a ship, by the way. We'll have to change that."

"So, wait...you've been in the ship for hours then?" Taj asked.

"Indeed. You should let your emotions out more often. That groove you wore in the floor will be hell to buff out."

Taj raised her head to the ceiling and screamed. The crew stared at her, grinning broadly.

"See? That's much better, isn't it?" Dent asked once she was done. "Always good to get it out so your diodes don't rust."

Taj groaned. *This is gonna take some getting used to.*

Still, it was far better than the alternative.

"Well, since you're all better, Dent, how about you plot a course to the nearest Federation planet, outpost, space station, *whatever*, and we can get on our way before something else pops up." She watched as the smiley face on the view screen melted away, leaving behind a swirl of distorted pixels that vaguely resembled a squashed banana. "Uh, you *are* okay, right?"

"Better than okay," Dent answered. "Lina and Gran Verren fixed me up perfectly. I'm as taco as I can be."

Taj slumped into her chair and clasped her head in her hands before it exploded off her shoulders.

"I'm only kidding," Dent assured her, a strangely metallic laugh filtering through the comm.

"Rowl, save me," she muttered.

"Now I'm hungry for meat rolls," Torbon muttered. "*Thanks,* Dent."

"Me too," Cabe agreed, licking his lips. "Some nip would be nice, too," he muttered, licking his lips.

"Let's raid the stores!" Torbon and Cabe shouted in unison, jumping up and racing through the open bridge door. "Meat rolls for everyone," echoed through the halls.

"Does this mean we're stuck with you?" Taj asked.

"Forever and ever," Dent replied.

"Then if that's the case, give me a view of the stars and let's get to moving before you wear out your welcome."

"Aye-aye, Captain! A course is set for Federation space, and we are on our way."

Captain?

Taj replayed the word in her head a few times.

She had to admit, she liked the sound of it.

CHAPTER TWENTY-FOUR

Hours later, the excitement of Dent's constant travel monologue and the sheer distance they needed to travel to reach the Federation outpost the AI had pinpointed as their destination having worn off, Taj excused herself and crawled back to her tiny quarters.

She'd only been there long enough to peel her uniform off and crawl into the stiff cot, her head barely having landed on the pillow, when there was a quiet knock at her door. Taj groaned and dragged herself to her feet. That she wore nothing but underclothing didn't deter her from staggering across the room, undoing the locks, and flinging the door open.

"What?" she asked, snarling.

Cabe grinned from the other side of the door. He cast a furtive glance at her, taking her near-nakedness in, before returning his eyes to hers. The flutter of his whiskers and the slight blush at his cheeks chased away her frustration at being hauled out of bed.

"So, uh...I was..." he started, and Taj grinned at his sudden tentativeness.

She chuckled. "You need something, Cabe?"

He sucked in his lower lip, and his eyes narrowed. Whatever he'd come to her room for had slithered out of his brain the moment he'd seen her. She couldn't help but smile at that.

The two had danced around each other for years, but their latest adventure had pushed them even closer. Taj stared at him as he hemmed and hawed, clearly trying to organize his thoughts, but she'd had enough of it.

"Just come in, gack it," she told him, grabbing him by the ear and pulling him inside the room.

He gasped as she pushed the door shut behind him with a solid *thump*, and then shoved him against it. She leaned in without waiting for him to calm and planted a kiss on him.

That was all it took to break the frost between them.

He leaned into the kiss, returning it, their lips pressed together. He reached up and pulled her into him, wrapping an arm around her, his hand settling on the small of her back. His other hand played at her fur, stroking the back of her neck.

Taj groaned and let him hold her up, leaning in so tight that, if it hadn't been for the door at their back, they would have tumbled to the floor in a flustered heap.

The air grew warm around them as Taj flushed. She shifted her kisses from his lips to his cheek, kissing her way across his face, loving the flutter of his whiskers and the soft exhalation of his breath in her ear.

Then it was over as quickly as it had begun.

A roaring whoop resounded in her cabin, the room lights soaked in a sudden red.

"You have got to be gacking me," she groaned, feeling Cabe pulling away with a muttered complaint. "What could it possibly be now?"

Cabe glanced at her, clearly unable to muster an answer, as he slid away from the door, putting a disappointing space between the two of them. He reached up and triggered his comm, snarling the entire time.

"What the gack's going on?" he asked, growling into the communicator.

Dent's reply came through crisp and clear. "There are two Wyyvan scout ships closing fast on us," he reported. "I've responded, giving us as much time as possible before they reach us, but these ships are designed to be faster than this leech craft. There'll be no outrunning them."

"It never ends," Cabe spit out with a bark.

"How do these gacking lizards keep finding us?" Taj complained as she marched over to where her uniform lay on the floor, scooping it up.

"I suspect it's the tracking device installed aboard the Discordant," Dent answered matter-of-factly. "It's broadcasting our location on a continuous cycle."

Taj stiffened, still bent over and clasping her uniform. She straightened and stared at the ceiling, never completely sure of where to look when speaking to Dent, then back to Cabe.

"There's a tracking device onboard?"

"Yes," the AI replied. "There is."

"How long has that been there?" Cabe asked.

"Systems say it's been active since you acquired the

ship, according to the data logs." There was a short pause, then Dent cut back in, "You should probably disable that thing unless you enjoy Wyyvan ships surprising you at inopportune times. Seems less than optimal, if you ask me."

"You have no idea." Taj bit her lower lip, snarling. "But no, leave the tracker on for now," she told the AI. "I'll be on the bridge in a moment." Taj cut the comm, shoving her feet into her uniform in a huff.

Cabe threw his hands in the air. "Why wouldn't you rip that stupid thing out right away?"

Taj zipped her uniform up and went to find her boots. "It doesn't make any kind of difference right now," she answered. "They know where we are already."

"But what if more show up?"

A feral grin spread across her lips. "Oh, don't worry about that. The next Wyyvan ship that follows the beacon will get a nice surprise." Suited up, she stomped past Cabe and flung the door open, letting it slam into the wall. "Now, let's go see what we're up against."

The journey to the bridge was quick, her steps fueled by the fury swirling inside her.

The first real moment she'd had Cabe to herself was ruined by the arriving Wyyvan ships, and now she'd learned they'd been broadcasting a signal to the universe, telling the murderous lizards exactly where they were every second of the way.

No wonder they had found them on Kulora. Then just a

short distance from Bolot, there they were again. Now, she knew exactly why.

Her bootsteps echoed loudly as she marched onto the bridge, a storm blowing in. Lina and Torbon stared at her, wide-eyed, and S'thlor just stared. Jadie hovered in the background, quietly observing the scene. Cabe arrived a moment later.

Taj went to the captain's chair and plopped down, glaring at the image of the two Wyyvan scout ships plainly visible on the view screen. An awkward silence settled over them until Torbon finally broke it.

"So, a tracker, huh?" he asked. "That would explain a few things, I'm thinking."

Taj let loose a ragged chuckle. "It would indeed."

"We probably should have shut that thing off a bit sooner," he went on.

"It's not like we weren't a little busy," Lina defended, despite clearly knowing Torbon wasn't being entirely serious. "Not to mention the whole language thing and learning how to fly and alien ship and all that. Oh, and the trying not to die stuff."

"This is nobody's fault but mine," Taj cut in, not in the mood to tolerate the crew's back and forth, "and I should have realized a society as cruel and controlling as the Wyyvans wouldn't trust their people to have complete control over a ship with no way for them to track it down if it went AWOL. No, I should have known better, but I let myself be bullied and blindsided into reacting instead of taking charge." She grunted, still staring at the incoming scout ships. "But that's okay because I'm gonna fix that problem right now."

She spun in her chair and waved to Jadie. Torbon's aunt came over, eyebrows raised, expectant.

"Do me a favor, go and collect Captain Vort and bring him to the bridge," Taj said. "And make sure you have a few people with you to help out."

Jadie nodded. "What about Dard?"

"Leave him," Taj replied. "I just want the head lizard."

"On it," Jadie replied, spinning on her heel and running off to do as she was asked.

"What do you want to do about these scout ships?" Lina asked once Jadie left.

"How long before they catch us?"

"By my estimate," Dent answered, "we're looking at ten minutes, tops. We can accumulate a few more if I press the ship harder."

"No, let's not do that. Don't want to run the risk we burn something out at the wrong time." Taj shook her head. "Anything nearby we can use to better our tactical position?"

"Afraid not," the AI replied, and Taj could imagine him shaking his head, the giant eyes of his previous android body staring forlornly. "There's only open space as far out as my scanners reach."

Taj grunted. "Then I guess we're gonna have to do this the hard way, huh? You up for it, Cabe? Dent?"

"I most certainly am," the AI called out.

Cabe shrugged. "I guess."

"Confidence, I like it," Dent complimented.

Taj only nodded as they prattled back and forth, brainstorming tactical ideas as they awaited the arrival of the

Wyyvan scout ships. She, however, was fixated on one thing. A few moments later, that *thing* arrived.

Captain Vort strolled onto the bridge with an arrogance out of place with his situation. Jadie escorted him in, three more Furlorians behind him, hands at their weapons.

Vort's gaze went straight to the view screen. "I see you've gotten yourself into more trouble, Furlorian," he told Taj. "I'm guessing you need me to get you out of it... again." He raised a questioning eyebrow at her.

Taj offered him a cold smile. "Oh, we definitely need your help, Vort," she replied, getting up and going over to where he stood. "We can't do anything around here without you."

Vort stiffened, his eyelids narrowing to slits. "I sense a bit of hostility in you, Furlorian. I had thought we were over all that."

"Oh, you are absolutely right. We are very much over all that. In fact, we're over pretty much everything between you and I."

She leaned forward and jabbed a finger into his chest, reminiscent of how he'd done to her when they'd faced off in the makeshift cell.

"For instance, I'm completely over the fact that you tricked us aboard the *Discordant* so that my people wouldn't have any food or supplies to get by." She offered him a sharpened grin. "I'm also over the fact that you conveniently forgot to mention the tracking device installed in the Discordant, more of my people being put at risk because you wanted to sow chaos to see how it benefited you."

Vort straightened to his full height, meeting her fiery

gaze with a forced smile. "You'll have to forgive me, but I assure you, I knew nothing about a tracker."

"No?" Taj asked, nodding and glancing up at the ceiling. "Think that's true, Dent?"

"I don't believe it is," the AI answered, his voice echoing around the bridge. "In fact, Vort and his commander were discussing that very thing in their cell not too long ago."

The captain stiffened, eyes darting left and right, obviously looking for the android.

"Oh, did I forget to mention that Dent survived Rath's attempted execution back on Bolot?" Taj asked, staring at Vort. "No? It probably slipped my mind. Anyway, yeah, Dent's alive and well and serving as the Discordant's AI. He's got ears almost everywhere aboard the ship."

"Oh, they're most definitely everywhere," Dent corrected.

"And on top of that," Taj went on, "he's dialed us in with coordinates to a Federation outpost nearby. We're on our way there now," she said. "Isn't that wonderful, Vort?"

He said nothing, but Taj watched him swallow hard, his throat bobbling.

"We couldn't have done it without you," Taj told him. "And don't you worry, we'll make sure the Federation authorities know exactly how invaluable you've been so they can reward you appropriately."

Vort's eyelids narrowed even farther, so much so that Taj could only see the barest sliver of his eyes glaring at her.

"What's the matter, Vort? Cat got your tongue?" she asked.

Vort's tail lashed out, slamming into the deck with a

reverberating *thump*. Jadie and the others jumped back, reaching for their weapons. Vort took advantage of their momentary pause.

"You worthless rodent!" he screeched, darting forward faster than Taj had thought possible.

His meaty hand encircled her neck, and she felt the pressure immediately. He whipped her about, turning her to face the armed guards who'd brought him. The world was a blur, the blood and oxygen flowing to her brain already being cut off by his brutal grip.

And then there was a bolt pistol pressed to the side of her temple, cold steel biting the flesh. Taj didn't have a clue as to where he'd pulled the weapon from.

"Back off, rodents," Vort warned Jadie and the others, his grinning teeth right next to her cheek. She could smell the fetid nastiness of his breath as he spoke.

"Hey!" Cabe shouted, darting forward only to stagger to a halt as Vort tapped Taj in the temple with his gun.

"Stay calm, lover," the Wyyvan captain warned, "or you'll be burying yet another of your kin." He motioned to the rest of the crew with his eyes, maneuvering so no one stood behind him. "All of you, move over to the wall there by the view screen, if you don't mind."

The crew hesitated, and Vort chuckled.

"Have I given you reason to believe I won't shoot your precious little leader here?" he asked. "I've plenty of Furlorian blood on my hands, if you recall. And if we're being honest, it's a bit addictive. A Wyyvan could begin to love the feel of squeezing the life out of you little rodents." He lifted Taj so her feet dangled off the ground.

He squeezed Taj's throat harder, eliciting a choked

gurgle from her. He grinned at the sound, and the crew shuffled to the wall as ordered. S'thlor went to stand, but Vort stopped him.

"No, stay where you are, my blind comrade. I'll need you there."

The world grew darker as the seconds passed, the edges of Taj's vision closing in on her. Her hands ignored her commands to reach for her weapon, her fingers wrapped tightly about Vort's hand in an instinctive bid to break free.

She watched as Cabe and Torbon shook with rage, both desperately seeking the opportunity to pounce and free her. Even little Lina trembled with anger, her cheeks gleaming with furious redness. More so than the Toms, she looked ready to leap to Taj's rescue.

"Now, if you don't mind, and even if you do, place your weapons on the deck and kick them behind me," Vort told the crew.

They hesitated only until he shook Taj, drawing out another gurgle. This one was quieter, less throaty, and even Taj knew what that meant.

Her world grew dimmer by degrees.

Weapons clattered to the floor and were launched across the bridge, all while Vort chuckled.

"And you, our troublesome AI," the captain went on, "I need something from you, too."

"Let her go," Dent argued.

"No, I don't think we've come to that point yet." Vort shook his head. "Now, I suggest you do as I ask or we'll all find ourselves in a bad spot." He gestured to the view screen with his eyes. "My *friends* out there are getting closer and are nearly in firing range, as you well know. It won't be long until we're smoldering ash floating in space and, to be clear, I'd rather not have that happen."

"Do what he wants, Dent," Cabe called out. "Taj doesn't have time for this." He inched forward and Vort warned him back.

"Too true, rodent. Your little lover here will soon fall unconscious, and then things will only get worse for her as her mental integrity becomes more compromised the longer I deprive her brain of oxygen. Hesitate or waste my time and you risk her dying, or worse, living on in a horribly deficient manner." He shrugged. "Your choice, of course."

Laser fire flashed across the bow of the *Discordant*, the view screen adjusting its angle to show the two Wyyvan scout ships closing in fast. More fire flew past, Illuminating the bridge.

Vort growled, and Taj realized it wasn't just *her* time running out, it was all of theirs. "First, you need to tear that wretched AI from the Discordant's systems. Then, you'll retrieve my second in command and bring him here, then you will recluse yourself from my bridge." He snarled the last.

"There's no time for that," Cabe argued. "You're killing her!"

Right then, Taj felt the vice-like grip around her neck loosen the tiniest bit, but there was still no breaking free. Her brain swam in the pool of her skull, and her limbs tingled, ready to go numb. She couldn't feel her hands against the lizard's any longer. Her legs hung limp beneath her, and her arms were next, she could feel it.

"Then I'd suggest you hurry," Vort warned. "You will do

as I say or she dies, then all of you."

Cabe hissed. "Gack it! Lina, shut Dent down now!"

"I need to be at my console," Lina said, and Vort nodded. She shot off without hesitation, flopping into her seat and pounding out commands as S'thlor conferred with her as to the best way to do what was needed quickly.

"As to my other demands…"

"I'm on it," Jadie spat out, spinning around and marching off the bridge.

"Don't do anything foolish," Vort called to her back, watching her leave.

"Now let her go," Cabe told Vort. "We're doing what you want. There's no need to hurt her."

The captain shrugged. "Says you."

Taj's head lolled in his grip, and she knew she had a few more seconds before she blacked out. Her arms had fallen to her sides at some point, but she couldn't recall it happening. They swung as if boneless, floating below her as if they were someone else's limbs.

She bit her lip, drawing blood, the pain the barest of sparks in her awareness as she struggled to stay awake.

Captain Vort smiled as more shots careened across the bow, scraping along the *Discordant*'s shields with a flicker of light and a slight rumble vibrating the floor.

"They're getting closer," Vort warned. "I'd hurry or we'll all die here, disappointed."

"Almost done!" Lina shouted. "I'm locking Dent out of the system in three…two—"

"As our Furlorian friends say so often," Dent said, cutting into the countdown, "gack it!"

The *Discordant* roared into a dive.

CHAPTER TWENTY-FIVE

Taj *hurked* as she was ripped from Vort's grasp, the leech craft whipped into a tumble by the AI.

The crew and Vort were flung about the bridge like so much debris in a sparkstorm, bodies flying and crashing everywhere. Everything not tied down flew right along with them. The loose weapons clattered and smashed into the consoles and crew with equal cruelty.

Taj heard the screams of her friends as the leech craft spun out of control. Like them, she flopped about, bouncing from floor to ceiling to wall and back to the floor, the rotation of the *Discordant* flinging them all over.

Vaguely, her thoughts beginning to coalesce and come back together, she could see the terror and pain of her friends as they were tossed about. Blood covered a few of their faces from the impacts, and Torbon looked to be unconscious, Taj getting a fleeting glimpse of him as he whipped by.

As she toppled along, she spied Vort clinging to the

captain's chair with both his arms and tail, his weight warping the back, but he was managing to remain in place. He hissed, his tongue flailing from his mouth.

"S-sorrrry, foooolks," Dent called out, his mechanical voice fading as the AI lost control of the *Discordant's* systems, Lina's program shutting him down and locking his mind into stasis.

Numb from the loss of oxygen to her brain, Taj could only feel the blows in the periphery of her mind. She wasn't being any less injured by being hurled about the bridge, but her brain hadn't yet remembered how to sort the signals.

That's why it took her a moment to realize she was no longer spinning but lying face down on the floor, her cheek cold against the steel. Dent had pulled the ship out of its tumble as his last maneuver before going silent, she realized.

Moans and groans resounded all around her, her people clambering about in confusion, and she heard a loud *creak*, the sound drawing her attention. She glanced in the direction of the sound to see Vort clinging to the captain's chair and desperately trying to get to his feet. Another few seconds and he would succeed.

Her synapses beginning to fire once more, Taj was determined to beat him.

She scratched at the ground, her gaze fluttering about, taking in the wreckage of the bridge as she fought to rise.

Torbon remained where he'd fallen, blood leaking from a gash in his head. Lina was nearby, rolling about on the floor. Her face was green-tinged and her eyes unfocused.

Jadie and the other Furlorians were in a jumble of limbs

in the far corner of the bridge. They struggled against each other, like serpents in a nest, but none of them slithered from the pile.

S'thlor rested against the bridge door. He sat there breathing heavy, each inhalation looking pained and difficult. Around him lay a cluster of weapons, several of them caught up under his bulk.

Taj pulled herself to her knees as Vort reached his feet. He let loose a barking laugh and staggered in the blind Wyyvans direction, favoring his right leg and using his tail to help him balance and walk.

"Taj?"

She heard Cabe call out and followed his voice, finding him bent awkwardly between the pilot's chair and the console. His leg was twisted at a bad angle, and Taj hissed at seeing it. There was no doubt it was broken.

Their eyes met.

"I'm sorry," he muttered. "I couldn't...couldn't..."

She shushed him as Vort reached the fallen weapons, and she shifted his way. He knocked S'thlor aside with his knee, clearing the way. Then he bent to grab one of the bolt pistols. He picked it up and growled, discarding the gun.

Taj spied its twisted barrel as it clattered to the floor, the captain claiming a second gun and doing the same. He sorted through the rest, grinning as he found the only one that appeared to be in working order.

The *Discordant* rumbled as the closing scout ships battered the shields.

"Seems we're all out of time," he told Taj as he rose to his full height, displaying the pistol in his hand.

Then he shrugged.

"Some of us, however, will die sooner than others." He turned around and tottered toward Cabe. "I'd like to think you'll remember this moment, Furlorian," he said to Taj as he made his way across the bridge, "but that's not going to happen given that those scouts ships will likely end us before too long." He offered up a lazy shrug. "At least I can work my way through your crew before that happens. That will have to satisfy me."

The *Discordant* shuddered under the continued attack.

Vort grabbed Cabe by the scruff and hauled him from between the console and chair. Cabe hissed and yowled, resisting as best he could, but Taj saw how weak he was. There was simply nothing he could do to stop the captain.

That wasn't the case for Taj.

"I think you're forgetting something, Lizard," she told him as she stumbled to her feet.

Vort spun slowly and stared at her, an amused grin pasted across his green lips. "And what is that, little Furlorian?"

She returned his smile. "You're not the only one with a gun."

Vort stiffened as Taj whipped her bolt pistol out from behind her back where she'd concealed it after drawing it from her holster when she got to her feet. His eyes went wide, and he went to raise his own weapon, but Taj fired from the hip.

A bolt of greenish energy tore from the barrel and crashed into Captain Vort's wide face.

He didn't even have time to scream.

His body spasmed, realizing it was suddenly headless,

and twitched once, twice, and then collapsed, falling forward to the floor with a *thump*.

Cabe crumpled to the floor beside Vort, still in the clasp of the dead Wyyvan, his arm pinning the wounded Furlorian down. He stared up at her, then toppled forward, unconscious.

As much as Taj wanted to run to his side and comfort him, pull him away from the disgusting lizard and draw him into her arms, she knew she had something else to do or they'd never get the chance to embrace again.

She raced to the pilot's seat as quickly as she could, shouting all the way, her voice raw and ragged. "I need you, Lina."

The engineer grunted, clearly still fighting the vertigo that had struck her down, but she climbed to her knees, doing her best to get up.

"I need Dent back online right now," Taj shouted as the ship shook, the scout ships taking advantage of the *Discordant*'s sudden discombobulation.

Jadie appeared at Lina's side. Though she had blood coloring one side of her face, the fur there matted and sticky, she helped the engineer up and started dragging her toward her station.

"I've got you," Jadie mumbled to Lina, though she didn't sound a whole lot better than the engineer.

Taj took a second to familiarize herself with the pilot's controls, glad that S'thlor had simplified them. She wasn't anywhere near the pilot Cabe was, but she didn't need to be at that moment. She only needed to be good enough.

She engaged the engines as the Wyyvan scouts reached close range and began pounding the *Discordant*. She groaned as she swung the ship about. With Lina struggling to gather her wits and pawing at the console, and Dent offline, there was no good way to adjust the shields to better ward off the enemy's blows.

That meant the shields wouldn't last much longer, especially not with the scout ships so close.

Just give me a few seconds longer, Rowl, she begged, casting her prayer into the ether.

She angled the ship toward the Wyyvan scouts and pushed the *Discordant* forward.

"What are you doing?" Jadie questioned, eyes wide as she held Lina in place. "There are no guns!"

Taj nodded. She'd known that.

With the engineer on the only console with any real control options outside of the piloting aspect, her flailing efforts focused on bringing Dent back to life.

Taj was on her own.

She pushed the engines for all they were worth, catching the scout ships by surprise. The first of them still managed to veer off, changing directions to avoid the charging leech ship that flew right at it.

The second wasn't so lucky.

The *Discordant* cut through its shields with its hull and clipped the rear hull of the scout ship. The *Discordant* shuddered at the impact, and Taj drove the ship into the other as it adjusted to pull away, keeping the leech ship's nose driving into the other ship.

The blow hadn't been significant, but it had stalled the scout ship for a moment, which was all Taj had hoped for, the *Discordant* now hugging the scout ship's aft. The second scout circled around, trying to find an angle to blast the leech craft without striking its companion.

"I need Dent, Lina!" Taj screamed. "I need him now!"

She fought the decay of her controls as the *Discordant* and scout ship ground into one another, Taj struggling to keep them locked together while the enemy pilot attempted the opposite.

A moment later, she lost the battle.

The scout ship yanked free with a thunderous roar that reverberated through the hull of the *Discordant*. Taj hissed as the Wyyvan ship angled away, trying to put some distance between them. It was succeeding slowly.

The second scout ship closed on the barely moving leech craft, drifting into position, obviously wanting to pummel the *Discordant* at a range where its shields would be effectively useless.

Then Lina giggled, the awkward sound echoing across the bridge.

"Looks like you could use some help," Dent said a heartbeat after, his voice spooling up and growing stronger with every word. "What can I do?"

"Oh, bloody Rowl!" Taj shouted, happier to hear the AI's voice more than anything in the universe right then.

She forced the *Discordant* into a sideways spin.

"Activate the tubes," she ordered.

Dent didn't question, immediately doing what was asked.

The boarding umbilicals shot out on the starboard side, two of the three crashing into the Wyyvan scout ship, magnetic clasps locking on.

"You know, I don't think it's safe to try and board a ship while yours is spinning about," Dent advised.

"Wasn't planning on going anywhere," Taj answered, her eyes locked on the view screen.

Then there was a sudden jolt, the tubes stretched to their limits, as both ships waged a war of momentum.

The *Discordant* won out.

The scout ship, unprepared for the forced shift in direction, did exactly what Taj had hoped it would do, thinking, like Dent had, that she meant to board. Its engines flared to get back to speed and break away from the leech craft, but Taj had already changed the angle of its nose.

"Release the tubes!" she called out.

Once more, Dent did as he was told without hesitation.

"Oh, that's...devious," he complimented, realizing what she'd done.

Unfortunately for them, neither of the scout ships realized it anywhere near as quickly.

The captured scout ship shot away the instant the clasps released, then barreled directly into its companion.

The two ships collided, their bridges warping together as if their hulls were made of molten steel. There were flashes of explosions, sparks that died out before they could truly form, and the two ships tumbled away into the bleakness of space, forever joined in a ruined heap of armor filled with broken lizard bodies.

Without celebrating their victory, Taj jumped from her seat and ran to Cabe's side, pawing at him and pulling him from under Vort's dead body.

She cradled him to her chest and planted a kiss on his

forehead. He groaned and forced his eyes open, staring up at her.

"We win?" he asked, the words barely a whisper.

She grinned and hugged him tighter. "We sure as gack did."

CHAPTER TWENTY-SIX

S everal days later, Taj stood on the bridge of the *Discordant* and watched the view screen as Dent guided them toward the hangar bay of the sprawling space station *Corzant*.

A flutter of excitement prickled the fur along her arms. "This is them?" she asked.

"Not exactly," the AI answered. "This is a Federation-aligned outpost, one of just many havens where the locals support the Federation, helping to expand the frontier."

The gaping mouth of the hangar bay swallowed the view screen, and Taj couldn't help but be awed by the moment.

"How do we know they want anything to do with us?" Torbon asked from his station. The white bandage wrapped around his head stood out in sharp contrast to his fur.

"Because I radioed ahead," Dent replied. "The local authorities have granted our request to dock, and a representative of the Federation has offered to meet us. Uh, well, meet you, more precisely, seeing how I'm stuck in the hulk of this ship."

Torbon shrugged. "Better than being a short alien with bug eyes, right?"

"That is quite true," Dent agreed.

The *Discordant* drifted into the bay and turned about, the station's automated docking system having taken control and settling the craft in its assigned berth with barely a metallic *thump*. The engines wound down as the magnetic clamps locked the leech ship into place.

"At least here we don't have to worry about those gacking lizards showing up," Jadie said, obvious relief on her face as the ship quieted.

Torbon burst out laughing. "We don't ever have to worry about those guys again," he said. "I still can't believe you did that, Taj."

She shrugged. "Well, we needed to get rid of Vort's body and the tracking device. It seemed a waste not to do them both at the same time."

"Yeah, but launching his body out the torpedo tube with the tracker attached… That's cold," Torbon said with a wry grin.

"It would have been much worse had she done it and he wasn't dead," Lina countered.

"That was the plan before everything went sideways," she admitted, grinning so wide it hurt.

"What about Commander Dard?" Jadie asked. "What are you going to do with him?"

"I figure I'll offer him up to the Federation's people," she replied. "He's got to be worth something to them."

"Too good an ending for him, if you ask me," Torbon stated, "but whatever, I'll be glad to be rid of him either way."

"Me too," S'thlor concurred from his new seat near the back of the bridge. Bruised and battered, the Wyyvan leaned to his right, favoring his ribs. "I kind of like being the only alien aboard."

Taj smiled at him, then glanced away, spying a small ground vehicle approaching on the view screen.

"They're here."

"Those would be the locals," the AI clarified. "I suggest you don't keep them waiting."

Taj grunted an affirmative and cast a glance around the bridge. Lina grinned at her and started over, only a few scrapes and scratches still visible as reddened lines under her fur. Torbon followed a moment after, and Jadie flopped into the engineer's seat.

Taj waved to her and the three started toward the bridge door. It hissed open before they reached it.

Cabe stood there, leaning against the wall. "You weren't planning on doing this without me, were you?"

"Never," Torbon replied.

"They most definitely were, Cabe," Dent stated, "Torbon specifically."

Torbon sighed. "We're gonna have to have Lina program some kind of discretion filter into Dent before he gets me killed," Torbon muttered, biting back a laugh.

Cabe grunted and hobbled over alongside the others, his leg in a plastic cast Gran Verren had provided. He reached out and clasped Taj's hand, and she entwined her fingers in his.

"Care to help a cripple?"

Taj smiled and planted a kiss on his cheek. "Let's get you to the transport before you fall over. Wouldn't want to have to carry you."

Cabe laughed, and the crew made their way out of the *Discordant* and down the gangplank, to where the transport waited.

"Welcome to the *Corzant*," a lean, wisp of a woman called out as they approached, her voice soft and ethereal. "I am Eliarar, spokeswoman of the Ooror people. We are honored to make your acquaintance."

Pale and willowy, she looked as if a strong breeze could carry her away. She wore bright white robes that flowed around her, making it look as if she had wings. She smiled, her teeth even whiter than the rest of her, and she ushered them into the transport.

"Please come," she said. "You are right on time."

The crew thanked her, and she climbed into the vehicle after they did, gracefully settling in across from them. Then the transport shot smoothly across the hangar bay.

The trip was short and uneventful, but that didn't stop Taj from gawking out the window. After what they'd been through, even the most mundane of scenery was a thrill she was grateful to have.

Not more than a few moments later, they had come to a halt and Eliarar waved them from the transport. With a bright grin, she led them from the hangar bay into a broad corridor that seemed to stretch on forever. The crew followed her as she swished ahead of them. Cabe's casted foot thumped along behind, Torbon chuckling at the sound every time it happened despite Lina shushing him.

They arrived at a pair of open double doors, and Eliarar waved them inside the meeting room beyond.

"Please, sit," she told them, gesturing to the table set in the center of the room, chairs strung out around it. A large view screen covered the far wall, its face reflecting their arrival in its off state. "Refreshments will be served shortly."

The crew made their way into the room and settled in. Eliarar saw herself out, offering a pleasant smile as she shut the doors behind her. The crew sat there alone, looking about.

"I thought someone was gonna meet us here," Torbon complained.

"And someone is," a roughened voice sounded from the view screen as it wavered and brightened, coming to life.

There appeared a tanned face with a shock of dark hair on top of the creature's head, silvered at the temples. Two penetrating eyes watched her.

Taj caught herself staring at the view screen, having never seen a human before. She didn't know what to make of the older man staring back at them. He wasn't all that different from them, minus the fur and claws.

"My name is Lance Reynolds," he told them, "I have the inauspicious task of managing the Etheric Federation," he introduced himself. "We heard you've had quite an adventure trying to get here."

The crew grumbled their agreement with the statement, and Taj offered the man a smile. "It was...interesting, to say the least," she told him. "But we're glad to be here and grateful that you were willing to talk with us."

"Taj is it?" he asked. She nodded. "Pleasure to meet you

and glad to hear you and your crew are healing up and recovering from your ordeal. Your AI, Dent, told me quite a story." A slight smile broke across his lips as he mentioned the AI. "He wouldn't happen to be related to Arthur, would he?"

Taj raised an eyebrow. "I...uh, really wouldn't know," she answered.

Lance broke into a quiet laughter. "No, I don't guess you would. Earth humor, never mind," he explained. "But anyway, I understand you want to join us and find a home for your people, right?"

Taj nodded. "Yes, that's correct. I'm sure Dent provided the details of our forced exile so I won't make you sit through that again, but we are seeking sanctuary, somewhere to settle and rebuild our lives," she answered. "We'd be happy to volunteer our services in whatever capacity is needed in exchange for such an opportunity. We've also information regarding a substance that might be advantageous to your people, as well as an enemy captive, who just might have some information you can use."

Lance looked upon the crew for a quiet moment, examining each in turn, though for what, Taj couldn't fathom. Finally, he nodded and offered a friendly smile.

"I'd be happy to provide you with sanctuary. We can discuss the finer details of what else we can do for each other at a later date."

Taj brightened, straightening in her chair, raising her hands to the screen. "Oh, thank you so much! This means so much to my people." She wanted to throw herself across the universe and give the man a massive hug.

Lance nodded. "Glad to help, Taj," he said, not even

trying to match her level of excitement. "I'll be in touch soon. Eliarar will take care of you in the meantime. Take care."

The crew muttered their appreciation as Lance Reynolds waved goodbye, looking down as he went to kill the feed. Then he paused, glancing back up at the Furlorians.

"By the way," he said. "Welcome to the Federation."

AUTHOR NOTES - TIM MARQUITZ

WRITTEN AUGUST 18, 2018

Hey, all,

Here we are again. A little late, but not overly so, but I apologize for not hitting my marks. Glad you stuck around.

Turns out, the JIT beta readers caught some glitches with the early story, my horror and darker (and weirder) fantasy habits breaking through, so we pulled back and reevaluated. In the end, I feel it was the right choice, and the book is so much better for it, and I appreciate the feedback. I love learning.

In the end, we write these books for you and all the ego and attitude has to get tossed to the wayside so that the reader gets the best experience possible. I'm grateful for the opportunity to do exactly that, provide you with what I hope is the best follow up possible to Any Port in a War.

Thanks to Craig and Michael and Steve and all the LMBPN and JIT folks, as well as Mia Darien for her edits.

Thanks to Steven Ott for his constant support. And thank YOU, yes YOU. Wouldn't be here without y'all.

Tim Marquitz

AUTHOR NOTES - MICHAEL ANDERLE

WRITTEN AUGUST 18, 2018

(Craig Martelle, standing in – this message was approved by MA)

Woohoo! You're still reading because you are awesome! We wouldn't be anywhere without fans, you good people who buy our books or borrow them through Kindle Unlimited and read them. You are the absolute best. Thank you. If you can also drop us a review on Amazon, that is icing on the virtual cake.

What is there to say about this fine story? It took a couple shots to get it polished appropriately for prime time. The story was always sound, but some of the bells and whistles weren't singing in harmony. The Just In Time readers identified some issues and we pulled the story back. Tim embraced the feedback and made great things happen.

What you read here is 16,000 words longer than the first version, and the flow is simply superb. The story moves along from start to finish at a nice clip. You get to learn more about the characters and become one with their plight and most importantly, their hope.

What do we have without hope? A very dark place that we refuse to go to. We see the best in humanity. Life is worth embracing and living well. Even if humanity looks like a pack of cats that are running for their lives.

Tim Marquitz continues to be an amazing writer, telling stories that people want to read. If you haven't jumped into his other stuff, I recommend his Demon Squad series. You'll get a kick out of that one – it moves fast from start to finish. I'm sure there are some of you who can read the current ten books in three days.

Have I thanked you for still reading yet? Well, thank you! I can't say it enough because you mean that much to me. We tell our stories to entertain and you in turn are entertained:) It is heartwarming and floats our goats.

I have to sign off now – so many stories left to tell and I need to tickle the keys into submission. Thousands of words before I sleep.

Semper Fi, my friends, or as Michael would say, Ad Aeternitatem.

Craig Martelle

BOOKS BY TIM MARQUITZ

Also Available from Tim Marquitz

The Demon Squad Series

From Hell (Novella)
DS1 - Armageddon Bound
DS2 - Resurrection
Betrayal (Intro short to At the Gates)
DS3 - At the Gates
DS4 - Echoes of the Past
DS5 - Beyond the Veil
DS6 - The Best of Enemies
DS7 - Exit Wounds
DS8 - Collateral Damage
DS9 – Aftermath
DS10 – Institutionalized
To Hell and Back - A Demon Squad Collection (books 1-3)

BOOKS BY TIM MARQUITZ

The Blood War Trilogy

Dawn of War
Embers of an Age
Requiem

Clandestine Daze Series

Eyes Deep (novella)
Influx

Standalone Fantasy

Dirge
Witch Bane
War God Rising

Sci-fi

Excalibur

Dead West

Those Poor, Poor Bastards
The Ten Thousand Things
Omnibus 1

Horror

Prey
Serial

Skulls
Heir to the Blood Throne: Inheritance

Collections

Tales of Magic and Misery

Non-Fiction

Memoirs of a Machine – w/John MACHINE Lober
Grunt Style: The Blue Collar Guide to Writing Genre
Fiction

Anthologies

Blackguards (Ragnarok Publications)
Unbound (Grim Oak Press)
SNAFU: Survival of the Fittest (Cohesion Press)
SNAFU: Hunters (Cohesion Press)
SNAFU: Future Warfare (Cohesion Press)
SNAFU: Black Ops (Cohesion Press)
In the Shadow of the Towers (Night Shade)
Neverland's Library (Ragnarok Publications)
At Hell's Gates 1&3 (Charity)
American Nightmare (Kraken Press)
Corrupts Absolutely? (Ragnarok Publications)
Widowmakers (Charity)
That Hoodoo Voodoo, That You Do (Ragnarok
Publications)

BOOKS BY MICHAEL ANDERLE

For a complete list of books by Michael Anderle, please visit:

www.lmbpn.com/ma-books/

All LMBPN Audiobooks are Available at Audible.com and iTunes

To see all LMBPN audiobooks, including those written by
Michael Anderle please visit:

www.lmbpn.com/audible

Craig Martelle's other books (listed by series)

<u>Terry Henry Walton Chronicles</u> (co-written with Michael Anderle) – a post-apocalyptic paranormal adventure

<u>Gateway to the Universe</u> (co-written with Justin Sloan & Michael Anderle) – this book transitions the characters from the Terry Henry Walton Chronicles to The Bad Company

<u>The Bad Company</u> (co-written with Michael Anderle) – a military science fiction space opera

<u>End Times Alaska</u> (also available in audio) – a Permuted Press publication – a post-apocalyptic survivalist adventure

<u>The Free Trader</u> – a Young Adult Science Fiction Action Adventure

<u>Cygnus Space Opera</u> – A Young Adult Space Opera (set in the Free Trader universe)

<u>Darklanding</u> (co-written with Scott Moon) – a Space Western

<u>Rick Banik</u> – Spy & Terrorism Action Adventure

<u>Become a Successful Indie Author</u> – a non-fiction work

CONNECT WITH THE AUTHORS

About Tim Marquitz

Tim Marquitz is the author of the Demon Squad series, the Blood War Trilogy, co-author of the Dead West series, as well as several standalone books, and numerous anthology appearances. Tim also collaborated on Memoirs of a MACHINE, the story of MMA pioneer John Machine Lober.

Website: www.tmarquitz.com

Follow Tim on Facebook and Twitter.

Subscribe to Tim's newsletter and get up to date information on new releases as well as an Excalibur prequel story (exciting sci-fi) and Dawn of War, the first novel in the Blood War Trilogy (Epic Fantasy)!

http://www.tmarquitz.com/contact

Michael Anderle Social

Website: http://kurtherianbooks.com/

Email List: http://kurtherianbooks.com/email-list/
Facebook:
https://www.facebook.com/TheKurtherianGambitBoo
ks/

Craig Martelle Social

Website & Newsletter:
http://www.craigmartelle.com

Facebook:
https://www.facebook.com/AuthorCraigMartelle/

www.ingramcontent.com/pod-product-compliance
Lightning Source LLC
Chambersburg PA
CBHW020358110726
47899CB00006B/1765